LOVING DAUGHTERS

Olga Masters

LOVING DAUGHTERS

W·W·Norton & Company
New York   London

Copyright © 1984 by Olga Masters
First American Edition 1993

Printed in the United States of America

Manufacturing by The Courier Group.

Library of Congress Cataloging-in-Publication Data

Masters, Olga, 1919–
    Loving daughters / Olga Masters.—1st American ed.
        p.   cm.
    I. Title.
    PR9619.3.M289L6   1993
    823—dc20   92-4248

ISBN 0-393-03498-4

NWst
IADZ5243

W. W. Norton & Company, Inc., 500 Fifth Avenue, New York, N.Y. 10110
W. W. Norton & Company Ltd., 10 Coptic Street, London WC1A 1PU

2 3 4 5 6 7 8 9 0

The lovely lady, Christabel,
Whom her father loves so well,
What makes her in the wood so late,
A furlong from the castle gate?
She had dreams all yesternight
Of her own betrothed knight;
And she in the midnight wood will pray
For the weal of her lover that's far away.

Samuel Taylor Coleridge

For Charles

LOVING DAUGHTERS

1

Evelyn, the mother of Small Henry, succumbed to a kidney disease and died hours after he was born.

The doctor from Pambula was there, and the Reverend Colin Edwards was sent for when death was imminent.

George Herbert, an uncle of the newborn, rode to St Jude's rectory in Wyndham to rouse Edwards from sleep. He helped harness Edwards's surprised and shivering horse to his sulky, then cantered off, the ring of hoofs on the dustless, winter road emphasizing the quiet, rather than disturbing it.

Edwards followed at a slower pace. He tried to utilize the time composing a suitable prayer, but barely got his brain working when Honeysuckle came in sight.

The doctor's car moved off before Edwards pulled the sulky up, which suited both drivers, the doctor feeling responsibility for the death, the minister social inferiority for not owning a car. They were happier avoiding an encounter.

Inside the house there was little activity, except for the Herbert girls, Enid and Una, in the clothes they wore to evensong eight hours earlier, moving lamps and bringing in tea. Their bodies apologized when they lapsed into normal, brisk movement. The lamp wicks were lowered, dimming the room, so that only white clothes stood out.

The newly-widowed Henry, the child's father, stood drooping at the window near the fireplace.

His father, Jack, was in a straight backed chair, his easy one empty, a token of mourning.

Henry's older brothers, Alex and George, were on the couch sharing a private shame that their main regret was the approach of daybreak and no sleep possible before farmwork began.

Violet, their aunt, the wife of Jack's brother Edgar, having brought the child into the world, was still on watch by his basket. He was still now and sleeping, having shown them he was alive by swimming motions with his arms and legs, as if he did not believe himself yet free of the waters of his mother's womb, and unlike her he had no intention of drowning.

As soon as he decently could Edwards left, pacing his horse quite swiftly for him, feeling the room clinging to his back.

He felt free of it only when he unharnessed the horse under the big gum, both of them dimly-shaped in the reluctant dawn. He slapped the horse's rump to acknowledge the errand done. The horse took two or three steps as its acknowledgment.

The scene at Honeysuckle returned to him when he was between his hairy blankets, the sheets pushed to the foot of the bed by his agitated feet.

The funeral! His first! He had seen little of the girl, turning on those rare occasions in embarrassment from the great egg shape that made a shelf for her hands. God, you have designed things in the strangest way. Our Father which art in heaven, he prayed in hasty repentance.

He punched a hollow in his pillow for his head and turned over away from a corner of the room, where a girl's slim shape had cut itself into the shadows.

He shut his eyes, but it returned. The blouse it wore had dark spots on white. Or was it all white with fine pleats gently stretched where the buttons ran from neck to waist?

Miss Enid was in the spots, I think, he said to himself, giving the pillow another punch. He remembered one of them in the kitchen, tumbling loaves of bread from tins onto the table, a face absorbed in the task, sorrow left in the living room.

They're making use of this extra time, he remembered thinking, wondering if they were grateful for it. Eyes and ears constantly bent towards the kitchen, he heard a rush of water from an emptied dish onto a plant outside the back door.

That would be Miss Enid, he thought, pleased with his observation. She was the gardener. Put me to sleep, Lord. Sunday service is only a few hours away. (I will see them both!) Lord put such foolishness out of my mind. Better that I think of the dead girl.

He would be expected to say something from the pulpit. The pews, more full than usual, would be eager for it. He might not say anything to nark them! (Lord forgive this wicked turn of mind.) Our sister has departed this life. A gentle soul.

He supposed she was gentle. At seventeen she would scarcely be any other way. He thought she looked trapped, like a large grey uncomplaining rabbit with round, watery eyes, and two teeth in front constantly pinning down her bottom lip. Her hair was gingerish, pulled back from her face, as if she wanted to emphasize its skimpiness.

Enid and Una had erect heads, crowned with brown hair, one more abundant than the other. Which? Go to sleep!

Tomorrow I will have all this nonsense out of my head. I promise You.

2

But no.

Una sat in the Herbert pew given to the church, and he knew she was twisting her hands in her lap by the movement of her arms near her shoulders, although he couldn't see past the second button of her black jacket (he marvelled that she and others had so quickly found black clothes to wear) due to the Robertsons in the next pew tending towards obesity.

He had a foolish fear in his head that he would not reach the door in time to shake her hand, and when he did he assumed a severe expression he didn't intend. To chase it away he asked about the baby, wishing too late that he had used the word "child".

"With Aunt Violet," Una whispered, and he was aware only then of Violet Herbert missing from the Herbert pew. He watched Una's back go down the wooden steps, and had to jerk his eyes away when he saw a question on a rotund Robertson stomach.

No one need ever know, he said to himself, shaking hands with an energy that surprised those in his grip. Bravely unconcerned he lifted his chin at the sound of the Herberts' motor starting up but allowed himself a brief glance that way, rewarding himself with the knowledge that Una was a good inch taller than her sister and had a straighter back.

It was his practice on fine Sunday afternoons these past

few weeks to put on his wide brimmed clerical hat, tuck his Bible under his arm and take a long walk.

It was both good exercise and a means of exploring the district. He varied the direction, although limited to the way to Candelo and Pambula and two or three turn offs, some no more than cart wheel tracks.

Last Sunday he had gone Honeysuckle way.

"Under the circumstances . . ." he murmured, giving the Burragate turn off an apologetic look as he strode past it. He walked with his head down to save the wind catching the underneath of his hat and blowing it away into the Hickeys' paddocks, bare and still like lakes rising one on top of the other until they reached the house sitting among fruit trees on top of the ridge. A Hickey was riding by the fence next to the road and Edwards bobbed his head so that his hat brim bounced a couple of times. That was good enough. The Hickeys were Catholics.

Honeysuckle came up on his right. It sat like an elderly lady surveying her surroundings. Refined though she was, she smoked a pipe, but it was a gentle dreamy smoke drifting away to rest on the barns and dairy well back from the house. She wore a bright skirt spread to one side, quite gay for her age, hinting at a reluctance to let go of her youth. The honeysuckle vine, which gave the farm its name, was piled thickly along the fence separating the house from the orchard. The old lady's colourful skirt was on the other side. This was Enid's garden.

Her mother, Nellie, when she was alive, had kept the honeysuckle trimmed and planted violets in clumps by the steps and lilies and other bulbs by the edge of the verandah, and found this enough to manage.

Enid at eighteen had coaxed Jack to fence a generous area on the kitchen side of the house, taking in some orange and lemon trees. Her garden, colourful and ordered all the year round, often caused buggies and cars to stop and spill out gaping occupants to spread against the wire admiring, until a driver strode away annoyed at the delay and honked a horn or rattled reins.

Enid's heart thumped with pride on these occasions, glad she had won a battle with Jack to have wire not palings, although he continued for some time to complain about the cost.

Edwards smelled something now heady and sweet, unaware that it was wallflowers spread at the base of rose bushes so the bushes appeared to rise from the centre of thick brown and gold patterned bed quilts.

While he smelled and looked at the shut face of the house, a curtain fell back into place at a window on the side nearest the orchard. He paused long enough to admire a stretch of fruit trees so still against a light grey sky he wondered if they were dead until he saw bumps like tiny breasts along the bare limbs. His face warm, he went up the steps and knocked on the door.

Henry opened it. He was in the process of rolling a cigarette and went on quite expertly with the job using one hand while he held the door with the other. Henry had round grey watery eyes rather like those of his late wife. Edwards looked into them for tears. There were none but a spark that said Henry was by no means done with life.

"Yep," he said using a slang term he had brought from the city with the new wife six months earlier. "Nothing to keep me here now."

Edwards glanced towards the hallway leading off a corner of the room, where behind one of the closed bedroom doors he suspected the young wife's body to be. He listened in the creaking silence for something that might say she approved or disapproved his plan.

Perhaps Henry listened too. He looked down at the cigarette between fingers resting on a knee.

Edwards raised his head and listened for the child, then realized Violet would have him. Her house was quite close to the rectory. It came as a shock to Edwards that he actually had a new neighbour. His spirits lifted at the thought and this surprised him too.

They remained uplifted for at that moment Una came in with a tray of tea and cake cut with slices overlapping each other, yellow and tender, breathing freshness. Here was Una! She's come! It might have been Enid, or neither might have appeared, but Una was here. He looked with gratification at the open door which gave her to him. The tea she poured was tan, and the cups were decorated with pale pink flowers. The pink matched Una's cheeks and the tea her tannish eyes unlike any other coloured eyes he had seen. Even sipping his tea and looking into the liquid he kept seeing Una's eyes, which were no longer around for she had slipped away with a jug of roses from the table. Would he not see her again during the visit? The disappointment turned the cake dry in his throat. But she returned to put the roses back, having removed one or two limp ones and given the others fresh water.

"Your roses are beautiful, Miss Herbert," he said.

"They're Enid's," she said.

"I'm sorry, I should be saying Miss Una."

He laid his cup on its saucer as she went out, thinking it best that he did not look after her.

"Yep," Henry said. "Nothing to keep me here now."

I will leave before I hate this man, Edwards thought, standing up. He asked Henry to thank Miss Una for the tea, so happy at saying her name aloud twice in ten minutes he was walking rapidly up the road before he realized it.

The four mile walk to the rectory took Edwards to tea

7

time, for the evening meal was never called dinner in those parts, most families eating largely at midday.

He threw off his hat and coat, made up the fire in the kitchen stove and put the kettle on. Often he made tea without the kettle boiling, it took such an interminable time, and then he would sit over it bluish with leaves floating about and drink it with a pained expression as if doing penance for a wrongdoing.

He decided now to walk outside thinking this might have the effect of boiling the water faster. But outside there was no garden, just rough grass with a track worn between the back door of the house and the back porch of the church. He surveyed it miserably thinking of the Honeysuckle garden. Then he went inside and looked through his window at the darkening sky above Violet Herbert's home where the small baby was, and wondered at it looking the same.

The baby reminded him of the funeral tomorrow. Good, he thought before he had time to stop himself. Then in repentance he dropped on his knees by a chair to pray and was there when Wilfred Watts arrived with a can of fresh milk.

Wilfred jumped in fright when he saw the big soles of Edwards's boots just inside the kitchen door causing some milk to splash on the doorstep. Wilfred, who was eleven and the son of Mrs Watts who cooked and cleaned two days a week at the rectory, stared at the running milk and clutched the can hard in the crook of his arm as if to avoid a further spill. Edwards flung a cup of water on the step and both of them watched the milk turn pale blue and gather dirt as it raced away to trickle into the grass. Edwards took the can and emptied the milk into a saucepan, his only jug being half full of soured stuff from the last delivery.

He set the chair firmly against the wall to dispel any thoughts Wilfred might have of a resumption of the prayer.

"Somebody died," Wilfred said accepting the rinsed out can.

"Yes, my boy," Edwards said, thinking not of the dead girl, but the alive and lively Una.

"Mum said the Herbert girls'll be glad," Wilfred said.

He tapped the can against a knobbly knee while he shared this reflection.

"Well, death is said to be a happy state," Edwards said.

Wilfred steadied the swinging can. "Why do people bawl then?" he asked.

Edwards remembered a shadowy girl's shape at the kitchen dresser with half a back visible from the living room. A head bowed briefly while a handkerchief was tucked into a cuff. Yes, Una had wept.

"God blesses those who weep," Edwards said.

Wilfred, embarrassed to hear God mentioned in conversation this way, stared at his bare sprawled feet, the cracked soles beginning to invade the uppers with brown threads like rough darning.

Edwards sat sideways on his chair.

"Come to church and you'll understand," he said. "Perhaps."

"One day Mum'll get us all new boots," Wilfred said trying to push his feet deeper into the grass.

"God wouldn't worry about the boots," Edwards said.

"The people would, though," Wilfred said.

As if there were no argument against this Wilfred spun the can a couple of times then turned and sped off home.

3

After tea at Honeysuckle Enid made a wreath of wallflowers and daisies and laid it in a tub of water on the wash house floor. There it rocked about, hitting the sides of the tub as if there was something disturbing it. Enid stayed until it was still, holding a lighted candle and the edges of her blouse together at the neck. Cecil Grant, the undertaker from Bega (who had an eye on Enid), had brought a coffin late the previous night. Cecil, his rumbling hearse and the girl's body would pass the night at the Wyndham hotel, the cost included in the funeral charges. The wreath had the effect of returning the body to Honeysuckle just as Enid had it thankfully out of the way. She felt now she should leave the candle burning in the wash house. Oh what foolishness, she said to herself, shutting the door with a brisk little click. It may well burn the house down and bring us more trouble.

She went to the bedroom she shared with Una, passing the kitchen, which was settling itself for the night under the heavy smells of food cooked for the meal when the funeral was over.

The bedroom was once Jack and Nellie's, Jack taking a smaller room when both girls finished their education at boarding school and Nellie by that time dead several years. It was a showroom at Honeysuckle, up a step from the living room and on a level of its own. It had been Nellie's sanctuary furnished with mahogany pieces shining like dark brown silk. There were two chintz-covered chairs, thick hooked rugs on the floor and a double bed with a handsome crocheted quilt and pillow shams. Enid kept it immaculate, constantly straightening the clothes in the wardrobe, and wiping out the jug and basin on the marble washstand after every use. Lately she had emptied a drawer in the dressing table for the creams and powders Una had taken to using, to save a clutter and spillage on the unblemished surface. Enid saw three of Una in the dressing table mirrors for she now had a dress spread on the bed intended for the funeral. It was a black moire silk, plain except for a pale blue piping at the high neck and wrists of the long tight sleeves. She touched the trimming as if willing it to disappear. Enid glanced at it while she removed the pillow shams and turned the quilt back.

"Perhaps it could be unpicked," Enid said. She sewed but did not have Una's talent with the needle.

"Tonight? Sunday!" Una said with round scandalized eyes. "Mother would die!"

Not Mother, Enid thought, taking out the black dress she wore to the last Bega races, thankfully untrimmed except for a large pale apricot floppy cotton rose which she now unpinned from a lapel.

"Wear your black suit then," Enid said receiving her answer from Una's face. Wear the same dress two days in a row? With him to see!

"I finished the wreath," Enid said. "There were more flowers than for Mother's. But I made it smaller."

Una approved but both faces were washed briefly with shame at the discrimination.

Una put her nightgown on, full below the bust with lace and tucks. She went to the mirror and brushed and coiled her hair.

Enid in bed blew out the lamp so there was only a fluttering candle on the dressing table to turn Una into a bride.

4

Violet's dream of turning her house into a hospital was reinforced when she took Small Henry home. His wailing through Sunday afternoon and a greater part of the night did not worry her too much. It was rather like an orchestra playing in its rightful setting.

It worried Ned a great deal. He lost an eye in the Great War and had a glass one in its place, and he turned both, one ahead of the other, on the white bundle Violet carried about, then looked through a door or window as if directing her to take it there.

This is a good way of breaking him into the idea, Violet said to herself, binding a screaming Small Henry into a napkin large enough for a young calf.

Violet was a nurse when she married Ned, giving him that name in preference to Edgar, and being a woman of authority, the family followed suit.

Since she and Ned remained childless, she continued to take cases, or home confinements in Wyndham and nearby.

Lately there had been a dwindling of numbers, due both to a growing trend, and slightly improved roads, to travel to Bega or Pambula to private hospitals there.

Here there were certain disadvantages of which Violet was well aware.

Few timed their trips to arrive with the imminent birth. Most went days or even weeks in advance, enjoying for a while the luxury of sleeping late and meals in bed. Then husbands at home with an added workload and reluctant relatives caring for other children, soured on the arrangements. The women grew heavy with guilt as well as their unborn children, as hours stretched into days and they watched the arrival of other patients, moaning in labour as they staggered up the hospital steps.

How they envied them, longing for their own pains to start, turning their cheating bodies in shame, even from the lowly maid who brought their food. Many tearfully begged to be taken home, adding to the trauma by returning almost immediately, narrowly escaping giving birth in the hired car or family buggy.

Violet's scheme was to turn her two front rooms, one a sitting room and the other the bedroom she and Ned shared, into wards for a maximum of six cases. One of the other smaller rooms also opening off the hall would be the labour ward, and the opposite one would take most of the sitting room furniture and double as a waiting room. She and Ned could make a room for themselves at the end of the front verandah, already partly closed in and presently sheltering some broken furniture and empty tea chests that held their wedding china while Ned was at war.

The tea chests (and Violet) were housed at Honeysuckle while Ned was away. Violet had her uses there, nursing Nellie through her last illness, then sharing the housework with Enid, and later Una when both left boarding school. She was restless without nursing work, for there were few confinements with the men away at war. She tried the patience of Enid, who as young as eighteen was eager to be in full control of the Honeysuckle household. Violet constantly gave advice on cooking and cleaning, although she was slapdash in most culinary skills. She criticized Enid's plans for her garden, causing Enid to go behind the locked door of her bedroom to write to a Sydney nursery for seeds and seedlings, and make sketches of beds and borders. Violet talked at length about enlisting as a nurse and following Ned to England and later to France. (Enid often wished she would, but was too well brought up by Nellie to say so.) It was soon too late anyway, for Ned's eye was shot out and he was invalided home before the war ended.

Violet and Ned named their cottage Albert Lane after the site of that skirmish with the Germans. It was the first built in Wyndham in many years and was Violet's idea, she being passionately opposed to their moving onto Ned's farm, Halloween, where there were suitable share farmers named Hoopers. Let them stay and Ned go there and potter about as the mood took him. A new house was just the thing to rehabilitate him. It was directly opposite the new war memorial too, of which Violet was greatly in favour (then) although part of Wyndham opposed it. Save the money, many said, and rename the public hall, which was next door, the Wyndham War Memorial Hall. Violet threatened to give a piece of her tongue to the source of this proposal, and Ned's good eye watered liberally and his glass one took on a drowned look as well. His hands, growing pale and weak looking, clutched at his knees, for he was either on the kitchen couch or a verandah chair, as if the hands were shouting the words working inside his throat.

But when the pink and grey marble monument was finally up, enclosed with a metal chain suspended from smaller pillars, Violet had less enthusiasm for it than Ned. He would sit on the verandah recounting the opposition to it, now blamed on Eric Power, who in Ned's few trembling words never heard the crack of a bullet, or lived for weeks on end in wet and rancid clothes, but was most of the time at home in a feather bed, the fruits of which were ten children, considered by Eric to be the superior war effort.

By this time Violet was ready to defend Eric. Sitting near Ned, sewing a dress, biting at a thread impatiently and trying to decide whether to carry on or bundle it up and take it to Una to fix, she informed him, not for the first time, that Eric Power had tried to enlist but was discovered to have flat feet.

Violet kept fowls and ducks in pens not far from the back door. She had in the beginning a modest dream of killing and cleaning the poultry with Ned's help and sending it off for sale to guest houses in the seaside towns of Pambula and Merimbula. She was enthused by the arrival of new life, yellow and tender and fluffy.

But the ducks grew old and scruffy, and the pens dry and brown like the sad eyed occupants, and Ned seemed to wither too, standing staring at them through the sagging wire. After a while, the squawking, perhaps reminding him of French farmhouses at the other Albert Lane, sent him scurrying into the bush where he would remain for hours.

In the early days when the Herberts were pioneers of Wyndham, an old Herbert woman named Phoebe had been found dead in a hollow tree after she had been missing for weeks. Violet, fearing a similar fate for Ned, would stand on the edge at the bush, only her beating heart breaking the silence.

Later she grew less patient and less fearful, talking aloud to her angry footsteps in the otherwise silent house, saying he could finish up like old Pheobe for all she cared.

But she was not yet brave enough to openly announce her plans about the hospital, warning Enid and Una, who were in her confidence, not to say anything in front of the "boys" in case word got back to Ned.

"He'll come round in the end," Violet said on this particular occasion, about two months before the birth of

Small Henry, visiting Honeysuckle and gossiping with Enid and Una in the living room.

The annual Wyndham picnic races had been held the week before, so the projected hospital had to be shared with that major event as a talking point. Priority was given to the food tent operated by Wyndham's meanest woman, Mrs Ena Grant, wife of the Wyndham storekeeper.

Una flung away the petticoat she was sewing and pantomimed, with exaggerated movements of her slender body and long arms, Mrs Grant removing portions of food from plates filled by other helpers. Then Una became the helpers and put the food back, and Mrs Grant removed it again, and after a while Una's body became a flurry of movement and her head rapidly swung from left to right in pursuit of her opposition, until she was jerking and spinning like a mechanical toy.

Enid with twitching lips got up and straightened the tablecloth when Una had flung herself back in her chair, and Violet used the inside hem of the dress she was altering to wipe the tears of laughter from her eyes.

"You should take it on," Violet said to Enid, as she had been saying for the past two or three years, referring to the operation of the food tent.

What followed each picnic races was equally predictable.

A few days after the event the workers gathered for their meeting, ranged on a wooden plank in the public hall, sharing the Herbert women's view that Ena Grant should be removed permanently from the food tent. They waited for Ena's arrival, stern of expression and resolute of mind.

"If anyone feels they can do a better job, they have only to speak up!" Ena said opening the exercise book containing her figures, one damaged in transit from the warehouse, but charged to the committee at full price.

16

No one spoke up although Enid, proud of her skill for management, wanted to. But leaders of charity work in Wyndham were matrons or established spinsters, and Enid at twenty-one might have been verging into spinsterhood but was not yet ready to draw attention to it.

Now Violet, Enid and Una each lifted their chins, like birds anticipating a scattering of seed, something with a taste they knew and favoured.

The food tent! Who gave what and who cunningly covered their donation to take it home untouched? Who dodged the job of stoking the fire under the tins boiling the water for tea, and spent their time flirting with the men leaning on the counter between races?

But there was no time for a burst of words from lips hastily moistened for an easy passage. At that moment Henry's wife drifted into the room, light and ghost-like in spite of her bulk. She took a straight backed chair near the piano, folding her hands one above the other on her thighs and looked down on them past her stomach under the stretched cloth of her dress.

She had not been included in the outing to the races, but left to drift about the big, cool, empty house where she did no more than wipe a few dishes left by the washing up dish, not putting them away in their rightful places, and Enid, clicking her tongue at the sight of them, felt immediate remorse, for the isolated, misshapen heap reminded her of the girl herself.

Enid felt remorse again now at the sight of the girl's misshapen body in her unsuitable dress, and wished she and Una had made her something loose and full to wear. Nellie, if she had lived, would have insisted, in spite of the shame and embarrassment the hurried marriage brought.

It was hardly worthwhile now, a waste of good material,

17

and Enid shrewdly suspected the birth was closer than the date given.

The conversation stopped, the expressions on the faces of the Herbert women slipped into a coolness, not quite a frown, not totally a lost smile, but features rearranged as in a schoolroom when a loved lesson is over, and the next one is of a more perplexing kind.

Violet, deciding she would do no more to her dress, jabbed the needle through the cotton on the reel and rolled both together on her lap.

She stroked quite gently for Violet at the blue and white spotted muslin.

"Where would you rather be confined?" she said, and the girl started at being addressed, certain as usual that she would not be capable of answering a question from a Herbert woman, whatever it was.

"Confined at home or in hospital?" Violet said, now at liberty to frown as deeply as she wanted to.

"Aunt Violet is thinking of making her house in Wyndham into a small hospital," Enid said quite kindly as she saw the terror in the girl's eyes at the ordeal ahead.

"Not immediately," Enid said in answer to the wild look the girl sent around the room.

Violet stood and stuffed her sewing into a basket and flung it over a stout arm. Small hospital indeed! And not immediately! But she had time only to pout in Enid's direction, for there was the rumble of the mail car in the distance and she had to be on the roadside to hail it for a ride home. She tossed her head huffily to the Honeysuckle doorway filled with Enid and Una as she climbed into the car.

Henry's young wife went off too before Enid and Una had left the doorway. She took the same vague direction Henry had taken earlier, on the pretext of looking at steers in a far paddock. She came upon him prodding with a stick at the edge of a dam and when he saw her with the side of his face, he dropped the stick and picked up some stones and sent them skimming across the water.

"Watch this one," he said as the girl dropped onto a log, grateful that her presence was known to him. The child thudded and tumbled inside her and she steadied it with one hand and put the other on the space beside her, wishing for him to come and join her. But he turned from the dam after a while and picked up his coat from a stump, checking that his tobacco had not fallen from a pocket and, putting the coat on, lowered his head and walked rapidly off.

She thought he might be having a game with her, that he might turn and run back, but he went on, growing smaller as he went over the first rise, and she saw only his head bobbing in the hollow as if swimming, and he sailed up the next hill like someone clinging to the crest of a wave. The grass all around him was like a sea too, a whitish waving sea soon to swallow him completely.

She put her hand on her stomach for comfort.

"He will be different when the baby comes," she whispered. "I know he will."

5

In the Honeysuckle kitchen Enid stoked the stove and Una, at a corner of the table, sliced carrots and turnips to go with boiled beef for tea.

"I'll make an onion sauce," Enid said, clearing space at the other end for her work, but distracted by some squeaky giggles from Una. Her face was pink and the hair on her bowed head had slipped heavily onto her forehead and her small white teeth and her small pink chin were shaking as she clenched the vegetable knife with its point among the peelings.

Enid, marshalling her features into severity, began mixing her sauce. Una collapsed on a chair eventually, flinging her arms behind her over the back.

"Where would you rather be confined?" she said in a fair imitation of Violet's voice. "I thought the other one was going to say 'underneath the big gum in the corner of the cow paddock!'" She took up her paring knife and a turnip. "Henry is such a fool!" she cried.

When it was time to find a saucepan she clapped the lid on as if boxing Henry's ears.

"Now do that properly," Enid said. "The water in first and have it boiling, then the vegetables. And remember the salt."

Una sewed and sketched with painstaking care, superior to Enid in these skills, and Enid took every opportunity of asserting her authority in the areas where she excelled.

Una left the stove to go to the window and look out. It

was a long stretch for her body to the sill, across the top of a line of tea tins, empty of their original contents and now used for biscuits and buns. Her protruding bottom, round as a pumpkin in an old tweed skirt, drew the hem up above the dip in her knees. Enid, frowning on the sight, suggested she go and set the dining table in the living room.

"It will make it look as if tea is closer," she said, a logic learned from Nellie.

She was annoyed with herself for talking so long in the living room with Violet and felt a temporary envy of Violet with only herself and Ned to cook for. A meal for two! What would it be like, she wondered, reminded then of the changes to be faced when the baby was born. She saw her kitchen in chaos, with napkins drying by the stove, and a bath tub on the table. It would not do! The girl did not like the country, you could see that plainly. The three of them should go back to Sydney as soon as she was fit to travel. But if they stubbornly stayed . . . !

Enid's face went hot and her throat tight, and she clasped her nose which had a tendency to turn red when she was agitated. She rushed to the mirror through the kitchen door in the hall to stroke at her nose, only emphasizing the redness with streaks of flour from her fingers. She turned away and scrubbed her face with her apron, and had her breath back in its rightful place when there was the sound of notes struck on the piano, coming from the living room.

That Una! Enid ran, then stopped to walk normally through the door. Una had the cloth on the table but was at the piano, standing sideways, striking notes, her chin on her neck and her hair against her cheek and neck thick as a horse's mane. The loose hair both offended and frightened Enid.

She took a handful of cutlery from the sideboard drawer and began to lay the table, eyes down.

"Go off and do your hair," she said.

Una threw back her head, loosening her hair still more. She lowered the piano lid, holding her fingers inside as if she might crush them if her feelings overtook her. She stayed so long with her small pert face directed towards a corner of the room that Enid looked too, although aware of nothing there to hold her gaze.

Enid took up the cruet and swinging it from two fingers walked, almost sauntered, to the kitchen to refill the vinegar. Her profile over her shoulder said see this relaxed body, free of the tension tying you foolishly in knots! Go and do your hair like a sensible girl!

But in the kitchen Enid went to the window giving her the best view of her garden and did not know how tightly she held the sill. Evening was coming on and some oranges and lemons high on the trees burned like small soft lamps. How glad she was she had insisted on keeping the trees, deaf to the Wyndham view that fruit trees belonged in an orchard and flowers in a garden. The fruit had once been small and sour, tossed in disgust to the pigs. Cattle had thrust their heads into the foliage spoiling the symmetry. But when the trees became part of the garden Enid planted ivy at their roots, and it was as if the trees looking down drew comfort from this token of companionship and burst into blossom, then bore bright gold and pale yellow fruit and appeared like crowned royalty, ruling their subjects with a gentle hand, more by example than direction.

Those who thought the trees out of place and Enid better employed inside the house, and said as much to Jack, changed their view as the garden developed into something close to a small, well kept park.

They praised the elder Herbert girl to soured wives

immersed in motherhood and small, dirty houses. The wives' envy turned to dislike of Enid as they waited darkly hopeful for her life to become a pattern of theirs.

Enid watched the may bushes toss their heads about above a bank of salvia, losing its fiery red to the approaching dusk, and a border of white daisies, their navy blue centres no more than a blurred hole.

Yes, I am pleased with you, she said to herself, feeling the tightness around her heart melt like a dish of butter on a hot window sill.

She turned to see Una, binding an old shawl to her shoulders with tightly folded arms, slip through the hall and pass out the back door, off walking to the old race-course before tea. Well, let her go, Enid thought, taking a stack of plates to warm by the stove. She saw her garden again glancing sideways from the dresser.

She hasn't got what I have.

But she did not know which was the stronger emotion, pity or triumph.

Two weeks later Edwards came.

6

A legacy from a bachelor who grew up in Wyndham and later became a successful seed merchant in Bega brought Colin Edwards to the church and rectory of St Jude's.

There was no resident minister during the war years, a man coming from Candelo or Bega once a month to take a service.

The seed man left the legacy for the appointment of a minister to St Jude's, and the sum covered a single man's stipend for two years.

It was considered providential by the Bega Parish Council that Edwards was available, his arrival in Australia known to one council member through a relative, a high ranking Sydney churchman, with whom the member kept in touch, adding an aura to his own humble post.

This was enhanced by taking Edwards in and boarding him for the few weeks spent in Bega adjusting to the new environment.

Edwards came out from England with a shipload of returned soldiers at the end of 1919. He avoided large packs of diggers on the journey, conspicuous in his clerical dress among the khaki uniforms. It was the robust soldiers unmarked by the war who made spitting motions with their lips and snorting noises through elevated noses when close to him. Those on deck chairs with frail hands clutching sticks, and faces hardly less white than their abundant bandages, appeared humbly grateful when he sat by them to talk, although there were padres (in uniform like the soldiers) who were carrying out counselling duties until the ship docked.

(These he avoided too.)

Edwards's only brother James was lost in the war. He had risen to the rank of captain and died in Egypt. The event brought great stress and grief to the family, particularly the father in charge of the fashionable parish of Kensington.

Colin had secretly believed he would be pleasing his father greatly by joining the church.

But it was clearly James who was favoured. He studied law, took a degree then joined the Army at the outbreak of war. He died tipping from his horse, like a child playing war games.

Colin, struggling with his studies at theological college, returned home to help ease his parents' grief, or so he believed. When he walked between his father and his mother in the drawing room, his father ran cold eyes over him as if he were a stranger yet to be introduced whom he was sure he wouldn't like.

His mother turned her drowned eyes to the window to give him no view of her face, only her little plump hand holding a sodden handkerchief on her knee.

His father said little about the opportunity of going to Australia. But it surprised Colin to hear how many of his father's colleagues told him he would do a fine job in a new country where there was a shortage of young men trained for the church.

Colin allowed his eyes to say briefly there was no less a shortage in England since the war had taken so many, then he lowered them as was expected of him in the company of his superiors.

His mother wept openly as he was boarding the ship, but he could take little comfort in this manifestation of her love for him (although she may have been weeping for James as well), aware of the stiff shape of his father, intolerant of emotional behaviour.

He suspected that enlisting would have pleased them both. It might have helped avenge James's death for his father and he had heard his mother blurt out to a woman relative, who was on a visit to offer sympathy, that she was so proud of James's legs in their beautiful shiny leggings.

But I am no good at killing and that is all there is to it, he said to himself, watching the great sheet of sea from the ship's deck, surprised that he saw no beauty in it, and came close to hating it for its contribution to his loneliness.

He dreamed of rising to great heights in the church in Australia (a bishop no less — that will show him!) and greeting his parents in his fine house on their visit to Australia.

The dream was disposed of fairly quickly when he got to Wyndham and found the church let the rain in and the damp crept up, staining the wood at the base of the altar and causing mildew on the strip of carpet by the pulpit.

"I will think of it as God's rain," he said, leaving it to go into the rectory where the rain had also come in to invade the recess that held the kitchen stove, so that the iron claws of the stove appeared like the feet of a stubborn black steer, guarding his territory with head down, determined to remain, whatever depth the water reached.

Edwards turned some wet wood over, plucking splinters from the short alpaca coat he wore when not in the cassock. It reached to the top of his boots, which he favoured, liking the idea of people knowing immediately who he was, for aside of pride in his status, he was still a little shy at introducing himself.

A little money had been spent furnishing the rectory with a bed and cedar chest of drawers for the bedroom, (other bedrooms were left empty) a couch, two chairs and a table for the living room, and a dresser, safe and chairs and table for the kitchen.

"Quite enough for one," Edwards said, humble and grateful when he saw it. "Quite comfortable. Thank you."

He wandered about the rectory with an air of ownership when he was alone, the councillor with whom he boarded going off in his old brown Studebaker to Bega. The councillor was glad to have the house to himself, as he put it, although this was scarcely so, for his mean wife ran the house and interfered in the butchery business as well, not serving choice cuts at her table, as you would think, but mutton scraps, pork knuckles and bacon that had been oversalted and had to be soaked in water so long it emerged like old thin grey socks and tasted much the same.

Edwards unpacked his case and put his brush and comb and the circular celluloid box for his clerical collars, a gift from his mother, on top of the chest with a mirror in a wooden stand.

He interrupted his task to glance through the front and side windows although the view was the same from both. No buildings could be seen from that part of the house, although there was the corner of an apple orchard, indicating life somewhere not too far off.

Edwards wondered if apples on the kitchen table had come from that orchard, unaware that every farm in Wyndham had several trees bearing a January fruit, a dullish red on the green skin, hard and tough of flesh, needing an effort with jaws and teeth to draw juice into the throat.

He did not know as well, but was soon to learn, that the orchard belonged to a Presbyterian family named Tunks, intolerant of other denominations, and unlikely to contribute to largesse delivered to the rectory for Edwards's arrival.

He walked about his living room, glad to see through the windows there the Wyndham Post Office, hall and monument and a corner of the Ned Herbert home. But the silence and the creaking floorboards frightened him. He stepped from one to another, the squeaking under his boots like some protesting mouse. Even leaping across three or four boards it seemed that those he was about to land on set up their squeaking in advance. He sought safety at length on the rug before the fireplace where he stood sweating slightly and clinging to the mantleshelf.

"Well, it's something I can do, I suppose, when things get too deadly dull around here," he said making his way to the kitchen, aware that his voice was squeaking too.

A fresh nervousness came over him there, realizing so little of his life had been spent in kitchens. He had gone to boarding school and then to college, spending only a few months assisting his father's staff before leaving for Australia. He remembered standing in the kitchen doorway at Kensington, looking past a cook and maid working at the table with lowered eyes, waiting for his mother to bring him shoes warmed at the hearth, hurrying in her fluttery way, lest his father come upon them.

Here was a kitchen he was in charge of, and good heavens, what was he to do with it? He stood by the table, grateful for the sturdier floorboards, setting up no protesting squeak. With the apples on the table was butter in a dish, the dish inside a flat wooden box lined with sand. He felt the butter through the damp muslin covering it and touched the wet sand. Keep sand wet, was written in untidy letters on the side of the box. I hope I do, Edwards thought, nervously prodding at the sand, should it dry up under his eyes.

His glance took in the other goods, jam and jelly in tall, thin glasses, pickles in a sturdy jar, a teacake wrapped in a serviette and bread smelling so fresh he glanced about him to check that the donor was not lurking somewhere in a corner.

Also on the table was a little pile of linen, and Edwards laid his hand on the fresh crispness of tablecloths and towels.

Topping the pile were two hand towels, embroidered near the hem with the words St Jude's.

The apostrophe separating the last two letters was so perfectly done, it was as if paint in a rich satiny blue had been dropped from the tip of a brush and fallen in a tear shape.

Edwards touched it to prove there were stitches.

Handsome indeed, he said to himself, I wonder who sewed that?

Una had.

7

Edwards decided to punish himself for looking forward too eagerly to the funeral by allowing himself only an occasional glance at Una. He tried to be stern with his face in the mirror when he saw it so lively, and turned away to brush his cassock. When he laid his surplice over his shoulders the white caused such a flash from the mirror he turned to almost purr in appreciation of his shape and Mrs Watts's excellent ironing.

I will give of my very best to the service, he told himself, groping for a humble attitude but overruled by the thought of "Abide With Me" and his voice raised above the others (for Una's ears).

His eyes did keep fairly clear of Una up until the graveside service when a wind came up suddenly and flung itself among the ladies' gowns. Most pressed black gloves to their thighs but Una used both hands to hold a little hat with upturned brim. A tweed cape, pale blue to match the trimming on her dress, lifted and came over her hat so that she had to shake it back, keeping a grip on her handbag and prayer book.

Edwards, saying the last prayers, had to keep his eyes on the tipping edge of the coffin, taking earth with it as it grazed the edges of the cavity, and he had to fight an urge to smooth Una's cape back in place. In spite of the chilly mid-winter day, he felt a film of cold sweat at his collar and a moisture on his hands which he hoped Una would not feel through her gloves, for he was looking forward to shaking hands with her, although this was still some time off.

It being his first funeral he had not thought of an invitation back to Honeysuckle for refreshments until it came from Enid, and he forgot himself to look hastily Una's way and see her with her gaze on a bank of distant oak trees and her fingers like scissors holding her cape to her waist, even narrower than Edwards thought at first.

The older one asks naturally, he thought, noting that even this gave him a small shiver of pleasure. He thought of his mother's mouth approving and her anxious eyes on his father begging his approval but ready to go neutral if he didn't. Why am I thinking of Mother now, he wondered, hurrying to his horse and sulky, then having to loiter to allow the Herberts' Austin to get away to avoid the humiliation of it passing him.

There was an air of urgency about it, due perhaps to Enid, who sat forward in her seat ready to leap out and fly into the house when the car pulled up. She mentally ticked off the order of jobs to be done, eyeing the dreamy Una and deciding not to rely too heavily on her for help, and grateful she had made extra scones and jellied brawn, in the event of a buggyload of Turbetts, distant cousins who lived six miles the other side of Burragate.

But only May Turbett and her daughter Jinny came by sulky, Jinny at twenty-two being closest in age of the unattached Turbett females to the newly arrived Reverend Colin Edwards.

The Turbetts pulled over now to let the Austin have the middle of the road, Alex in his peaked tweed cap raising a free hand. The startled horse tipped the sulky backwards when it jumped with all four feet together, and looked wildly back beyond its blinkers wondering whether to step out and try and keep up with the odd contraption or take to the side of the road and shiver there with head down until the strange and frightening noise died away in the distance.

Inside the Austin the Herberts were quiet. Alex very privately was grateful to his late sister-in-law for this opportunity of showing the car to a fairly representative gathering of Wyndham people. George, between his sisters in the back seat, felt a sense of inferiority at his inability to drive, and the way Alex was in full possession it seemed unlikely he would have a chance to learn. He sided with his father that a new silo should have priority, but Alex, of whom Jack was a little frightened, got his way, and the car was one of only three or four in Wyndham. He talked so much about it the others wondered what he found to discuss before it came.

Jack next to him sat with a fold of purple jowl over his collar. The boys wore shirts with soft attached collars, but Jack clung to the stiff ones over which Enid toiled to get the shine he liked. Jack's eyes were on the road and his hands on both knees, pressing them hard, expecting the car to stop any moment. He tended to lean forward as if urging it to keep going, and Alex leaned back to show his confidence in the motor, and the more Alex leaned back the more Jack leaned forward until Alex shouted in anger.

"Sit back against the seat! That's what it's there for!"

Jack, infrequently receiving a command, obeyed in shock.

"Some people can't move with the times," Alex said, changing gears with no more than one or two quite mild jerks.

"Just look at it! You'd think it had a brain of its own," Alex said as the Austin sailed sedately on.

"I wouldn't mind a go at driving," George called out.

"Then sit in the front and watch me!" Alex said, "I don't make the seating arrangements!"

Enid as much to protect Jack as for any other reason put her face near his rapidly reddening neck.

"Please remember where we've been!"

They all remembered. Una remembered Edwards in the wind, it tearing his cassock backwards so that his thighs were clearly outlined. Enid was troubled at the memory of Henry climbing in the hearse, a converted Ford with a coat of new black paint. He should not have taken a seat beside Cecil Grant, but should have travelled home with them in the family car. She only saw his back and thought it rebuked them for all their aloofness to his dead wife. Enid moved her shoulders under her moire silk, but this did not shake off the guilt which stuck and rubbed at her skin as if the seams were weighted. Jack's good Chesterfield overcoat was weighted too, as if the dead girl sat there. He saw her again, wistful of eye when brave enough to meet his, which blinked intolerance and found something else more worthy of his gaze.

"I do not feel it has gone off all that well so far," Enid said in the kitchen, stacking extra china on a tray to almost race with it to the living room.

Una raised questioning eyebrows above the scones she was buttering, keeping the rest of her face dreamy.

"For one thing, Henry should have ridden home with us! The chief mourner!" Enid was back unstacking the big meat dishes which would take the boiled fowls, their greyish white sweating skins to be scattered with parsley she picked from the garden soon after dawn that morning.

Una rushed to the stove flinging her apron over her head, pretending she was overcome by smoke, when in fact she was overcome by uncontrolled giggling.

The chief mourner! Oh, dear me I'll explode, she

thought. Enid saw the crossed straps of her white apron shaking over her black back.

"I also thought your blue cape was wrong," Enid said. "Blowing about like it did."

Una smoothed her apron down and tipped her chin up, a snap in her brown eyes.

"I'll pin it to my waist for the next funeral!" she said.

"Curb your disrespectful tongue!" Enid said. "The Turbetts are here already!" Their horse, rough bred and rough coated, had outpaced the sleeker animals, and Enid had to show them to the bedroom to wash at the china basin. They slid their eyes from left to right to take in the details of the room, sniffing both in appreciation and disdain at the French soap Enid had set out for the visitors.

Back in the kitchen Enid peeled off her apron.

"Henry and Cecil Grant are drinking rum as you would expect!" Cecil had noted the apron with a hungry eye. No one else would see it!

"Nothing seems to be going right!"

Una took off her apron too. She found joy in the fresh sight of her dress gathered gently across her bust, fastened with jet buttons. He would see it without the cape!

There were many more in the front room now and their voices reached the kitchen as the door slapped to and fro with the girls going in and out.

Like the creek after rain, Una thought of the babble. She saw it brown with scattered foam, flattening the reeds at it rushed along. Had he seen it?

She saw them together on a high bank looking down with the bush all around them fresh with wetness, their sides nearly touching.

Enid put the two big teapots on a tray, the signal that this was the last job, and looking the kitchen over for defects, for there would be eyes looking for them when the washing up was on, told Una to bring the milk and follow her.

He was standing with Jack, holding his hat, with his face a little ruddy from the cold or the fire George had got going, leaping and crackling as if it was another person adding to the talk. Una suspected he saw her for he turned quite abruptly giving more of his attention to Jack and moved his hat further up his chest. Una and Enid saw the hat at the one time, Una lowering the milk jug and Enid the teapot, excusing herself to May Turbett and her raised teacup, and going to Edwards she took his hat to lay it on a music stand, giving it a distinction above the others piled on a table inside the front door.

Una, pouring too much milk in May Turbett's teacup, splashed some on the table when Mrs Turbett jerked her cup away, and Edwards, surrendering his hat to Enid, saw Una move the tray to cover the splash and was torn between a desire to smile at the little face she pulled and to pay closer attention to Enid's eyes, thoughtful and grey green in colour.

He saw more of the eyes for they came closer to his own when she moved him and Jack to a tapestry-covered lovers' seat near a chiffonier and seconds later was back with plates of meat and buttered bread and tea expertly handled.

"Thank you, Miss Herbert," Edwards said. "But you shouldn't be waiting on us with so many to look after."

Jack gave a small but telling snort. "Bring the pickles, Enid," he said a trifle tersely.

"Of course, Father," Enid said finding them on the table and after spooning some on Jack's plate, held the spoon, a question mark like her eyes, above Edwards's plate.

"Thank you," he said, although he didn't know whether he wanted them.

Her face looked a little sad, he thought. Of course it would be. A family death! Although you would hardly believe it, scanning the faces in the room. The people's throats, unclogged after a rapid intake of meat and Enid's good bread, were sending forth a spatter of words, and sometimes a sharp cackle of laughter which caused Enid to stretch her quite long neck until it appeared to rise above everyone else, simmering the noise down, like a boiling pot removed from high heat.

Mrs Ena Grant, still in a glow of satisfaction on being asked back to the house, was making a good meal to save on tea, and should Cecil Grant call in before returning to Bega (he was a cousin on her husband's side) there would be no need to offer food after this. Violet wasn't here, she noticed, although she was at the church. What would become of the child? Henry, by the mantlepiece, seemed to be handling his grief well, talking to a former girlfriend Lila Johnstone, now bethrothed to one of the Power boys. Henry seemed already to have shaken off responsibility for the child, judging by his habit of lifting his shoulders now and again, and giving a lot of attention to the cigarette between his fingers. Ena could not see him taking the child back to Sydney to his mother's relatives, even if Jack supplied an escort in Enid, Una or Violet.

As soon as she decently could she would ask, but it seemed safe to assume the child would stay with Violet. If passed over to Enid and Una that would put a spoke in their wheel, dressing to kill as they did and off to the Bega races and the Sydney Show and anything worth while at Candelo and Pambula. Ena with her hand temporarily empty of food picked like a small brown dusty bird at the crumbs in her saucer, and inhaled a new smell from the kitchen which was doubtless another cake, slipped into the oven since the meal started. They were a capable pair, the

Herbert girls, no denying it, but she wouldn't want their grocery bill, thank you very much! She put her feet out from under her chair admiring her new shoes of brown leather and looked at other women's feet. Jinny Turbett was in large clumsy lace-ups. She would never catch a man in footwear like that! When Ena had the chance she would mention to May Turbett the new stock in for spring, beige and light tan, slender with narrow straps at the instep, in Jinny's size.

"I don't mind if I do!" she said when Enid came by with the new cake. Trying not to eat too fast she looked the company over. The men were bright eyed with their talk of spring crops and new cows coming in, for it looked like a good season. The flowers at the burial showed that frosts had not been too heavy. There would be money around and Ena would get her share across the counter of the store.

You can say what you like, she said to herself, accepting more tea from the pot Una held. I quite enjoy a good funeral.

Edwards was the last to leave, having hoped for another chance to speak to Una, and wanting the cars and superior buggies and sulkies out of the way before he set off. He was troubled by this pattern of behaviour, feeling the day would come when he would have no choice but to depart with a gathering of faces staring at the wobbling wheels and peeling paint of his sulky and his horse's rump, resembling coarse dark sandpaper worn thin in places.

"Wherever and whenever it is I pray for a good sharp bend to get me out of sight as quickly as possible," he told himself (speaking aloud too) on numerous occasions.

Had he been aware of Una at the kitchen window, he would have been grateful there were no early bends on the road back to St Jude's.

Una was at the end of the small table with her face between the window frame and the edge of the blind, not causing even a flutter of the curtain. She smiled to herself at the comical picture he presented, for he was still new to handling a horse and sulky and did not hold the reins confidently on his knee but had them raised in the air and his head inclined to one side in the listening pose that was becoming familiar to her.

She dreamed on for a moment when the road was empty then turned and found Enid, who had slipped into the kitchen for the broom to brush crumbs from the precious living room linoleum.

Liquid eyes black as treacle slipped over Enid and grey green ones surveyed the top of Una's head.

Enid just slightly swung the broom as she went away.

8

Violet was angry at missing the best part of the funeral. She was able to leave Small Henry only long enough to go to the church, a five minutes walk from her place. He should sleep throughout the half hour service, and if he didn't a cry would do him no harm. She frequently told her patients this but did not take her own advice with ultimate confidence.

Before leaving she lingered by him, looking with concern not love on his mauve coloured face, even in sleep wearing a pinched look, not completely trusting, which was communicated to Violet.

"I don't trust the little bugger," she said aloud, having shouted around sleeping babies all her nursing days, believing them to be insensitive to sound.

He merely drew a deep breath that shuddered his frail frame and slept on under Violet's gaze as she stood in her black mannish two piece suit she favoured for the air of professionalism it gave her.

Ned heard her from the kitchen and coughed. The cough said see if there is anything I need before you go off, for he was not going to the funeral. He had not said so for Ned had little or no use for words. While Violet laid out her suit and cream silk blouse, answering Ned in his own language, he put a second flannel on with old khaki trousers and dragged on old military boots almost white with age. Violet took her best black shoes from the wardrobe and dropped them angrily by a chair. Ned could buy some good clothes and be there today as smart as any of the other Herbert men! She flung her head back at the mirror and dabbed perfume under her rather heavy jaws, thinking her good creamy skin would draw its quota of admiring glances.

Damn Ned if he was fool enough to wallow in self pity for the rest of his life! But she felt a need to mention Small Henry in addition to leaving his door wide open by way of saying he was there if there was a fire and would Ned oblige by snatching him and making a dash for safety.

Ned built up big fires in summer and winter in the kitchen stove and front room. Often he sat close enough to set himself alight and dozed off with his newspaper (one from a pile Violet saved while he was at the war and wished she hadn't) tipped dangerously towards the flames. The crackling of the fire would startle him and in the early days Violet would put his head to her breast and stroke passionately at his hair, trying to erase the memory of the gunfire when Ned reared up wild eyed and agitated.

Now she rebuked him for the kind of wood he was bringing from the bush.

"That wattle farts like a bullocky, Ned!" she said. "Get some box for goodness sake, or something that burns without waking the dead!"

She was ready to go and the service was about to start and all she could do was push the logs together in the grate with the toe of her shoe and say in a loud voice she would be back (unfortunately) before you could turn around.

"Of course," Ellen Power said, nodding under her fake fur hat when they were all about to go to the cemetery and Violet had to turn and go the opposite way. "You are the right one to have charge of the poor young thing!"

Part of Violet bristled at this — Wyndham deciding it was she who would take Small Henry and rear him!

Another part accepted readily this tribute to her status and capabilities as a nurse.

But she looked with resentment at Enid and Una climbing unencumbered into the Austin to go to the cemetery. Violet had not seen the cemetery since Nellie's burial. All denominations used it, the cost of the land being shared between Catholics, Anglicans and Presbyterians, there being too few Methodists in Wyndham to bear a share, and needing to change their religion on their deathbeds or have their bodies bumped over many miles to Candelo or Pambula. Wide strips of grass were planted to divide the sections. But Wyndham grew careless of tending it and allowed growth to run riot, so that Michaelmas daisies, a favourite of Kathleen O'Toole, struggling weakly on her grave, flung their seed onto the grave of Dora MacDonald where they grew luxuriantly, mocking the barriers of religion and the fact that Kathleen and Dora were bitter enemies in life.

Violet would have liked to see where Henry's young wife was buried in the Herbert plot. Quite a distance from Nellie, she would reckon, and as far towards the edge as they could get her. They would be out there with their sorrowful faces fooling everyone (mostly the Reverend Colin Edwards) into believing they were mourning the girl, when their thoughts would be with Nellie.

Violet saw again the girl's face white as the bed sheets. She had turned it from them, weak as she must have been, lowered lids on those protruding eyes, as if glad at last to be able to dismiss them. Violet had slapped the child to life, causing it to scream lustily, and Una to clap her hands to her ears with her face almost as pale as the girl's. Well, they had a lot to learn and God help the child if it was left in their care, although nothing was settled by any means.

Leave them to stew on, while she enjoyed their sucking

up to her and their new respect at her handling of Small Henry. His motley legs were a sign of good health, she had said, towelling them hard enough to break them, and she was openly scornful of Una's fear of touching his pulsing scalp under hair like the wet fur on a kitten.

Violet plodded on home, nodding to Tom Grant opening up the shop under instructions from Ena to close it, as a mark of respect to the dead, only during the church service, and pay no heed to Rachel Holmes shutting the post office for the day. Rachel was a Herbert cousin, widowed in the war, with her husband's name on the new monument, and a healthy appetite for socializing. Violet's anger simmered stronger at the thought of Rachel on the Honeysuckle couch eating largely of good Herbert fare.

Never mind, never mind, none of them know what's around the corner, Violet said to herself seeing Ned in the dim hallway of Albert Lane as still as a monument raised to himself. He had closed the door of Small Henry's room but the child's shrieking was audible and Violet, to fuel Ned's agitation, took her time in getting out of her good clothes and into the kitchen to mix a bottle.

By the time Violet had the teat in Small Henry's mouth Ned had gone towards the bush, past the pens where the fowls set up a squawk rivalling Small Henry's, and threw themselves frantically against the wire, unable after more than a year to accept the fact that Ned had never tossed even a breadcrust their way.

Ah well, I should be grateful for a bit of a racket, God knows it's deadly quiet around here most of the time, Violet said to herself holding Small Henry well down on her lap to feed him where other women might have pressed him to their chest.

He sucked eagerly, eyes squeezed shut, moving a tiny ear in his greed and Violet's anger ran from her tight chest downwards to die under the weight of the tiny body. She fell to dreaming about the hospital. More shelves here, she said to herself, taking the bottle from an outraged Small Henry's mouth and pointing the teat towards a corner of the room. George can run them up for me, Una can hem the sheets and napkins, Enid can pass over some of that glut of vegetables she often had.

Money! I will need money though. She had very little of her own left over from confinement cases (some debts were still outstanding) as she liked new clothes, and, when shopping in Bega with Enid and Una, was easily carried away on the tide of their enthusiasm.

Ned's war pension went into the bank barely touched, for there was the monthly cheque from Halloween, and they lived cheaply as it was fast proving a waste of time and money cooking for Ned. He would turn away from the meat and vegetables she served him saying he saw nothing like that for months on end "over there."

"Well, you're over here now Ned," she would answer, tipping his plateful onto hers, and cursing him later when her stomach tightened with wind from the turnips and cauliflower. "And if you die of malnutrition, that's your lookout!"

She knew she would have no such ready answer when Ned refused her request for a hundred pounds to set up the hospital.

She stood suddenly, Small Henry having finished his bottle and fallen asleep. The violent movement should have unleashed the contents of his stomach and flung them down Violet's back. But Small Henry in response to the rubbing she gave his back, hard enough to dislodge a portion of his skin, opened his lips to belch, then tucked them up again, moist with a trickle of milk and settled back into a deep, sighing sleep.

"Listen to that!" Violet cried, binding him in his blanket and ignoring the flopping of his head from side to side. "I drag the wind out of them if it's the last thing I do!"

In his room she laid him in his basket sitting on an old deal table and shoved it noisily against the wall, standing by Small Henry's head to survey the rest of the room.

"Three cots, more shelves and the table," (kicked with her foot) "will be for bathing them on!"

She flung up both windows for the chilly winter air to rush into the room as if there were already a roomful to breathe it, and closed the door behind her.

She looked down the hall imagining people trooping in, women heavy with child, men tiptoeing nervously on the linoleum, herself straight of back in her blue and white striped cambric uniform, severe and unsmiling to let them know at once she would tolerate no blubbering nonsense.

I feel it all coming closer, she said to herself, turning towards the kitchen and allowing the vision to disappear for the present.

There was Ned inside the back door, his clothes carrying damp patches and twigs from his tramp through the bush, and his eyes on Small Henry's door, asking if he had been returned to Honeysuckle yet.

Not as bloody close though as I would like, she went on thinking, flinging a cloth on the table for dinner.

9

Violet walked to Honeysuckle next day, seeing inside the open front door a packed suitcase. As she looked Henry appeared with another. He lowered his eyes on seeing Violet as if to shut away the sight of Small Henry in the crook of her arm. With his foot he pushed the cases together. Violet knew his wife's things were in the smaller one, and he was taking them to Sydney to hand over to her brother living in the slums with a wife who would receive them with no small degree of pleasure, having a brood of children and an unreliable breadwinner in her husband.

Violet remembered then that this was the first day since the funeral the mail car was going all the way to Nowra, the nearest railhead to meet the train to Sydney. No one had taken the trouble to let her know, but what else would you expect, Violet thought, lifting Small Henry to her shoulder with a swooping motion so that Henry's eyes were drawn for a second to his shawl. She threw Enid's arrangement of cushions on the couch roughly together to make a bed for Small Henry, and Enid coming into the living room saw and winced. Una came in behind, her face brightening at the sight of Violet and the baby who in some vague way she connected with Edwards.

She took the piano seat and Enid temporarily suspended her job of turning out the room where Henry's wife's body had lain, the last chore in restoring the house to its former order. Violet took a chair at the foot of the couch, not too close lest she give the impression of a deep bond of affection between her and Small Henry, but close enough to show at this stage she was in charge of him.

"Has he been behaving?" Enid said, uncertain that this was a suitable question.

"Crying all the time, like most newborn babies!" Violet said.

Enid felt the beautiful peace of the house.

"And how is Ned?" she said, actually seeking information on Ned's reaction to the intrusion of Small Henry.

"The same!" Violet said sharply. They all blamed Ned's condition on the war, and one day pretty soon she would say right out that Ned hadn't found old Pheobe's tree yet, but he was getting terribly close.

"Just as well I came," she said testily to Henry on a chair, smoking with his elbows on his knees and his eyes mostly on the floor. "You wouldn't have seen him before you left!"

He's not seeing too much of him now, Enid thought drily.

Henry got up and carried his cases to the verandah. Una followed, standing on the verandah stonework while Henry sat on the edge. Many times in the past she had stood and he had sat, in similar poses, waiting for the car to take her back to school. Her black clad legs were long and thin and her clothes had always seemed too big for her, particularly the mushroom hat with a binding of ribbon at the edge, brown like her eyes, slits of rebellion under a forehead of thick hair.

She had followed him about in the holidays, mostly to the racecourse where dead and whitened tree trunks, narrow as a woman's body, had been made into seats and a stand for judges to watch the races, and a counter to serve beer on, and logs jammed together and bound with leather at either end. The timber was weathered smooth as silk, particularly that making the rough ladder they climbed to the judges' stand, he following, wondering at the mystery between her legs where they disappeared under the hem of an old cotton holiday dress, and when they sat together, she studying the back of his neck, tanned by the sun, except where his fair hair grew in a duck's tail, pushed about by his collar.

Now at nineteen and twenty-three the gap had widened between them, although her heart was soft towards him, and she might have cried before the car came, had she not kept her teeth together and her chin up. She had joined her hands together behind her and was beating them gently on her rump as she used to do to steady herself waiting for the mail car to school.

When she slid her eyes around cautiously to look at him, she saw his head down and only a piece of fair cheek and a red ear visible above his overcoat collar, giving him an air of innocence as great as when they climbed the racecourse ladder.

They heard the mail car rumbling towards them, and Violet and Enid came onto the verandah.

Una looked for Small Henry, but there was nothing to show of him except the crumpled front of Violet's grey morrocain dress where he had lain. Only that to show Small Henry had been born! Una looked back to the living room, longing for him to wake and cry for the sound to follow Henry, who was climbing into the car. Something for him to carry away!

But he was gone like the grass seeds she had watched from the racecourse ladder, blown by the wind to rest somewhere. Like a grass seed too, Henry had stopped to give roots to the child, and now he was blown away again.

Jack, Alex and George, working in the corn paddock, watched the car carry Henry off. They were not close enough to each other to speak. There was no reason to pause in their work either, for they could look and listen while they tore the corn from the stalks, now dank and smelling of mould, the long silken tassels turned to dead strings.

Alex compared the sound of the engine to that of the Austin. The mail car was a Ford and both Bob Twyford the driver and Cecil Grant (with his Ford hearse) had tried to persuade Alex to buy a similar make. Well, listen to that engine, growling and straining like a mongrel dog on a leash! The Austin purred like a well fed kitten.

Dinner would be in an hour and he would look in on it on his way to the house. As a boy Alex had dreamed of finding an old chest and tearing it open, half blinded by the jewels inside. His Austin was like that inside the old dark shed, when his eyes could pick it out after the bright sunlight outside. Bright as a jewel with its deep green paintwork and cream wheel spokes, warm brown polished wood inside, blending with the finest leather. If Henry had stayed he would be hankering for a licence to drive it. He was gone now! Even straining your ears you could barely hear that labouring engine. There was Jack with his back to the road, just slightly slower in stamping the corn stalks into the earth. The old geezer didn't like Henry going, not that he gave too much away!

Jack put Henry to one side to think of the girl. It was all her fault, dead as she might be! She would have told Henry on the quiet she wanted to go back to Sydney when the baby was born, he going ahead to find a job and somewhere to live, apart from their former squashed existence in her brother's rented rooms in Surry Hills, which became intolerable and brought them to Honeysuckle for minimal living costs and Violet to deliver the baby for nothing.

Jack had been prepared to restore Henry's former wage and give them the old house he and Nellie had lived in before Honeysuckle was built a mile away close to the new road.

Jack came upon her once sitting on the narrow little verandah rubbing her feet gently into the earth. He had pulled his horse up, hidden by a thicket of eucalyptus, and watched the girl get up and clear a window of cobwebs to look in. Not much to see but four rooms and a fireplace that would take a stove and had a chimney still in working order. Nellie had made a home of it! He was beginning to think grudgingly that the girl might too, when she moved to the end of the verandah, standing so that her big stomach became a silhouette. Jack wheeled his horse then and cantered away, too angry to care whether she had seen or not. Those stomachs on women offended him! The girl had trapped Henry, there was no doubt of that. He was glad he did not have to look at her that evening at tea, for she had gone to bed with stomach cramps, he overhead Enid say, and Henry went off to play cards at the Hickeys.

George blamed the girl too, but had envied Henry, mostly at night, George's room being next to theirs. He heard, or imagined he heard, the thud of Henry's body leaving hers, and the stirring of bed springs as he gathered the bedclothes around him for sleep. A woman with you in bed! Violet next to him! He needed to rub his face into the pillow to rub her away. The girl spoke little in the daytime in the Herberts' company, and he listened hard at night for her voice, thin and wispy like her hair.

She had a short cut, one of the few in Wyndham, convincing Jack that here was another reason why she got herself in trouble.

Girls with long hair wouldn't be free with their favours, Jack thought, with his mind on Enid.

George had to keep in mind Violet's haircut. But that was different, she was a nurse and it was convenient with her cap.

She had given them a demonstration when she returned from having the cut in Bega. Even Jack did not turn at once from the sight of the starched white cap sitting as easily as an upturned cup on Violet's thick hair, black as ebony and showing all that lovely white neck.

George tipped a bag of corn into the dray causing it to tip and Dolly in the shafts to shake her harness by way of telling him to steady on.

"Steady on yourself", George said. "I might find some other use for your useless legs after this!"

He had just thought of it, but there might be an excuse to go to Wyndham in the sulky after dinner and call on Violet to drink tea with her and eat of the cake she kept for him, a bit rough on the outside, not professional like Enid's but full of sultanas and peel inside, just to his taste (rather like Violet). There would be no more work on the corn, for Alex was moving steers to the south paddock and Jack was off to the share farm where a famiy called Skinner with six children were tenants. Jack needed to keep an eye on the place. Skinner was lazy but not so his wife, who had a hard, lean body and unusually long arms and legs. He had seen her with a foot and a hand steer a great bristly boar into a pen, the pig blinking a hateful eye but doing no more than grunt low as he scrambled over the rails. They were in need of repair, as you would expect, but Skinner was waiting for George to come and do the job.

Here was Jack now pulling his braces over his shoulders, a sign they were leaving for the house. George would go ahead to open up the shed where the corn was stored, feeling his way inside with hanging harness slapping his face and rats and mice scuttling for safety. Alex would look in on the car in the neighbouring shed, opening the back door and scraping at the floor with his fingers to remove any twigs and fragments of earth left there by shoes after the funeral. They were a pretty careless lot!

Alex stayed there until the corn was in the shed and Jack was unharnessing Dolly and George made his way towards the house. The fire in the living room was burning well judging by the smoke from the chimney. George knew there was curry for dinner made from the meats over from the funeral meal. He felt the hollowing out of his stomach to take it and the taste buds in his mouth at the ready. He hoped no one had called right on dinner time, as sometimes happened. Enid thinned the helpings out if she had not cooked more than enough and it was his plate that was lighter than Jack's or Alex's. What was this? There was someone there, a shape with Enid and Una in the garden looking down at the flower beds. But it was Violet! He had thought with that baby to care for he would hardly see her now. But there she was! Violet! Staying for dinner! He clicked the back gate open louder than was necessary and she was the first to turn her face. It softened too and the mouth stretched at the corners digging into her creamy cheek. She was pleased to see him, though the others weren't, pulling faces at the thought of having to go inside and dish up the dinner. Violet could have most of his!

10

But George was not happy through dinner, although he got a good helping of curry and the pudding was trifle, using up some of the cake left over from the funeral.

The baby squirmed and whimpered throughout the meal and Violet had her body screwed towards it a lot of the time. Enid suggested putting it in a bedroom, in the washing basket with pillows (already the good cushions were getting creased with all that writhing). But Violet set a stubborn mouth. Let them see what she had to put up with and what could be their lot if she decided to pass him back to them. Back to their ordered ways as if nothing had happened! Look at the sparkling clean house and hers littered with napkins and nightdresses and basins for sterilizing bottles, as well as Ned's mess. (But she was a poor housekeeper at any time.) Wait till she got the hospital though! They would see then the real meaning of cleanliness and order.

"Why don't you feed him?" Enid said coming in with freshly made tea when Una had taken the pudding plates away, and Small Henry was squealing in an alarming way.

"It's crying with flatulence," Violet said for she tended to use medical terms when she had an audience. "Feeding it would make it worse." She looked at the grandfather clock in the corner and Una's alarmed eyes rivetted on it too as if willing the hands to move faster. "It's a good half hour to its feed time."

Another half hour! The news hit them with such force,

Jack and Alex rose from the table simultaneously, and George would have got up too if Violet had not stayed where she was, her tea tucked between her elbows supporting her chin. She was not bothering to look back on the child now but allowing it to bellow on, fighting its way out of the constricting blanket. Una was afraid Small Henry would smother and her frightened eyes ran from what was visible of his purple face and neck to Violet's unconcerned profile.

"You're finished, George!" Una said as if she had to order someone to do something. George pushed his chair back, although he felt he had eaten nothing. He had seen many kittens and puppies newly born, but they mostly lay sleeping, squirming gently when awake, murmuring with a thin sound as if grateful to be alive.

This was something different, this shouting at the world as if it was not to Small Henry's liking, and someone had better set about effecting a remedy or he would squeal himself to death.

Violet got up suddenly and lifted him from the cushions. He stopped crying, and Enid lifted a relieved face from the cups she was stacking and Una brought her hands together in a clap under her chin and left them there in a praying pose.

"Nothing in the world wrong with him," Violet said, binding him in his blanket from the neck down and moving to lay him down again.

"Don't!" Una cried. "Let me have a go!"

"A go at what?" said Violet, poised with Small Henry in the air, his face dropped sideways and his eyes closed.

"Well, he might cry again!" Una said.

"A fat lot you could do if he did," Violet said, taking a spare blanket from her bag and tucking it over Small

Henry and under the cushions, as if there was a danger of his escaping.

"Well," Una said looking at the clock. "It's so close to his feed time shouldn't we keep him awake?" (Five minutes had gone by.)

"I'll mighty soon wake him when it's feed time!" Violet said, returning to the table and pouring herself more tea.

Small Henry snorted and squeaked and was silent a couple of times, fooled into thinking the edge of the blanket was a bottle teat. Jack and Alex left for their rooms, like soldiers sneaking away before the firing started up again. Enid noiselessly tidied the music inside the piano stool and Una sat where she could get a full view of the clockface.

George by the fireplace marvelled at the changes in the room. The tablecloth was askew with Violet turning so often to look at Small Henry, the blind was down nearly to the window sill above his head when it was usually thrown high to let in what winter sun was about and the sight of a passing rider on horseback, buggy or car. There was only a small glow from the fire. He should put more wood on, but lifting his head he saw as much as felt the quiet. Small Henry had fallen asleep again. He dare not make a noise with the dropping of a log, and putting out a foot gingerly put some ends together sweating gently and catching a heavy frown from Una.

Blast Henry to bring them to this! Look what he left behind this time! Usually it was a big bill for tobacco at Grant's store, and heaven knows there was plenty said about that for weeks afterwards.

Even Violet was still thoughtfully marking the tablecloth with the handle of her teaspoon. Enid was now pulling the cloth from under the cruet and the few odd things left on the table without even a tinkle of silver and Una moved up silently to help. Violet took the cue and raised her cup from her saucer so there wasn't even the tiniest grind of china.

He couldn't stay here, his joints would creak, his stomach would rumble, he would be responsible for a noise that would waken that small ruling king with his purple face faded now to the beauty of a pale mauve plover's egg. He had seen one in a nest once and stared barely believing the life inside it. Small Henry was a living thing, no doubt about that.

George would get outside, escape this oppressive atmosphere, it was a woman's world, in spite of Small Henry, no place for him just now! He took large jerking steps to the front door, but Violet turned on her chair when he cupped the knob in his hands only inches from Small Henry's head. She frowned on his hands so he dropped them and resumed his giant jerking footsteps, walking with heels raised, fearful of a squeak from the linoleum, to the door leading to the hall past the bedrooms — left open by Jack and Alex thank heavens! — and outside into the back yard.

There the cold hit him and he shivered against a verandah post while the wind laid flat the short pale grass around Enid's roses, for she had a new planting in beds adjacent to the back verandah in addition to those in the big side garden, and would, he sometimes felt, extend it all to the dairy half a mile away if given a chance.

He took a spade from the garden shed to warm himself with some digging of the vegetable patch. Looking up he saw through the window Una in the kitchen mincing about mocking him with his tweed cap on, imitating his gait.

George put his head down and rubbed the dirt from a carrot he had sliced through.

"Eat it up, George," Una called. "Never mind the dirt since you must be starving!"

Enid came past her and put her head out the window.

"You can drive Violet home if you like, George!"

Well that was more like it! He swung wildly into the digging hiding his joyful face from them, not allowing them to see his great wide grin, although it almost set his ears twitching and sent sparks of delight from the back of his neck.

Una threw George's cap to land expertly on a peg in the hall, then sauntered to the other window to beat her knuckles on the edge of the table below and stare onto the garden, or more likely the empty road. Enid, not sure why, wanted to cut across her thoughts whatever they were.

"You can bring in some of the clothes," she said. "The sheets were quite dry when I felt them earlier." The washing was not done on Monday as usual, but a day late because of the funeral. It threw the week's routine out and Enid would not feel totally comfortable until things were right back to normal. Una slipped into the hall and taking an old coat from a peg shrugged herself into it. She was moving fast for a change. "Take the basket and don't dump the things on the ground now," Enid said, hoping the words would cause Una to turn her face and Enid to read her expression. A baffling girl! Una went without the basket and Enid opened the back door to call her, but she was walking swiftly under the clothesline and through the sliprails of the house paddock, up the short rise towards the dairy and soon would be out of sight.

The wretched girl! thought Enid, angry enough to forget the sleeping Small Henry and make quite a clatter with the washing up. She poured water on crockery almost without sound, though, when Violet slipped into the room, soundlessly, as large women often move, to set about mixing Small Henry's bottle.

Una will miss seeing him fed, that's good! I'm glad! Enid decided she would leave the things to soak and find something to do in the living room if Violet fed him there. Violet was swirling milk inside the bottle now and Enid noted the bluish tinge not full strength. How did she know these things, she wondered feeling inadequate, a new experience for Enid. How did people know what to do with small babies? Given Violet was a nurse, she had never raised a child of her own, and here she was, eyes on the kitchen clock and the too hot bottle on her morrocain knee cooling to the right temperature — what would that be? — for Small Henry's mouth.

"Una's gone wandering off," Enid said. (Surely the bottle was ready now!) "She'll do it once too often and I'll be speaking to Father!"

"Perhaps she's taken the track to the rectory," Violet said. "Then there'll be good reason to speak to Father!" She had her back to Enid, sauntering off to Small Henry, leaving Enid to guess accurately the malicious smirk on her face.

It took a while for Enid to gather her thoughts and when she did she was in front of the hall mirror, angry that her nose had gone red. She pinched and slapped at it and wished for a comb to do her hair. It might not be so noticeable then! She rebelled anew at Una, leaving her with all the afternoon work to do, and no time to wash and change her dress and shoes. You never know who might come!

After a while she went into the living room to set a small table in case Jack wanted his afternoon tea by the fire.

That done, she rearranged some daisies in a brass jardeniere that had arrived too late for the funeral. She didn't have the kind growing so would save some for seed when they were ready to throw out. A peppery smell was in her nostrils — from the flowers or Small Henry? He was finished feeding, spread out like a frog on her cushions, the navel of his egg-shaped belly moist and bloody, legs no thicker than pipe stems, feet too long for them. His genitals lay like a mound of used tissue paper and Enid thought they might detach themselves the way Violet was ruthlessly wiping around them as she put him in a dry napkin. Of course she had set him crying again! She was too rough with him, showing off perhaps, how dare she? The small innocent thing, the victim! She felt the beginning of a small ache somewhere around her wrists and elbows, and then dropped her arms to her sides quickly lest Violet see them partly outstretched. Violet bound him in his blanket and flung him over her shoulder to go to the kitchen and gather up anything left there. Enid saw Small Henry's small squashed face on Violet's shoulder sailing away from her. She turned back to stroke the creases from her cushions in an automatic way.

A smell rose from them. Of warm flesh and urine and newness, that peppery smell again. And faintly of blood.

And tenderness and terror.

11

George put on his best trousers to take Violet home. Enid kept the smell of Small Henry close to her when she carried the bag with his wet napkins and bottle to hand it to Violet in the sulky. He was lost to her almost at once due to Violet's bulk. She's nearly as wide as the sulky seat, Enid said to herself going inside.

The sulky purred along and so did George. The air was rushing past them clear and cold, making Small Henry's face a deeper purple. Fresh air was good for him according to Violet, who told her mothers to get their babies out in the air for some time every day and not swaddle them too much or have them close enough to the fire to catch alight.

This thought reminded her of Ned. He might not be home though, out of the way in the bush somewhere and she could sit with George over the kitchen table in intimate talk. The news of her hospital was banked up there in her stout chest and George's red ear was close by, ready for a stream of words.

George was pacing Dolly out swiftly, not such a good idea in one way if he got to Albert Lane and found Ned at home. But he was dreaming of driving the Austin with the side curtains up and Violet beside him, the child somewhere else. He slapped Dolly into top speed, swaying the sulky as the Austin swayed so that Violet needed to put the arm not holding Small Henry along the back of the sulky seat and George's tingling back came in contact with her fingers.

"Well, the place hasn't burned down at least," Violet said, although irritated at the difficulty of getting out of the sulky. She couldn't see the iron step past her skirt and might miss it.

You couldn't see down at all with this great bulk to hang onto! George leapt out and went around Dolly's head (keep steady while this is on, you perverse old nag!) to help Violet down. She handed him Small Henry instead and his surprise was so great he nearly dropped him, looking up and down the street fearing someone would pop from a door or window and see him. Was he expected to go into the house and face Ned this way? But Violet, taking her time in hooking her bag onto her arm, hoisted Small Henry onto her own shoulder and George, turning hot then cold, was so confused he overlooked tying Dolly to a fence post, until Dolly took a warning step forward, suggesting he watch out for the consequences if she was a free agent.

Ned was in his corner of the kitchen couch, smoking and staring at the stove fire as if his one mission in life was to keep it going. Violet, having dumped Small Henry in his basket in the bedroom and closed the door, flung up the blind to show on the littered table the newspapers Ned was reading to tatters, a heel of bread he had been eating and a cup tipped over with cold black tea swamping the dish of butter beside it.

She made an angry show of cleaning it up, embarrassed that George, in spite of an association of many years, might make a comparison between her housekeeping and Enid's, and even irritated by George remaining standing with lowered head.

"Sit down, George!" she said. Here was another exasperating man needing directing all the time!

George sat and Ned went shuffling to the front room,

tucking his papers under his arm, as if they were all that was worth salvaging.

"Let him burn himself and his wretched papers to a cinder there if he wants to!" Violet cried, throwing a dipperful of water into a kettle that had puffed itself dry.

She sat at the table overcome with rage, trembling and with both hands before her face.

George longed to but didn't dare reach out and touch her wrist.

"George!" she said suddenly uncovering her face. "I'm going to open a hospital!"

George had the strange and foolish thought that she wanted somewhere to admit herself.

Or Ned?

Violet brought both hands down — slap! — upon the table and the heel of bread, overlooked in the clean up, bowled itself over. Question marks hung invisibly in the air between the two. "A hospital for midwifery cases, George " Violet said.

Where? said George's round eyes, grey like well water unfit for drinking, but useful in emergencies.

He looked down the back towards the fowl pens and down the hall to the closed front door as if the hospital would suddenly spring up for Violet.

"I need some help to get it started," she said, taking the lid off the teapot for the dipper of water in the kettle was already near the boil.

"Money?" said George, and Violet gave him a smile for his cleverness.

George had a bit put away. Alex had some steers of his own and George had pigs and when these were sold the returns boosted any savings from wages. (Jack did not pay too generously.)

The girls received no regular wages, but gifts of money

from Jack for clothes and occasional visits to Sydney or to the seaside towns of Pambula and Merimbula.

George thought of the bathing costume Una bought with money for her birthday six months ago. She ordered it secretly from a catalogue, for Jack would not approve anything so brazen, and showed it to him in secret too. It was a lovely thing of dark green wool with bands of orange at the sleeves running right up to the shoulder and around the scooped out neck. In its box of tissue paper George saw it a tender and sensual thing and would have liked Una to put it on for him, so that he could picture Violet in it. Violet would have strained the wool and her thighs would have come out of the green legs like thickly poured cream. George put her in the costume now, her breasts nearly brushing her teacup filling their green wool nests.

Her face was soft and happy — if it could always be that way! She sipped her tea, cut more cake for George and talked on in low tones like music whispered from piano keys. She would miss out on the two local women nearing the end of their pregnancies and booked into Mrs Black's at Candelo. Mrs Black was not as good a nurse as Violet, giving more attention to the horses she kept than to her patients, and known to go off and ride in a show, leaving a woman in labour in the care of her daughter Stella and a drunk doctor.

Here was Violet saying something that made his heart jump. If she had a spare room — ward, I mean! — she would take the occasional broken limb. Or a bad case of boils. George saw himself with one of his heavy winter colds that irritated Enid and Una, and Violet putting him into pyjamas and a bed fragrant with eucalyptus.

"Nothing infectious, though," she said, dashing his hopes and rising briskly in good imitation of the efficient matron.

She attacked the washing up as if already practising the ultimate in hygiene, finding a clean teatowel for George to wipe up. (At home he left all this to Enid and Una.) The day was closing in, the lemon tree casting a great shadow over one end of the back verandah. George hung his towel on the verandah line and taking a dipperful of corn from a sack in the wash-house, with the air of one who was part of the household, flung it to the fowls, who immediately turned from sad little bundles to a great screeching agitated tablecloth with grain running into a score of crevices.

He came inside to find Ned back by the kitchen stove and Violet standing by a corner of the table. She might have told Ned about the hospital! It was their secret, he didn't want anyone else sharing it! He took up his hat, trying to read her expression and Ned's, whose eyes were on the scarlet line around the stove door and soft pale hands were holding up a khaki knee. No, she hadn't said anything for her brown eyes were melting toffee with the dream stuck to them. He spun his hat on his hand which was his way of saying he was leaving.

"I'll walk you to the door, George," Violet said loudly as was her habit when she wanted Ned to be informed too.

They were passing Small Henry's door when he gave two or three warning grunts and by the time they reached the front verandah his wailing was rushing under the door and through the skylight above it. Violet's face tightened and her eyes snapped and her fists were closed and beat on the verandah rail.

"Listen to that! What would they do at Honeysuckle if that was ringing in their ears all day long? I'm here bearing it all, and I'm not even a Herbert!"

(Neither she was, thank God, neither she was!)

She went ahead of him, flinging the gate open and causing Dolly to swing her head inquiring if Violet was to be carried home as well as George. I'm not in favour of that, said the violent jerks following the swing, and the stamping of a front hoof.

"Steady on there!" George cried to Dolly, and he might have used the same words in a more gentle way to Violet.

"I'm having that hospital, George!" Violet cried. "See if any of them can stop me! I deserve it George! You know I deserve it!"

George leapt into the sulky and turned Dolly around. He raised the reins and set her pacing off, as if he were leading an army into battle and the prize was a hospital for Violet.

12

At Honeysuckle they were all quiet during tea, so quiet that the scrape of spoons on the last of their soup set up a squeaking chorus that normally would have set Una giggling, but she bore traces of a mutinous expression, brought about by a tirade of angry words from Enid for returning right on teatime.

Enid had no help from her to carve the jellied brawn and whip the potatoes, for she had to send Una off to change her dress and shoes and comb the leaves and twigs from her hair before Jack saw her.

Eating his brawn, George wondered if Violet could make it, dreaming of the familiarity of saying "Make some brawn, Violet." He imagined helping Violet with the patients' trays in the kitchen of her hospital. By heavens, he could almost say "their hospital"!

He lifted his head to look around the table, pitying the others stolidly eating. Their faces were as dull as their lives!

Jack was heavy jowelled because of a discovery at the share farm. Mrs Skinner was expecting again, and an air of neglect had already taken over. He and Alex and George would need to give a hand there or the spring crops would never go in. Henry would have been of some use if he had stayed! He would be in Sydney by morning among those smoking factories and dark little dens, where men and women sat drinking cheap wine and the trams went screeching along with sparks flying from wires overhead. There was more life there than in the people! Every couple of years Jack went to the Sydney Show, sometimes taking Enid and Una. He wanted to return home after two days. But of course the girls trudged about the streets and went into shops buying stuff they didn't need. Una one night at the hotel dining table talked about staying and sewing for one of the big shops. He soon put a stop to that!

He watched them now, eating in small ladylike mouthfuls the way women should, Una dreamy as usual and Enid with her efficient, no nonsense face, getting up to bring in the pudding, for they had it at teatime, as well as for dinner, as Nellie used to.

That girl dying made him think a lot of Nellie, although the two were in no way alike. (What would Nellie have thought of her!)

A week ago she was at this very table, sitting farther back than everyone else because of that great stomach. He had not even then abandoned the idea of her and Henry and the baby moving into the old cottage, although he knew the girls wanted them right out of the way. As if that would remove the disgrace brought to them.

Now she and Henry were gone there seemed hardly anyone at the table. A foolish thought that!`

When the girls had gone to the kitchen Jack brought up the subject of the delicate condition of Mrs Skinner. And that wretched man had seemed pleased to tell him!

Alex appeared unaffected by the news, going off to his room to read. George almost rose from his chair in his excitement. He wanted to get to Violet and tell her! A patient for the hospital! He wanted to be the first to tell Violet, see her eyes shine and her face go soft. It would be terrible if someone else got in first with the news!

He went off in a glow to measure the space in the lumber room where Enid wanted a closet to keep the place tidier.

If it was started in the next day or so there would be an excuse to go to Wyndham for nails and screws.

Enid came back to the table to sit with Jack and offer him freshly brewed tea. Una snapped the door shut on herself in the bedroom and Enid looked pointedly at it, so Jack had a fair idea that Una was the subject for discussion.

What was coming now? Jack moved his bulky body in his chair. There had been enough lately. Couldn't they settle down again content with their full bellies? His thoughts swung to Mrs Skinner as he saw her on the woodheap rubbing her arms, for she seemed cold huddled there, but she got up when she noticed him and walked with a show of dignity into the house.

Skinner said she was crook all the time now, sounding quite proud of himself. Jack had enough of full bellies with that girl dying and now the child whom he had avoided looking at so far. He didn't want full bellies on these girls, wondering why he should be thinking this! Never Enid and not Una if they kept a close watch on her. What was this Enid was saying?

"She needs a little holiday, I think, Father."

Well, that was a relief. Nothing more than a little holiday! He would give them some money each before the spring, and they could have a week in Sydney or at the seaside.

Violet and Ned would come as they usually did, although it would be awkward now with that baby. He wouldn't tolerate a repeat of mealtimes like their dinner today. Nellie had always kept small babies out of his way until he was ready for them. He had quite liked walking about the farm with them occasionally, showing them flowers and animals, their fat little rumps jigging with pleasure on his arm.

Nellie would hold his other arm, looking down on her skirt swishing about her ankles, glad her stomach was flat, he knew that!

He thought of the women's skirts at the funeral, getting higher and higher, showing legs that were once never seen out of bedrooms.

Nellie would sometimes lie on their bed, behind the closed bedroom door, and raise her nightgown above her knees, then her white legs and ankles would be raised too. And she would laugh, not unkindly, teasing and joyful, at him, normally painstaking and ponderous, trying to shed his trousers with speed.

He needed to drag himself away from all that, back to Enid saying something with eyes lowered onto her teacup.

"I couldn't get away of course, now that Violet has the baby to care for, it would be too much for her here with Ned and you and the boys."

Here was a how-do-you-do! Suggesting Una go away on her own! But Jack's jowls settled down with her next words.

"She could go to Merimbula and have a week there with the cousins!"

Percy Herbert, a brother of Jack and Ned, owned and ran a hotel at the coastal town, less frequented by the family for holidays than the closer Pambula.

Percy and his wife Alice had six daughters. Percy got out of farming and into the hotel trade. With all those girls, could you blame him? The eldest was Enid's age and besides Sadie there was Clara, Sybil, Annie, Bridget and Linda. The hotel was full of holidaying guests in the summer and travelling salesmen and fisherman in the winter.

Percy had land behind the hotel and kept cows and poultry and grew vegetables. He boasted about how well he was doing and what a better choice he made than to remain tied to farming like Jack and Ned.

His girls, a buxom lot, though not as refined looking as Enid and Una, were kept out of mischief with all the hotel work, and Percy considered them providential.

After practically ignoring them as small children, he enjoyed making his morning rounds and watching them fling the clean sheets on the beds, one on either side, their sturdy arms and well developed busts moving in time with their talk rippling from room to room.

Percy had little more to do than spend an hour every afternoon with the hotel books in his smoking room, and Alice brought him tea there. He received her civilly now that all those girls she bore had become a bonus.

Enid and Una had stayed there two or three times since Nellie's death and Jack saw no reason why Una couldn't go now (since Enid thought it a good idea) and he would pay for her room and meals like any guest.

An hour or so later Una was not taking to the idea at all.

"Go to Percy's I will not!" she just about shouted, snatching a blouse from the bed, for she was studying it, with the idea of cutting a pattern from it. She stuffed the blouse under her arm and sprawled on a chair like a rag doll flung down and furious about it. Enid looked guilty.

"Well you might look guilty!" Una said. "You suggested this to Father!"

"Father suggested it!" Enid said, not fully conscious of lying. It was for her own good!

"There's nothing there!" Una said. (Did she mean there was no one there?) "Nothing but jerry pots to empty and that great fat Sybil stealing my talcum powder and trying to squeeze into my clothes! Helping make those millions of beds! Sleeping in that attic room, or trying to with them giggling all night about the boys they were chasing. And never caught, I might add!" (Was she thinking she had caught one?)

"That's all nonsense," Enid said. "Father would pay for you. You would be like a guest."

"Then come with me and be another guest!"

"Violet can't look after everyone here and the baby as well. You could see today what a handful he is!"

An image of Small Henry rushed to Enid. She put her arms out foolishly, then to use them pulled the shams from the pillows and plumped them.

She decided that next time Small Henry came she would give Violet these pillows to lie him on. She held one briefly to her face to smell the lavender, thinking of it mixed with the smell of Small Henry for her to fall asleep with.

Una was at the mirror with her head tipped sideways, brushing her hair then coiling it, frowning critically as if it was of great importance that it turn out well.

"I might take a walk to Violet's tomorrow for company for her for an hour or so," Una said.

"Remember the ironing! We're a day behind this week!"

"Of course! That funeral put everything out!"

"The funeral had to be!"

"One could scarcely leave a body lying around!"

"Una you most definitely need a holiday!"

"Well, I'll take a short one — to Violet's and back tomorrow. Leave my share of the ironing!"

She went out, no doubt, thought Enid, to tinkle away at the piano, rousing Jack's wrath whether up or in bed, for he was firm about the girls being in bed by nine o'clock.

Enid sat to take off her shoes. It seemed she was going to bed. She didn't want to. Her place in the bed did not look as if it wanted her.

Always she had been eager for bed, to lie in that gentle gully between waking and sleeping, knowing sleep would come as surely as a cloud races across the sky, only stopping when it reached a place that appeared waiting for it.

There it broke up, and when you looked a moment later it was all in pieces, frail as the wafers at communion that dissolved swiftly on a warm tongue.

She remembered his hands taking that cake yesterday. All that long time ago! She knew he was trying not to look clumsy, but to lift it expertly.

She stood putting her toes back in her shoes and pulling them together on the floor, her back to the alien bed.

She decided it would be foolish to go to bed with sleep so far off.

I'll find something to do in the kitchen, she said to herself. And should Jack find her there, she would explain that the funeral had put her all behind.

13

Edwards was not home when Una went to Violet's.

The rectory was deserted and the horse and sulky gone. Violet had seen him go towards Candelo after Rachel had taken him a message from the Post Office. She had been on the verandah giving Small Henry some air. He went about nine o'clock and it was late afternoon when he got back. Violet and Una missed him then! Small Henry was crying and Violet making tea in the kitchen, keeping an eye on Una hovering near his door. She didn't want a spoiled child on her hands constantly crying to be picked up. That was all he was up to, all of four days old he might be!

They did not hear the clop, clop of Edwards's horse on the road and when they went to the front gate, Una to go home, there was the sulky under the gum and the horse standing in a state of great boredom and Edwards obviously inside and not yet raised a window. (If he bothered to.)

Oh come on out, come on out! cried Una's heart, dawdling along while trying to give the impression of walking at a normal pace, for Violet was watching. A thin wisp of smoke rose from the chimney stating he was occupied with the fire. It seemed also to say Run along home, I'm busy! She wrenched at the flounces of her silk dress, as if it was their fault. He might have seen her if she had worn something dark. Her fawn tussore was too light for this time of year, but he had never seen it! And wouldn't now! She would soon have to break into a run to avoid freezing to death. The visit was a failure!

Edwards coaxing the stove to burn felt his was too. The message had come unexpectedly from the archdeacon in Bega who was visiting the minister in Candelo to talk parish matters with him. Candelo was midway between Bega and Wyndham, the same distance to travel for both archdeacon and Edwards, who in the archdeacon's view would benefit from the meeting. Edwards went eagerly. It was a chance to talk to the archdeacon on a matter closer to his heart than anything else. He must say something to someone soon or he would burst!

He walked the archdeacon to his car after a two o'clock church service with the most devout of Candelo turning up. The archdeacon hooked his thumbs in his vestments. He was the kind who would snap his braces if he wore them.

"My dear boy," he said, and Edwards was sure he put meaning into the word boy. "You know what St Paul said. It's better to marry than to burn!

"In your case you will have to continue to burn!"

Edwards's face did indeed burn.

"No, out of the question while you have that term at Wyndham. Your stipend can't be increased, and I wouldn't advise two trying to live on it."

In his misery Edwards was silent.

"Unless the girl is wealthy of course." Wealth in Wyndham! The archdeacon's short, breathing bark said this in telling scorn.

"Wealthy or not, the council decided on a single man for the Wyndham post. Single he must be!"

The archdeacon took his thumbs away and settled his vestments tidily on him.

Edwards allowed the dust to swirl around the back wheel of the archdeacon's car before he untied his horse, grateful despite his disappointment for that.

Adding to his misery was the fact that he missed Enid or Una — he didn't know which.

He now slammed the stove door shut on the fire, deciding he had done enough for it, and it would have to do the rest on its own or die (for all he cared) and went off to the bedroom to get out of his best clerical clothes. Bobbing down to pull off his trousers he saw through the window a small female figure about to disappear around the bend on the road to Honeysuckle. Una or Enid? She wore a dress of a light colour blurred in the afternoon light. The girls were not alike close up, but at that distance, both slim and neat, he couldn't tell which it was.

He stared at the empty road longing for a mirage to return her, then turned at last and sat on his bed which was not made. He got up, got into other trousers, straightened the sheets near the pillow, plumped it and smoothed at the quilt, only succeeding in showing up the rumpled blankets more. He thought of the Herbert beds he had glimpsed from time to time at Honeysuckle. There were folded eiderdowns across the foot, gleaming white quilts and pillow shams stiff with starch and lace.

He walked about the room picking up a towel and a dirty sock, for he had left in a hurry. He should have a housekeeper every day! The archdeacon had one, a comely woman, as he remembered her, for the archdeacon had been widowed ten years or more. He would like a wife for himself, perhaps the housekeeper to move into his bed? His cold grey eyes had gone colder and his lean hard jaw went in and out when Edwards had mumbled about marriage. A dog in the manger, most likely!

Then he dropped on his knees and put his head on the quilt in repentance. The image of the archdeacon's face stayed before him, so he put another head there. Enid or Una's. Which one had been to Violet's? Which one had he missed seeing? He rose and went to the kitchen with two circles of grey dust on his knees.

He made himself a meal of cold meat and some sliced cold potatoes and sat watching the black kettle stubbornly refuse to boil. The spout was the long nose of the archdeacon and the lid, a big archdeacon eyelid lowered on unrelenting eyes. He saw his dusty knees and went and sat in the front room brushing at them. Across the road he saw the light still on in the Post Office window for it was not yet closing time. He could go across for stamps and chat to Rachel. She might mention Enid or Una visiting Violet. Rachel sometimes baked him a pudding from left over mixture, for she was not yet disciplined to cooking for one. Remembering her husband's appetite for her apple cake and rhubarb pie she thought of him while mixing the ingredients and ended up with too much, so put the surplus in a small dish and when it was cooked carried it to Edwards or whisked into her kitchen for it when he called for his mail.

It would be nice if she had some pudding for him now, although he would have to look surprised if she produced one.

If there was pudding at the Post Office for Edwards he never got it, and he did not get his stamps either, for Violet waved to him from her front verandah, frustrated as she was by Small Henry whingeing most of the afternoon, then falling asleep right on feed time. Ned had gone off into the bush in his shirtsleeves, after sitting over a fire all day. The man was mad! Violet went angrily past Small Henry's door to look for diversion from the front verandah. She was rewarded. There was Edwards. She went to the gate and opened it for him.

Violet turned over a cushion on a verandah chair squashed flat by Ned over a week's intermittent sitting. She took the other chair. Let Small Henry sleep on and Ned go to Burragate, ten miles away, if he wanted to.

"You missed Miss Herbert," Violet said. "I think she would have liked to have seen you."

Miss Herbert the elder, or Miss Herbert the younger? These people were ignorant of the etiquette of using the Christian name of sisters other than the eldest. He might have expected that!

He looked expectantly on Violet's fingers gently tapping her chair arms but they gave nothing away.

"I was in Candelo," Edwards said. "Meeting the archdeacon there."

"Is he in good health?" said Violet who had seen him but once in her life.

"Very good health," Edwards said fighting a desire to have him terminally ill.

"Is Miss Herbert well?" Edwards said looking at his knees to which some dust was still clinging.

"Very well indeed!" said Violet. Oh, this was funny! He was bursting to know which Herbert girl was here, and she wasn't saying. There would be a laugh with George over this!

"Miss Herbert came to see the little child?" Edwards said. "Her concern is natural." He saw Enid's face bending over Small Henry, then changed it to Una's.

"We did intend taking a walk," Violet said.

Una's face had turned glum when she saw the sulky gone, and she lost interest in giving Small Henry some air.

If only he knew this! She sneaked a look at his face, a brownish jaw for he was out in the air a lot, not cooped up in the rectory. A healthy man! Feeling stirred around Violet's thighs. His were strong under the stretched cloth of his trousers, a grey pair he alternated with his black ones. Violet flicked her eyes away after running them over the fly.

"I need to see Miss Herbert soon," Edwards said.

Oh, do you? Violet thought, watching his face now on the Post Office where Rachel had pulled down the blind and was carrying the lamp to her kitchen.

"I want to start a kitchen garden at the rectory," Edwards said brushing his knees. "I'm sure with Miss Herbert's advice I could get one going."

"Now is the time to get the ground ready for spring planting," Violet said, wondering if it would be possible to get a spade into Ned's hands for what she was now calling in her mind her hospital garden. The thought was a brief one. Edwards thought it was Enid who came! She would keep this up!

"Enid remarked once that the ground behind the rectory would grow anything," Violet said. Enid said nothing of the sort. But it was true of the ground, lying dormant for years, and eager to give life. She saw them spading together, his masculine back and Enid's slim one. They were suited, she thought. She watched his face slyly for a reaction. His chin did lift a little. Yes, he had an eye on Enid, or maybe one eye on each of them!

"Have you had tea?" Violet asked. My goodness, things would change for him if Enid got into that rectory kitchen!

Edwards rose and said he had. He was nervous in Ned's company and he heard his footsteps in the back of the house. Violet heard them too. The steps were measured and dull, Ned was talking with them as usual. It's late, what are you doing out there? Oh, he can go to hell! Violet got up and stood with her back to the verandah rail as if she were a door closed against Edwards's threatening departure. She saw his face full on now, a softened anxious face like that of a retriever she had as a girl. She had teased it too, laughing at its begging eyes and throwing a bone she had for it unexpectedly to Foxie their old cattle dog. You don't deserve it bad dog! she had said, aware that there was no cause for punishing the retriever, only a desire to make her cringe with her chin on her paws and a great sorrow in her eyes.

"Have they provided you with any gardening tools?" Violet asked. I'll see how practical this man is and how serious he is about his garden.

"I believe there is something there," mumured Edwards. Something there! A pick and crowbar probably, in an advanced state of rust. Another useless man! (Ned had taken a few more steps in the kitchen.)

"Well, there are plenty at Honeysuckle," Violet said, and Edwards's face grew even softer.

"A pretty name that," he said and went down the steps, putting his hat on and taking it off to say goodbye.

More than the name is pretty down that way, Violet thought.

Edwards stood with his hand on the gate as if he might say more.

What?

Then Small Henry cried, a wail loud enough to drown out Ned's footfalls.

Edwards lifted the latch of the gate and got himself away. Violet stamped her way to the kitchen.

You don't stay happy long in this place, she said to herself, slapping the feeding bottle on the table.

14

On his way to the rectory Edwards looked in the shed for gardening tools.

He was supposed to keep the sulky there but, using it fairly regularly, he left it under the big tree, something not approved by St Jude's wardens who were complaining among themselves about the deterioration of paint and leatherwork and were clearing their throats to say something before too long.

Edwards looked hard in the gloomy interior. In a corner there was something shovel shaped with a very short handle and a rake with a very long one and big bent and rusty teeth. Not much could be done with those!

He did not bother examining them but went outside to survey the ground between the back door of the rectory and the lavatory where he decided the vegetable garden should be.

He could not picture any production there. The ground seemed hard, as if it would resist disturbing, and the short grass waving about looked as if it was in charge. There were some tufts of foreign growth. One was a wild rose, thorny and half lost in the grass and against the fence there was some foliage that he thought would be lilies and there were a few geraniums, not low and thick and studded with bloom as in Enid's garden, but grey stalked like miniature ragged trees and a smell of rankness hanging about them.

He went inside to find the fire had burned and the kettle singing. This cheered him and he made what he called some decent tea and sat in the warmth and drank it with some bread and parishioner's jam, thinking of a discreet time to go and visit Honeysuckle. The day after tomorrow? That left tomorrow stretching interminably.

His day started early for he rang the bell at seven o'clock for a church service. Only once in the six months he had been in Wyndham did he have a congregation, a traveller staying overnight at the hotel and up and waiting for the mail car long before it was due. He heard the bell and scuttled to the church, slipping into a back pew without a sound so that Edwards going through his swooping motions and bowing at the altar as he did when alone, almost slipped on the altar step when he turned and found him. The fellow turned out to be a nuisance. He followed Edwards into the rectory where the fire was out and made it plain that he expected to eat with him.

Remembering the occasion Edwards fell to thinking what a difference if Una (or Enid) had been there, marvelling that he did not give them a thought at the time. He imagined one of them now (which?) bringing tea and toast to the living room fire. He saw eyes shyly lowered and a mane of thick hair brushing a smooth cheek.

He got up sharply and went into his front room as if drawn there by the image. It was tidy, but cold and lifeless. Mrs Watts kept the brass fender polished and the table dusted but this chilled the room rather than gave it a homely look. He never lit a fire there, the kitchen stove being enough for him to wrestle with.

He raised the blind on one of the front windows. A cold and bleak outlook with only a pale light visible in one of the rooms behind the Post Office. Rachel was there eating a solitary meal and he thought if only he could go and sit with her, instead of allowing the cold road and cold outer walls of their houses to separate them.

But Wyndham would be outraged at a man unrelated to a woman visiting her alone after dark.

It would be no use anyway! He would put Enid or Una's face on hers, and listen through her words for a comparison to theirs.

The cold drove him back to the kitchen stove. How long did winter last in this country where he had been told the sun shone all the time? He lit the lamp and saw the glass chimney was dark with smoke, but the light was not so feeble that it did not show up his dirty cups and drying bread.

He should put his things away, he knew, but he was still not sure where they should go, and when he did wash his crockery he left it for Mrs Watts to deal with.

He never used the dishcloth hemmed by a parishioner good at plain needlework, but flicked crumbs from the table onto the floor and then pushed them out the door with his broom. Why did women (Enid and Una) do all these things with such grace it was good to look at them.

His milk was worrying him too. There were two lots on the table and Wilfred due tomorrow with more. Mrs Watts urged him to make cocoa at bedtime but the fire was usually dead out when he thought of it.

He should get a cat! A small thing with a grey heart-shaped innocent face sliding around his legs in the friendliest way. Honeysuckle would have cats to give away! He had seen cats there, he was sure he saw Enid once nursing one while sitting on a garden seat. He immediately gave himself a picture of Una with one on her arm, bending her head for her brown hair to mingle with the cat's fur. A pretty sight!

"That's an idea!" he said aloud startled to hear his own voice, silent since he left Violet's. The meowing would please him. It was far too quiet.

He took up the lamp and went to his bedroom. Early as it was he decided he would go to bed and read, not the Bible but a book of poems by Samuel Coleridge which his mother sent him for his last birthday. He found the sonnet about the Virgin Mary feeding the child Jesus and let the book fall on his own breast, savouring the words "She hid it not, she bared her breast" and thinking of Enid and Una with their white blouses ballooning over their breasts and the white lace running into the hollow between them. He often followed that with his eyes disappointed when it stopped.

He turned his attention back to the sonnet and began to think of Small Henry who had to kiss a rubber teat and not the bless'd breasts. Why could he not kiss the breasts of Enid or Una? It didn't seem fair.

He put the book down and blew out his lamp. He should fall asleep quite quickly after that long drive. The prickly edge of the blanket stroked his mouth. A rough kiss, that! He flung it back and laid a hand in the space beside him running it down to what he believed the length of a woman's body.

Tomorrow would not be too soon to go to Honeysuckle since there were good reasons for a visit. There was his kitchen garden, the cat, and another he just thought of — Small Henry's christening! It would not be out of order for him to introduce the subject to his closest relatives, Enid and Una, since Violet was not a churchgoer. Neither were the Herbert men, Jack showing him the most courtesy the day of the funeral, glad, Edwards suspected, to have him on hand to do the job, instead of bringing a man from Candelo.

Suddenly Edwards sprang out of bed and knelt on the floor. Never in his life before had he gone to bed without kneeling by it at prayer. He needed to punish himself and he would too by delaying the visit to Honeysuckle for a day. Tomorrow he would take the opposite direction. He would walk four miles along the Candelo road to visit the Grubb family. He was reminded today that he had only called on them once since coming to Wyndham, when he passed their little house close to the road with pot plants lining the verandah.

The Grubbs had many yellow legged children and on that first visit one had come close enough to him to lean against his thigh.

The contact with bone and flesh that seemed no thicker than woollen cloth had startled him at first. It felt alien and he waited for her to move. But she stayed and he found his flesh melting into hers and growing warmer, and he put an arm out and held her there, conscious of her slight waist moving a little for she had sunk her chin into the side of her neck and was giggling, with her eyes on a line of her sisters and brothers against the wall.

Mrs Grubb, a stout woman in dirty clothes she was ashamed of, frowned on their behaviour, telling them with her eyes to go outside and play.

He regretted now that he didn't lift the child onto his knee. I will tomorrow, he thought, warming himself by rubbing his body between the blankets, for his sheets as usual were nowhere to be found. He forgot it was a weekday and the Grubb children would be at school.

He thought of flesh on flesh, and whichever way he turned he saw a female shape slipping down the road out of sight, and even with eyes shut he strained them trying to decide which it was.

Dear God, don't let them slip out of my life forever, he thought, remembering the archdeacon.

He gripped his knees hard through his nightshirt, raising

them high against his stomach, and was that way until he fell asleep.

Next day was warm and unseasonable and Mrs Watts said she thought it would rain because the cats' saucers at home were black with ants.

These strange Australians! Edwards thought. In England the rain fell gently without surprise, as if doing what was expected of it, and dozens of times opening the door in Kensington to walk to the gardens he had found the street moist and black and the people amazingly in mackintoshes, although it had been fine only hours earlier. Nothing told you it was going to rain in England!

As if he were still there he told Mrs Watts he was visiting a parishioner, and when her eyes went round for information on the identity Edwards turned to get into his short jacket, as if he was off to see someone in the thick of Notting Hill who would remain nameless. I simply will not fall into the habit of telling everyone everything, he said to himself going off. He turned his back on the road to Honeysuckle (he knew Mrs Watts had an eye behind the window blind) and strode out, the sky clear above him with only a crow flying across it. *Aaah, aaah* it called, and Edwards thought *aaah* yourself!

The day was already part gone and he was bound to fall asleep quickly tonight after his long walk. Nine o'clock would not be too early to set out in the morning. He would not go too fast, detour a little down the Burragate turn off and stand on the little bridge watching the creek, winter brown and silent among the reeds. It would be hard to waste time though!

The visit to the Grubbs was not successful. The house was deserted although the front door was open and there were cats on the chairs inside. A dog rose from the verandah and barked savagely. When it stopped and lay down with head on paws, it growled in a way that was even more terrifying. Edwards was afraid to move lest the thing leap on him, and stood rivetted to the top step until Mrs Grubb came through the house with something that looked like scraps of hay in her hair and a long fork in her hands.

She seemed as frightened to see him as he was of the dog, which got to its feet and circled and barked and lowered its hindquarters and shook them, throwing its head about until Mrs Grubb flung a foot in its direction and it went growling over the edge of the verandah and towards the back of the house. Inside, Mrs Grubb sat with the fork between her knees and tried to make conversation with Edwards, who tried not to stare at her hair and make a game of distinguishing hair from hay, surprisingly alike in colour and texture.

In a very short while there was a voice from the back door of the kitchen which was down a step from the front room, obviously that of the elder Grubb boy at home from school that day.

"Dad said get rid of who it is and come and help before it rains," called the voice and Edwards got to his feet so suddenly the chair scraped the floor and the dog, fearful of an attack on Mrs Grubb, raced into the room barking around Edwards's knees. Above the noise Mrs Grubb explained that the hay stacks had been left uncovered during the dry spell and they had to be covered now that it appeared rain was coming.

Edwards got himself away quickly, sorrier for Mrs Grubb, who he expected would receive the rough end of Mr Grubb's tongue when she returned to the hay.

He would not let the incident trouble him, he told himself, hearing the dog's bark become fainter. By the time he reached the rectory he was in a cheerful frame of mind, especially when the stove, left warm by Mrs Watts, burned up obligingly with the wood he selected for it. He was improving, he thought. By jove he'd get the hang of things yet! He went out in the still afternoon to pray in the church, kneeling in a pew like an ordinary parishioner. "And make life easier for the Grubb woman," he finished up, not quite ready yet to include the husband and the boy.

Tomorrow, tomorrow, he thought, his head on a clean pillowslip. He slept so soundly he did not hear the rain.

15

Una, on the Honeysuckle verandah next morning, frowned on the rain splashing on the road. Her hands behind her back beat angrily on her rump. Enid was bustling about the living room getting it in order, trying through her noisy movements to get Una to come and do her share. Una's remote profile seemed to be looking through the rain expecting something to emerge. Enid, smacking cushions and putting them out of reach of Alex's head (which he had lately taken to liberally smearing with hair cream), felt a lightness of spirits not entirely due to the beneficial rain on her young oleanders. She's looking out for him but he won't be coming in this rain!

"It would be a good day to rearrange Henry's room," she called out.

"Rearrange Henry's room," Una muttered. She had taken lately to repeating Enid's sentences in a low voice with her face turned from her. She sat suddenly on the step drawing her knees up under her skirt and fondling the tips of her shoes.

"Put your legs down there, someone might go past!" Enid said.

"Someone might go past," Una muttered with her mouth on her knees.

"I thought of making a little sewing room and studio of it! Asking Father first, of course!"

Una laid a cheek on her knees and closed her eyes. "Asking Father first, of course," she murmured.

"Well?" said Enid in the doorway, looking at Una's curved back. How sad and dejected a back can look! Una's closed eyes were seeing a studio, but not of Henry's room. She could feel his hands on her waist, for he stood with her before a painting — of Small Henry! She sprang to her feet and turned with her back to the rail. "I'm going to paint Small Henry!" she said.

"Well, then have a nice little studio to do it in!" Enid said.

She transferred Small Henry's frog like shape from the couch where she had last seen it to Una's canvas. Blast the rain! She could have gone to see him if the day was fine. Una went yesterday!

Behind her was the disordered living room, vases together emptied of the funeral flowers and waiting to be refilled. She had planned to arrange pieces from her shrubs, as shown in the women's pages of the *Sydney Mail*, the editor concerned at the housewife missing the blooms of summer. Massed red and orange berries and green ferns. She intended gathering an armful when the rain eased a little. If it didn't she would have to put the vases in the pantry until tomorrow.

Tomorrow! It was too far away! The desolate room silently begged her to restore it to order.

Oh, blow you! She turned her back on it and went to the kitchen to stoke the stove and take bread from the crock for sandwiches. The men would be in for tea as usual in a few minutes, Jack having found something for them to do in spite of the rain. The bread was getting down and there was only one teacake left. Where did yesterday get to?

Suddenly she cried "Una!" surprised and frightened at the small scream edging her voice. Una came with a curious face. Enid's flushed cheeks and cold and red tipped nose was bowed over her cutting knife. Una took cups from the dresser quietly and with a grace Enid saw and envied. She wanted to sniff and use a handkerchief but avoided both.

"I can't do everything on my own!"

"If I go to Uncle Percy's that's what you'll be doing!" Una said.

"You said you weren't going!"

"You're making me a little studio instead!"

"I'm trying to make you happy, Una!"

"You are?" Una threw the words over her shoulder as she sauntered with a tray into the living room.

Enid felt a trembling inside her throat. This will never do! She must say nothing, nothing at all.

But Una returning said that Jack would not be too happy with the state of the living room.

"Then help me as you are supposed to!" Enid flared. She flung the knife down and ran to the bedroom, needing courage to look at herself in the mirror. If he saw her like this!

The rain slanted down past her window, but she didn't see it now as a deterrent. He would come if he wanted to!

She took the pins out of her hair and did it, and poured water into the wash basin, but it looked cold and uninviting to wash, so she dabbed at her face with the towel trying to take the redness away. She stroked some cream around her nose and dusted on a little powder. That was better!

Outside the window the rain fell hard enough to part the clumps of violets and send the pebbles on the footpath to gather under the gate. It really was too wet for an open sulky.

She looked back at the mirror standing erect and arranging her hands along the bedhead. She was not as tall as

Una but elegant and fine looking, as she believed people said.

She saw herself as a portrait hanging. On the rectory wall looking down on him at his desk. She lowered her eyes as if this was how she would look in the picture. My sister-in-law painted my wife, she heard him say, his brown eyes proud. The archdeacon was visiting, very pleased with what she had done to the rectory.

More suitable, much, much more suitable. (Of course I am!)

She moved her lips, wondering if she dared redden them a little as Una was doing.

Una put her head suddenly through the door and Enid jumped, caught out. She shook some hand cream from a bottle onto her hands and began to slide them up and down as if this was what she was there for.

"Please knock!" she said.

"Why?" Una said, leaving her face there for a moment before withdrawing it.

When Enid went to the living room, Alex was there in his motoring cap and leather gloves and George was finishing off the teacake alone at the little table. Jack with his jowls showing reddish displeasure was stoking the fire. His teacup was on the mantlepiece. Una, having taken her blue cape from the back verandah where she had it airing since the funeral, was fastening it over her breasts.

"Alex hasn't had the car out in the rain yet," she said. "We are going to see how it goes." Enid poured herself some tea, keeping her flushed face from them. Were they going Wyndham way? She put the pot down with a trembling hand.

Una's eyes were watching her hands, smoothing and straightening her cape. "If we went Wyndham way we could call and see Violet and Small Henry!"

Enid had no appetite for her tea. But he wouldn't come out of the rectory in this rain!

Alex pretended not to hear. He was going Pambula way. There was a hotel two miles this side where he could stop and show the Barretts the car. Una could sit in the parlour while he had a drink. The Barretts had the first wireless in the district, a feeble thing compared to his machine! There it was by the front gate waiting for them, defying the rain, crouched there with the water rushing under its wheels and down the side curtains. Not a drop inside! He couldn't wait to get in warm and dry with the chance of passing open sulkies and partly exposed buggies with bleak, damp figures angrily slapping at horses as if blaming them for the conditions.

Una was holding the car rug she had chosen in big green checks to match the paint and leather. Jack's face said plainly he had no intention of joining the motoring party. George's watery, bulbous eyes were on the back of Alex's neck, asking if he was going Voilet's way. Not that it would be much good to him. He would be lucky to have a chance to whisper to Violet about the Skinner woman above Alex wanting them to talk about the car and Una losing her head over that baby. Alex stood in the doorway with his back to them, which might have been inscribed with the words: "Come, if you're coming!"

"I certainly can't go gallivanting off," Enid said, throwing her eyes around the room and resting them longest on Una's bent head. Jack's face grew ruddier with pleasure. She would put the living room in order and he would look on as he liked to, seeing her hands moving among the vases and ornaments as Nellie's used to. "Feet up, Father," she would say cheerfully as she brushed the linoleum around the hearth then laid the rug back in place. Those were Nellie's words, for she often did housework after the

91

children were in bed, when the two of them did the milking alone.

Times were better now! The sound of the Austin moving off brought this sharply to him, going in the direction of Pambula. Enid lifted her head to listen and when she went back to her work he thought her face was soft and much happier. She was glad to have them out of the way, for George was in the lumber room working on her closet and the two of them were cosy together! She liked nothing better than making the place nice for him.

She wrapped her arms around her vases now. "I'm getting some ferns and things for the garden," she said. "And I'll bring us a pot of fresh tea. That was awful."

Of course it was. The flibbertigibbet was too fond of pleasure to attend properly to her work. The room brightened and he saw through the window that the rain had eased to a misty drizzle. Rain at the right time, just before spring ploughing! After his tea he would take Horse (a foolish name given by Una to the bay he bought as a foal that seemed to have been born overdeveloped) and ride to Halloween.

Ned was going there less and less lately and he had kept away too, what with Henry coming and going and the girl dying, there had been no time. He was a little uncomfortable about Ned, the only Herbert volunteering for service at the front. But Nellie had wept on his chest one night and begged him not to let their boys go. Alex might have done quite well for himself, but George, unable to slit the throat of a pig, would have been less successful. He would have thought Ned would have picked himself up by now, but he seemed sometimes to barely know where he was.

He would talk to Hoopers about their plans for the spring. He would do that much for old Ned, fourteen years younger than himself and not likely to weather the years as he was doing. The Hoopers were a strong pair, a bit elderly but there was the advantage of their not springing children out every other year.

Enid was back with his fresh tea, and she had toasted some bun just to his liking. He could watch her finishing off her flower arranging, a pretty sight with a mist of rain on her brown hair.

The rain had almost stopped. Nellie used to say if it stopped before twelve o'clock it would be fine for the rest of the day. His Nellie sleeping so close to that girl!

Enid there putting her head to one side to make sure the vases looked right. He and Nellie had worked hard and Nellie hadn't lived long enough to enjoy the better life, but it was good for Enid. Agitated he stood and took up his hat from the fender where he had dropped it. He would like to hold her hard against him, moving a leg up her hip and down again, hinting at more when the day was over. It was what he did with Nellie!

He was about to call to her, for what foolish reason he did not know, but her attention was taken by something visible at the edge of the window blind. He saw her straighten and hold herself upright with the tips of her fingers on the couch back. He strode to the window to see.

That minister fellow striding down the road! A bit bedraggled, his black clothes looking blacker in the wet and making for Honeysuckle it appeared. The fellow was here two days ago! That funeral job was done. What call was there to come traipsing back?

Enid was smoothing at her cushions in a distracted way. She had no time to entertain him. She had mutton to roast for dinner, she told him so! Jack's jowls grew very heavy seeing the fellow steer towards Honeysuckle gate.

"Don't worry, Father," Enid said, gently tipping her head towards him and closing her eyes, almost leaning upon him. "George is here. You can go off as you planned to!"

Her gentle voice concerned for him, her body nearly upon his! Confused, happy, angry he crushed his hat on and made his way across the linoleum to the back hall. Rest assured she would get rid of the fellow quickly!

Enid waited for the back door to slam, then smoothed her hair and her nose, brushed briefly at her skirt, glad she was without an apron, and waited half a minute — so long she was afraid he might turn and go! — before opening the door to his knock.

16

At Halloween Jack learned that the Hoopers were leaving. He saw at once the air of neglect around the place and Hooper and his wife Sarah sitting on the little verandah, obviously not going to put themselves out now their time was nearly up.

They started guiltily when Jack rode up but held their ground and Clem with support from Sarah said many of the things he had been thinking for a long time.

Ned gave them no help at all, and they were not going to face a new season as they did the last. They recounted, although Jack knew the story, their potato crop ready for digging and waiting in vain for Ned to turn up. There came a sudden downpour of rain followed by a burst of hot weather and the potatoes cooked in the ground. Sarah, who had a small brown leathery face and very few teeth, sank down on the pile of bags they had ready to fill and wept to see Clem's spade come out of the ground covered with thick white slime. Clem was angrier at Sarah's tears, the first seen in more than forty years of marriage, than at the loss of the crop.

Until Jack showed up though, this and other disappointments and setbacks had been put behind them. The two of them were indulging in the luxury of drinking tea at the little table on which there was hardly room for their teacups, covered as it was with an old washing basket into which Sarah had already put pieces of silver and china that had belonged to her mother, wrapped in linen from the same source.

They were going to a married daughter the other side of Candelo whose husband had a roadside hotel. They did not care for their bullying son-in-law, who had a ripe dark face, wet lips and bold eyes for women other than his wife. Perhaps he was improving in character for Marie did not complain, though they hardly ever saw her and the children. They were to have a room to themselves, something to which they could always retreat if relationships were strained. Clem was to be the yardman and Sarah to help in the kitchen.

She looked forward to that. The kitchen had a screen door to keep out the flies, a new and wonderful invention. On the one occasion they had been there, she had sat (ignored by the son-in-law) and marvelled at it clapping to when people passed in and out. She had been smiling at the vision when Jack rode up.

Jack did not know whether to ride to Ned's and tell him or go back to Honeysuckle. That fellow should be gone by now and he was hungry for Enid's roast mutton.

But Jack wanted to tip the news from his shoulders onto Ned's, its rightful place. What would happen to the cows and pigs when the Hoopers were gone? They looked ready to take off at any moment, and did not appear fussy about telling Ned. The only answer was to shut the place up and take the stock to join that at Honeysuckle.

It would be hard to find a family to succeed the Hoopers in the wretched little house of two rooms and a lean-to to bathe and wash clothes in. Ned was supposed to fix it up. Violet should have gone there and lived instead of wasting money on that house, which she called living "in town". Going soft like a lot of women wanting a shop at hand and people to gossip to! Nellie and Enid would have been prepared to live on a place like Halloween and make a home of it.

Jack dug his heels in Horse's sides and sent him galloping towards Albert Lane. Even that name was ridiculous, encouraging Ned to remember the war!

He received another jolt when he got there. Dolly and the sulky were there, which meant George was inside and not at Honeysuckle with an eye on that fellow! He might have driven him back to the rectory, although he thought not. It looked shut up with no smoke from the chimney. The fellow would hardly leave that soon.

Jack climbed from Horse, needing to tie him to a gum, an inferior position to that occupied by Dolly, who swung her head and scraped a foot on the ground to say Horse should keep this in mind.

He knocked roughly on Violet's door, which she opened with a frown and a head tilted towards the bedroom where Small Henry slept. Violet banged about herself while he was sleeping, but expected the opposite from others. Well it had its advantages, Jack thought. He didn't have to speak a greeting to Violet, merely remove his hat and inclined his head in such violent fashion you would expect the creases in his neck like a purple concertina to set up a squeak.

Ned and George were on the kitchen couch as if they had nothing to do in the world except sit in idleness.

"Did you bring that fellow back?" Jack said, setting up creases in the other side of his neck for he inclined it towards the rectory. George's bulbous eyes travelled around the kitchen as if the person Jack was referring to would emerge and answer for him.

"Is Alex back then?" Jack said.

"Might be," George said. "Should be. Soon anyway."

Jack clamped his hat on. He wouldn't tell Ned about the

Hoopers leaving. Let him go there one day and find the pigs squealing for food and the cows bellowing with painful udders, or gone dry as dead wattle bark. Enid was alone in the house with that fellow! Violet following Jack down the hall said so.

"Don't rush off. Enid and the reverend might be getting on very well there by themselves!"

"Hoopers are leaving. Did you know that?" Jack fired back.

"They're old and stupid and useless!" Violet said. "Good riddance to them!"

"You get a cheque every month you won't be getting when they're gone!"

"Two pounds it was last month! I'd spend a month at the Hotel Australia if I could get away!"

Jack stared at the latch on the gate. An efficient little contraption, which he had shown to Nellie when he got one the same for the front gate at Honeysuckle. The half hoop of steel lifted with the touch of a finger and the gate defied opening without a similar touch. Nellie was gravely ill then, her face yellowy with the liver trouble, and he saw again her smile running with a watery strength from her mouth to her frightened eyes. If Nellie was here now to spare him all this!

He showed Violet only the back of his neck while he untied Horse, who showed his delight at such a short visit with a toss of his head towards Dolly, who lowered hers and leisurely cropped at some grass to say waiting around had its compensations.

Violet was less pleased. Small thanks she was getting for taking Small Henry off their hands! She got the rough end of the stick every time. Old Herbert had left Ned only that miserable little place and the main property to Jack with the excuse that Ned had no sons and Jack three. The other brother, Percy, had been well provided for also in spite of no boys and six daughters.

She had half a mind to rouse the sleeping Small Henry and dump him on the saddle in front of Jack!

There was that monument in full view with only Ned's name on it to uphold the Herbert honour. Violet wanted to fling an arm towards it and shout out to Jack, who was putting a polished boot over Horse's back and allowing his well cut coat to settle easily on the saddle.

"There might be changes down there at Honeysuckle soon. Look out for them!" she cried as Jack galloped off.

17

They were eating dinner at Honeysuckle when Jack got there. Enid rose with a pink face and went to the kitchen for his. At first Jack was not sure the fellow was there, it was hard to pick him out coming in from the strong light, but he might have known for he was the one pushing his chair back and half standing in greeting. The fellow made a big thing of manners, but did not impress Jack who went to wash and take off his coat and kept Enid waiting by his chair until he was ready. The fellow did not sit quite as close to the table as before, Jack noticed through the steam flying off his food.

Una of all of them went on eating in unconcerned fashion, stabbing at her carrots and fussily cutting the fat from her mutton. She was pulling her little faces as she did when things did not please her.

When Edwards had arrived, Enid barely had time to seat him before George came in and said he was putting Dolly in the sulky and driving to Wyndham for nails from the store. He held up long nails in evidence of the authenticity of his errand, and both Edwards and Enid nodded gravely in agreement that they were quite unsuitable to put a closet together. George standing there on the linoleum dropped his chin to sit almost on his neck, and both Edwards and Enid were overcome with the dreadful possibility that George was going to suggest Edwards travel back with him.

Edwards lowered his eyes and prayed. He was here to

ask Enid about a vegetable garden, a pet cat and Small Henry's christening. Church work, all of it. When he opened his eyes George had gone and Enid was putting a cup of tea in his hands.

He stood with it and put his free hand out indicating the way to the kitchen.

"You have things to do. Don't let me hold you up," he said. She saw his slightly rounded shoulders with the black of his jacket stained a darker shade. Some rain had fallen on him on his way. She knew nothing would stop him from coming! She brought a sweater of Alex's for him, mulberry coloured with brass buttons at the neck.

"Put this on," she said, managing not to look into his face. At first he did not know he had to remove his thin alpaca jacket but he saw she was waiting to take it and when she did he pulled Alex's sweater on. He settled it at his waist while she put his jacket on the back of a chair turning the chair to the stove.

"You suit the colour," Enid said. "Look."

He saw across to the little hall mirror his brown face above the thick rich wool and smoothed his ruffled hair, pleased but a little ashamed of his vanity. He thought the little mound of potatoes on the table looked handsome too.

"Let me," he said.

He peeled them thinly enough even for her and peeled the pumpkin too, thinking the skin too thick and hard for her fine hands. He liked the way they flew among her measuring cups and bowls, for she was making a pudding using several large lemons, puzzling him as to how it would turn out while trying to look as if he knew.

They were in the living room, she setting the table, when the Austin pulled up outside. "Quick, this!" said Edwards, plucking at the sweater. She ran ahead of him to the kitchen snatching up his jacket, glad to feel it warm and dry. She took the sweater and returned it to the hall, seeing her face in the mirror disappointed that she could not smooth his jacket on his shoulders. He missed the comfort of the wool. His arms felt they were in mourning.

Una coming into the living room was about to fling her cape off, then, seeing him rise from his chair in the corner, held it together at her breasts.

"The rain stopped, thankfully," Edwards said, immediately regretting it for country people he knew never got enough rain. Alex sharing Jack's view that churchmen were a race apart ignored the remark and strode away to take his coat off.

Una's face was vivid enough to light the room. He had set out after the rain which had stopped less than two hours ago. His clothes were dry; he must have just arrived. He had to sit alone while Enid got the dinner. He did look pleased to see her!

"Take your cape off, Una," Enid said, coming into the room with things for the table. "We will have Grace and start without Father."

Edwards was wishing there was some way of letting them know he peeled the vegetables when Jack came in.

"George is not here," Jack said, spreading his napkin.

"In Wyndham for nails," Enid said.

Jack asked without speaking how long he had been gone. His measured forkfuls said the words as in the old days when the children had played in some forbidden area.

"He left just a little while ago," Enid murmured. (Well, it seemed no more than five minutes they were alone together!) "The nails he found were too short."

"Too long," Edwards gently corrected.

"Oh yes, much too long!" Enid said, and overcome with

a wild desire to giggle, she took the bread plate to the kitchen to refill it.

Instead she dropped it on the table and took a jug of cream from the cool safe.

He is wonderful, wonderful, she told herself.

He was even more wonderful on her return.

"I would have returned to Wyndham with George in the sulky," he was saying to the top of Jack's head bent over his mutton. "But I needed to discuss the christening with you all."

Jack saw the faces of Enid and Una take on a dreamy softness. Did they foolishly expect to have some sort of party here? The funeral business had been enough to do them for a long time!

"Violet can take care of all that," Jack said. "She's right by there!"

That was what he called the church, Edwards thought with a pummelling of spirits. How would he feel if one of his daughters —! Things will not be easy, he thought, though he felt a little cheered taking his pudding from Enid and seeing how well it turned out. Una took hers still with her dreamy air.

"Small Henry!" she said. "I wonder will we always call him that. It won't suit him if he grows too large!"

Edwards thought with a tenderness that surprised him of the shut eyes of Small Henry in his strange coloured face. When would he see him again?

"I shall call and talk to Mrs Edgar," Edwards said. Well, let him! Jack said to himself with an intake of tea. Violet was welcome to him. Nothing to do but visit people! How would he handle some real work?

As if needing to express this Jack rose with a boisterous movement of his body and went to the fireplace to stand and fill his pipe. A ripple of uneasiness went over the table, only Una playing with the handle of her teacup in unconcerned fashion, and Enid looking to see if Edwards was attending to his or observing Una's brown lashes resting prettily on her pink cheeks.

Alex moved his chair back slightly from the table, to let Jack know he was going out to the paddocks, though not necessarily at once. He had said far too little about the car! It slid with only a couple of barely noticeable dips to one side through a rush of water over a low culvert, just this side of Pambula. Una shrieked and raised her feet, obviously expecting the water to come up through the floorboards. A silly female! Some women were actually driving cars these days, but he would not have either of these girls behind the wheel.

"She took to the road like a duck to water," Alex said. It was the Austin he was referring to. Would they be stupid enough to think it could be anything else! He took a small tin from his pocket and lifted strands of greenish yellow tobacco to lay in the hand that held a cigarette paper between the fingers. Enid felt a rush of protection towards Edwards. He had no car and could not afford to smoke if he wanted to. Of course he wouldn't want to! She saw him looking with tolerance and interest on Alex's hands. But no envy. Of course no envy!

"A fine machine," Edwards said. "Indeed, a very fine machine!"

Jack clattered his pipe against the mantelpiece. Was the fellow angling for a ride home in it? Let him walk or drive his sulky, and not this way too often, if you please!

Alex decided Jack's agitated back was sending out signals to get him out to the paddocks. He got up, letting them see he was in no great hurry, and gathering up his tobacco went off to his room to change to work trousers.

Jack stayed. He was going to see that fellow away, or he

may well dig himself in for the afternoon. Una startled them all when she suddenly cried out.

"I know!" She jumped up and flew to the chiffonier, taking a large book from a drawer. She found a page and held it up to show them illustrations of baby clothes on fat infants.

"I'll make a christening gown for Small Henry!" She flung back the tablecloth covering the green fringed cloth, and frowned on the page.

"I need brown paper to cut the pattern. Have we any, Enid?" Enid rescued the cruet and cream from under the tablecloth and folded it rapidly before any damage was done.

"Look where it is usually kept," she said with a little smile for Edwards to see. See what a child she is!

"I'm going Enid,"Jack said knocking his pipe empty on the grate and stowing it in a pocket. These girls needed to learn how to dismiss people. He had finally taught Nellie!

Edwards stood and found his hat. A large pair of scissors drooped from Una's hand and Enid's unguarded face wore a wistful look, although she straightened her back and folded her hands hostess fashion at her waist.

Going down the steps he heard the door shut sharply.

He guessed accurately it was Jack who shut it.

18

Una returned to the table to stare at the open book and the only sound was the grind of the scissors as she absently cut nothing with them. The noise set Enid's teeth on edge so she slipped away to the kitchen.

How different it looked without him! There was the sweater hanging by the hall mirror, puffed up gently with the shape of his body. She would not pat it flat but leave it to look at with secret pleasure. She went close to it and saw her eyes were bright, and smoothing her eyebrows she thought she might pluck a few stray hairs from them with tweezers Una bought when last in Bega.

Enid saw Una's face come into the mirror too. She was by the kitchen table with the scissors, making their squeaking noise as she cut the air with them.

"Did you look for the brown paper in the lumber room on the bottom shelf?" Enid said.

"To the right or left, past the empty preserving jars or before them, beside the tin of flower seeds or next to the dead daisies you saved from the funeral?"

Enid pushed the words away from her by putting more wood on the stove and wondering what he would eat for tea. She could have sent something home with him, if Jack had not dismissed him so curtly.

There was time to work for a while in the garden before starting tea. She took an old woollen jacket from the peg close to Una, now studying her face in the mirror.

"We're off to look at the cabbages, are we?" Una said. "Look hard, there might be something inside one!"

I will turn the other cheek, Enid said to herself going out. He would.

She stirred the earth around the wallflowers and straightened poppies beaten by the rain and pushed clumps of pansies together, smiling tenderly at their black and brown and yellow faces smeared with tears of rain. She would have liked to dry them. She would have liked too to turn up her skirt and work in the freedom of her long woollen bloomers but Una was hovering about behind the kitchen window and there was George bowling home in the sulky. It brought Edwards closer.

Where was he when George met him? George would not think of turning the sulky around and sparing his legs for the last mile. She stabbed the earth with her fork as if it were George.

She finished the poppy bed and went inside, George eating bun and drinking tea at the table, for Violet had not been in a good temper after Jack left and had not produced the customary tea to fuel George for the drive home. Under cover of Small Henry's yelling he whispered in the hall that there was a baby coming at Skinners. Her reaction had been disappointing.

"I wish she'd ladle out three or four in the one go to make it worthwhile!" she said. "We live on that cream cheque from Halloween, and now there's an end to it!"

She saw George's unhappy face and was angry enough to want to make it unhappier. "I may not bother about the hospital, after all! Why should I work round the clock with groaning women and screaming kids to keep every seat in the house warm for his lazy arse!

"In which case I'll be sending that back to Honeysuckle too!" With snapping eyes she tossed her head towards

Small Henry's door. His yelling dropped to a pathetic bleat.

The pale sunlight outside enhanced the misery on George's face.

He put out a hand and touched Violet's wrist.

"You have your hospital," George said. "You'll be good at it."

"I've never lost a case, you know George!" (George knew.) "Up and down the coast there isn't a better nurse!"

George was certain there wasn't. Flying home in the sulky he was sorry for everyone in the world except Violet and himself. She would have her hospital and he would help her get it. He raised his whip in superior fashion to the straggling figure of Edwards making his way home. A poor and sorry lot was his!

George thought the lot of Enid and Una poor too as he watched them at work, Enid rolling pastry for jam tart for tea and Una faced with a pile of vegetables to peel and chop. He would liven things up for them.

"There's a new one coming at Skinners, you know," George said.

"Oh pooh!" said Una. "Who would bother counting heads there!" George was downcast for no more than a moment.

"You'll never guess where it could be born," George said.

"In Albert Lane Private Hospital!" Una said, giving a cabbage a hefty whack.

Enid felt a stirring at her thighs and groin. She must have gardened in the one position too long.

George's face fell and he had to turn to the fire so that he could blame that for his burning neck and ears.

"You'll have to do better than that, George, to liven up our dreary day!" Una said.

So she thought the day was dreary even though he came! I know now what they mean by a singing heart! said Enid silently to her singing heart.

George's was hurt and heavy. It was not his and Violet's secret after all.

"There's only Ned left to tell!" Una said. "He'll take to the bush and never return!" She slapped a saucepan heavily on the table and flung handfuls of carrots in.

"Not so rough there!" Enid said. She treats her vegetables like children, Una thought, pressing a half cabbage into another saucepan.

"She needs help to get it going," George said running both hands down over his pockets, indicating this was where the help would come from.

George loves Violet! Una thought, as if she were scratching the words on the smooth trunk of a gum tree. George is fond of Violet, Enid thought with a hot rush of love and pity.

"Hoopers are leaving, I suppose you know," George said.

They didn't! How did he?

"Jack came to Violet's while I was there and told her," George said, feeling he was ahead at last.

Enid took her tarts to the oven opening it with her foot. Jack would have known Edwards and she were alone in the house. That accounted for Jack's hostile manner towards Edwards. She saw herself between the two each desperate for her. Oh, poor Una! Poor, poor Una!

"I know!" Una cried suddenly sitting on a chair and throwing both legs out in front of her. The blushing Enid felt Una did know.

"Let Ned go and live at Halloween and Violet will have him out of her way!"

George reared a delighted head. Yes, yes! A great idea, that!

Enid, building the stove fire lest it cool off for her pastry, fixed blazing eyes on Una.

"That's no way to talk!" she cried. "Violet's job is to care for Ned, not discard him!"

She's talking like a wife, Una thought. Just like a wife.

George had been roused to leave for the dairy but Una on her feet called to him. "Put a saddle on Horse for me, George!" His halted back said "What for?" as did Enid's raised eyebrows.

"I'm riding to Violet's! I need to borrow a dress of Small Henry's to cut a pattern by." She saw George's back had turned sulky.

"We don't have to ask permission of you, George every time we go to Violet's!" Una was now in front of the hall mirror doing her hair, brushing at her skirt and putting on an old riding jacket hanging there. She slapped a pocket to check that a comb was there, and calling out that she would be back in time to set the table for tea, raced out the back door.

Well, let her go, Enid thought, the peace of the kitchen bringing him back. He loves me, I know. Nothing can take him from me. Nothing and no one.

19

Una sent Horse flying along the road. She pulled him up sharp just outside Wyndham, her eyes softening towards the roof of the rectory, and Horse finding a patch of short, sweet grass under a clematis bush which the frost had missed. He tossed an inquiring head when she slipped her feet out of the stirrups.

"Make the most of your cropping, for short and sweet it will be!" Una said with hairpins between her teeth. She shook her hair down over her shoulders, combed it rapidly, then rolled it into a bun lying like a glistening coiled snake on her white neck. She smoothed the sides over her ears and caught up the reins and with her feet back in the stirrups rubbed the toes of her shoes on Horse's belly and gave him some muttered directions.

"Walk, if you don't mind. Make a noise with your hoofs too, if that's not asking too much!"

He was at the rectory woodheap. Una was not sure it was he at first, for she had never seen him without a black coat. He had on a grey woollen jumper and was searching for lengths of wood that did not require cutting. She suspected his axe needed sharpening and he had nothing to do the job.

Horse, preparing for a walk to Violet's, was reined in sharply and sent flying up an embankment, through a patch of dead ferns which stuck into his knees. The next thing he had his neck over the rectory fence and Edwards, wood in arms, was coming towards them. Horse raised his neck, curved into a question mark at what came next. Una loosened the reins and patted his neck. Edwards put his free arm over the fence and stroked under Horse's mane.

There were the two of them, one patting one side of his neck and the other at work on the other side. Una jumped from the saddle and tied him swiftly to a post.

"He's had two big rides today. Poor old dear! Let him crop here for a while!"

Edwards became aware of the wood and embarrassed about it. Una looked up the Wyndham road.

"I'll walk to Violet's from here," she said. "I'll go through the back gate and surprise her!"

That meant passing through the rectory, or going around it. Edwards and Una walked towards his gate, one on either side of the fence. They both turned their faces when Horse shook his head and snorted. He was stuck among the roots of a wattle tree coming into bloom, with the pollen tickling his nostrils and the branches jabbing his rear. There wasn't a blade of grass in sight. Cropping indeed!

Edwards shifted the wood to the arm farthest from Una. Suddenly she stopped and picked up a branch on her way. Edwards murmured an apology that it was not he removing it. But surprisingly Una dragged the branch after her. "We'll break it into small pieces and it will get your fire going!" she said.

"Let me!" Edwards said at the rectory gate, and taking the branch from her they went side by side in the direction of the backdoor.

"You take the big wood in and I'll snap this into starting wood," she said. Starting wood! He had a lot to learn. He liked his teacher though.

Inside, Edwards as usual found his stove choked with ashes. He made a space for some crumpled paper and when he turned round, Una was there with an armful of her wood that looked eager to be alight.

"Let me," she said, dropping her load, and in a second had emptied the ash pan in the back yard and had it back in its place.

"If you had a garden you could put your ashes on it," she said.

She stood back while he built the fire. I will die of shame if it doesn't burn, he thought, remembering his past failures. Una went to the window and looked out on his barren yard. "I intend asking about starting a garden," he said. "You have such a fine one at Honeysuckle." (She would work in it too.)

The fire was catching. He would keep a stock of dry brambles on hand in future, he thought, putting the iron lids on the stove and watching with pleasure the orange glow in the cracks. But it would not be the same gathering them alone. He joined her at the window.

"A path to the what-you-call-it, don't you think?" she said. He blushed at the sight of the half open lavatory door, and wanted to rush out and close it.

"Could I get vines to grow over it, do you think?" he said.

"Grow over what?" said Una, looking about the yard and keeping her innocent expression from him. She felt his smile and saw briefly a stretch of red brown jaw.

"Vines grow over ours," she said gravely. They had one too! His did not look so bad now.

Una turned a curious but still merry face towards the door leading to the other rooms. Yes, he should take her to the living room. It was improper having her here in the kitchen. In spite of mooning about the house all the morning before the weather cleared, he had not made his bed and it would be seen through the half-open bedroom door.

There was also a good chance of a view of the chamber under the bed not emptied either. Edwards disposed of his slops only on the days Mrs Watts was due to come.

He went ahead of Una and pulled the bedroom door to and cleared a chair of books and writing pad, unaware thankfully of what she saw. She sat folding her hands prettily at her waist and he went and straightened the wrinkled rug before the fireplace, leaning there and reminding himself nervously of Jack. "I wonder how our fire's going?" Una said.

Our fire!

They saw it was going immediately they got to the kitchen, for it was fluttering and sparking and the big kettle was there gasping for breath. He realized he'd done it again. He seemed always to have full kettles on cold stoves and empty kettles on a hot one. He filled it, painfully aware now that he should be offering her tea. But he had no cake until Mrs Watts came tomorrow. He saw himself hacking at stale bread and trying to spread cold butter that curled into lumps around the knife and made holes in the bread. He could not rely on the kettle boiling either. In his experience they never hurried themselves when needed.

"I must go," Una said, and he felt relief in his pain. Letting her out the front door he discovered, with a fine shivering inside him, that he was closer to her than he had ever been. There was a tiny mark at the corner of her lips, formed there by that quirking smile, and fine creases on her brow from her frown. The little frown was at work now. She was not pleased about going! He walked with her to Horse, neither speaking, and he had a job keeping up with her rapid step.

When she climbed on Horse she looked at the sky. "The

rain's all gone, I think," she said and plunging down the embankment cantered off.

She had gone a quarter of a mile when she pulled Horse up so suddenly he turned himself right round, facing the opposite way with his mouth jammed against his chest. He lowered his backside in alarm, then needed to straighten up immediately for she dug her heels into him and sent him towards Wyndham.

"You crazy fool of a horse!" she cried. "You dumb, stupid, crazy thing! You knew I was going to Violet's! You turned your stupid head and went the wrong way! He will see me! The noise of your stupid clumsy hoofs will bring him running. You are no help, you know that?"

Edwards did hear, but was too disconsolate to go to his window, although he was fast falling into the habit of other villagers and shamelessly flinging open windows and doors whenever there was the sound of feet, wheels or motor engines.

He was in the kitchen, staring down at his fire.

It had gone out again.

20

Edwards buried a saucepan with an egg in it into the hot ashes in the stove and made himself tea from water in the kettle. It was not on the boil and tea leaves floated on the surface. He slapped them on the kitchen table and turned them into the letter *U*.

He wandered to his front door looking at the road, empty without Una, needing to look over his shoulder to where she sat, making sure she had been there.

Her hair had been curved over her cheeks, covering her ears like birds' wings. Different to her usual way. He had wanted to ruffle it. He stroked his hands across his grey jumper, as if it were her hair.

No, it was his mother's hair, grey too, wiry to touch. He took his hands away and went quite swiftly to the kitchen for his egg. He turned it out, barely set, and not bothering to sit at the table properly, but screwing himself to an angle, mopped it up with a slice of bread. A splash of yolk fell on his jumper and he brushed his hand on it, wondering what to do with the yellow on his knuckles and finally finding a tea towel to wipe them.

He went into the living room with the towel, holding it like a serviette, remembering his lonely nursery tea at home in England.

Everything around him was of enormous proportions, his chair where his legs did not reach the first rung, the table large enough for the ten children who belonged to the former rector, and his nanny with an apron white and stiff like the serviette he was expected to use, but was afraid to, in great fear of picking up the apron by mistake.

For on one terrible and memorable occasion he had flung himself up under her apron.

He had been standing by her as close as he dared while she was lighting a gas lamp on the nursery wall. The high backed chair in the corner, on which she usually sat to watch him eat, became a tiger; the claws at the end of the chair arms were waiting to spring out and crush him. There was nowhere to go. The cupboard next to the chair was locked and the sofa next to it sat an inch above the floor. He dived up under nanny's apron and clung to her belly, surprised at its hardness, and tried to wedge himself between her legs.

Her screams brought his mother running. He saw her take hold of one of the chair arms, since the apron had been tugged brutally from his head.

"Don't, don't!" he cried, still believing it was the tiger's paw.

"Don't indeed!" his nanny said. She looked with a great and angry knowing on his mother, protecting her belly with two spread hands. "He will get more than don't, I should think, when his father has been told!"

He held the corner of the table, putting his face there, waiting for the distance to close between him and his mother. He could not run and fling himself on her. But she could lift him up, past her thighs and belly, and he could hold her neck and raise his legs and bind them to her back, and her grip would be so tight and sure, there would be no chance of his slipping downwards to where he must not on any account go.

"His father should beat him, Madam," Nanny said. She was trembling, he supposed, for her words were trembling too. "He is not a happy child like his brother."

His mother let his father beat him. But afterwards when she went to him, sobbing on his bed, she pulled his stockings up over his legs striped pink and red with tears in her eyes too. He flung her hands off him and turned his head to burrow it in the pillow, wondering if he would be beaten for this too, not caring if he died, hoping he would.

Later in the day she took him to the park. He still hated her. She took him to the water, murmuring her regret that she had not brought bread to feed the ducks. This omission brought tears to her eyes again. He failed to understand it. He didn't like to see her cry, but saw no reason why she should. She had not been hit. He fiddled with his stockings, and she put a hand out to cover his, appearing to be afraid he would pull his stockings down and expose his welts.

Walking home she held his hand still, but he made it into a tight little fist, and left it that way while they went through the park gates and turned towards the rectory.

She stopped by the hawthorn hedge, near enough for the red berries to appear to be part of her hat trimming. He thought, even through his misery, they made her hat look much nicer. She saw his face less pinched and thought he might be starting to forgive her and squeezed the hard little fist. But she made her eyes sorrowful and her mouth severe.

"It was a very bad thing you did to Nanny, you mustn't forget that," she said.

When he turned away to look at the passing pedestrians and traffic — so urgent and unconcerned! — she tried to prise his fingers open.

"All boys get beatings sometime," she said, in a voice that surprised him with its note of pleading.

He wanted to tell her his brother James hadn't that he knew of but she began to hurry, and he had to take little running steps to keep up and clutch at her hand now, staying clear of her quivering bottom.

Nanny came to the front door to meet them. His father had apparently gone somewhere and was not yet back. His mother, breathing in fluttery relief, said, "Dear me, we needn't have hurried," and put a hand to his shoulder blades.

Do it, do it, said the pressure of her fingers.

"He is ready to say how sorry he is, Nanny," his mother said.

He imagined Nanny's white apron billowed towards him, but did not imagine one hand near her groin holding it down. He stood back very far and reached out a hand to shake her other one, stretching his body from the waist, like a bent black hair pin, his little white face the pin head.

"Quite the little gentleman, Madam," Nanny said.

"Thanks quite a lot to you, Nanny," his mother said, with feeling so deep her voice trembled.

He watched her lift her hat from her head — a dull thing without the berries! — and go off to put it away, concentrating on the bustle back of her dress, which he had not noticed when she wore it previously. Ashamed, he turned his burning face from Nanny's watching eyes.

Now he began to walk about his living room, touching a few odd things, still with the tea towel. He should take it to the kitchen and hang it there, but he was not good at doing that sort of thing, and Mrs Watts would come tomorrow.

He threw it crushed up on the table beside his writing pad and idly capped his ink bottle. He was reminded of owing a letter to his mother and uncapped it again, then squeezed himself into his chair, not pulling it out with a flourish, as he imagined was more suited to his station in life.

"Dear Mother," he wrote, "I have been thinking a lot about you today, possibly because I'm wearing the grey jumper you knitted me, which I thought would be too warm for this climate, but that is not so."

The words, very high on the page, ran quickly into the shadows. Dull, puny things escaping in their shame! He felt the need to escape too and went to look out on Wyndham merging into the dusk.

But it was grey too, all grey, the war memorial a blackish grey, the posts holding up the roof over Grant's store verandah, a washed out grey, the sky a nothing colour, but grey when you looked at it for any time, his staggering fence posts grey too, and the wattle tree where Una's horse had been tethered not the silvery grey of daytime, but cut out dark and sharp with hard decisive scissors, a guard for the road. A grey, grey road leading to nowhere.

He sat on his couch with his back to it. He remembered Una's small round buttocks settling onto the saddle. She had shaken them down as you would shake seed to the bottom of a bag, and made her back very straight as she pulled on one rein to turn her horse around.

He got up and went to the table, flicking his pen so that it rolled off his pad, leaving it a white and gleaming thing, relieving the dark, pleasing him as a soft light would.

Dear mother, said his mind, and he watched almost surprised not to see the words crawl along the lines.

You will be surprised to hear, since I paid no attention to young ladies at home, that I must make up my mind now to choose between two.

He should describe them next of course. Una first, or Enid?

The elder of the two is Enid. (I fancy you would like that

120

name.) A very capable homemaker, which would please you also.

The younger is Una, lively and lovely. (Both are extremely handsome.)

The room was quite dark now and he projected all three women into it, his mother leaving for a bedroom down the hall, a faint rustle from her dress, Enid with her back to him too, arms raised, attending to something on his mantlepiece. And Una. She had her hands on her hips, her back to him as well, but her head thrown provocatively over her shoulder.

He looked down on his writing pad, as if it were a face about to speak.

It was he who spoke. In the room, shadows swallowing all but the edges of his furniture, he threw his words, hitting the wall, loud and resonant, as if they came from the pulpit, in his most impassioned address.

"Both of them, Mother, have the most beautiful little bums!"

21

In their room at Honeysuckle Enid and Una slept with their backs to each other, the space gradually widening since the funeral. On the morning following Una's ride to the rectory, Enid rose first, as was her practice, and noticed Una did not roll to the middle of the bed, as was her practice, revelling in the luxury of the bed to herself, binding herself in the blankets and taking possession of both pillows.

She stayed huddled at the edge as if she had not been warm all night.

Enid got into her dressing gown, taking time settling her cuffs as if to say I am quite prepared to talk if you are. She went to the kitchen for a jug of hot water, for George was always up first to light the stove. When she came back, Una was sitting up with her dressing gown around her shoulders. Enid loosened the neck of her nightgown and pulled the sleeves up to pat her skin with the steaming cloth. She got into corsets as quickly as possible, embarrassed because Una wore only a suspender belt, grateful to pull on her warm loose dress and fasten the belt, pleased too with her slim waist. Una had made the dress. Both of them were thinking this.

"If I were not here to make your clothes how would you manage?" Una said.

Enid covered her dress with an apron that had been Nellie's.

"Why on earth would you not be here to do the sewing?"

she said, brushing her hair and frowning on her nose, daring it to turn red.

"I said make your clothes," Una said in a voice cool as the air coming through the window.

Enid pulled it down sharply.

"There's tea made in the kitchen," she said.

"Then bring me a cup here to sip in the gloom," Una said.

"You know how Father feels about food in bed when you're not sick!" Enid said, showing Una the back of her neck, almost to the door.

"You should ask Father how he feels about being love-sick!" Una said.

Enid had the stove stoked and the fountain, set into the side of the stove, filled before seeing the teapot under its cosy. She poured tea into a kitchen cup, one of her favourites, thick and white, remembering Nellie's hot tan tea that tasted wonderful after the blue grey stuff at boarding school.

It was just light enough to see the garden through the window and she stood watching the beds take shape and the shrubs separate from the fog.

When she returned after refilling her cup, she could see the yellow of the wallflowers, and the sight made her eyes fill with tears.

She let them run over her cheeks, wondering at the pleasure of taking liquid in, and having liquid flow out. More of the garden could be seen now, in particular the corner where there was a large flat rock. Jack had been surprised when she didn't want it moved. In crevices where the earth showed she planted vines that raced across the surface, and her centrepiece was a low growing shrub with feathery foliage that bore mauve, star-shaped flowers, coming out suddenly, as if fighting an inherent shyness.

When I made that garden I thought I was happy. Silly woman, I didn't know what happiness was.

She was pouring water onto oatmeal for porridge when Una came into the hall, and took a coat from the stand, muffling her face in the cloth as she put it on. Enid watched her through the back kitchen window, striding to the dairy to bring milk back for breakfast. That's not the way a clergyman's wife should walk, she thought, feeling happier.

Jack, dressed for a day's work outdoors, came into the kitchen and Enid poured him tea.

"Where's that one?" he said, looking towards the silent living room.

He sat at the corner of the table holding his hat, as if to put it down would contribute to time wasting.

"The dairy way — walking," Enid said, liking to have Jack think she was preparing breakfast without help.

"Walking! At this time of day! She's always wandering about leaving you to do everything. Now there's that car, she'll be riding in that if she isn't walking!" Jack swallowed a large draught of tea. "A mistake, that car! All the money it cost and you have to keep pouring more into it! 'To see how it runs in the rain'! You wouldn't need to try a horse out in the rain!"

He got up and slapped his pockets. "My tobacco and pipe, Enid? Where did someone put them?" Enid, slicing rounds of bread to warm by the stove for quick toasting, went to the living room and returned with the tobacco and a small smile.

I love him, I do love him, I love him helpless. And she lowered her warm face because she was not sure whom she meant.

"Alex's up, I hope," he said. (He would never go and look.) "He needs to be to make up for the time he lost yesterday." He got into his coat and Enid noticed he seemed slower than usual. Is he getting old? I don't want him old!

"You're worried about Ned's place and Hoopers going, aren't you Father?" she said.

How like Nellie she was! He turned his large red face from her. It's not only Ned's place I'm worried about, he said to himself, finding a place for his tobacco. She was still there by the table, her face soft. He hadn't seen her look like this before! She was usually bustling, with her arms working from the shoulders, rapidly moving across the table, reaching up to the shelves, with the cloth of her dress barely settled in one place before moving to another.

Now her shoulders were still, slightly bowed, her arms loose and her hands linked together, long fine hands, with fingers gently, not nervously stroking each other. Like Nellie at the altar where he found her after that clumsy walk, feeling such a fool! Then she turned with that lovely head at the end of her slender neck, tipped back a little to smile on him. Nothing overawed her! Enid, now returning the bread to the crock, lingered by the little table, looking at her garden. That was her pride and joy. She would never leave that! He saw her profile and a gentle absent biting of her bottom lip.

"George can do some digging for you today," Jack said. "I'll tell him at breakfast." He should get away, but felt compelled to stay. As if there was something hanging in the air unsaid!

She took porridge plates from the dresser and stacked them on the bricks beside the stove. That was for him, he liked his porridge in a hot plate and she never forgot. She was alright! She was back now at the window looking out. That flibbertigibbet needed to do more inside to give her more time in her garden.

"I thought I might go to Wyndham today for a few things from the store," she was saying now.

"Take Dolly and the sulky, or let George drive you," Jack said.

"I can walk, thank you Father, since the day seems to be fine."

"You can't go carrying great parcels," said Jack to her back for she was unhooking cups from the dresser.

"Just a few small things. I noticed we're out of nutmeg and darning wool." She stacked things on a tray with downcast eyes.

Jack felt disturbed, trapped, until Una came through the back door swinging a can of milk. There was a deep, black border of damp on her brown shoes and some leaves clinging to her skirt and stockings where she waded through the line of poplars.

"You go into Wyndham after breakfast," Jack said to her. "Your sister wants some things from the store. No need to take all day about it!"

His back was almost through the door when Una called out. "Certainly, Father!"

22

Una put on her tussore dress and cape and came into the kitchen to find the breakfast crockery piled by the washing up dish on the table and Enid on a chair by the stove with the big ginger cat Thomas on her lap, one hand buried in its fur. The warm skin sent comfort up her arm stopping short of her heart.

"Shall I help you wash up before I go?" Una said.

Enid raised Thomas to her shoulder almost totally obscuring her face. Thomas flashed slate blue eyes on Una. Rescue me, they said, with alarmed legs pushed at Enid's breast. This is most unusual.

"Father said to go after breakfast," Enid said.

"I know! But I must know what to get!"

Enid stared at the fire for several moments, loosening her hold of Thomas. He flung his tail up and leapt from her, racing for the back door, sliding through the opening, flying across the yard, scaling the fence and making for the sheds. Una wished she could escape so easily.

"Very well," Enid said, going to the dresser and taking a pad and pencil from a drawer. She sat at the table very straight and Una stood at the other end both hands holding her small leather bag, resting it on the table. Enid stared at the bag very hard for a while then lowered her eyes and began to write. Una had to crane her neck to see. She drew back sharply at the first item but said nothing. Enid wrote twelve pounds of sugar. Una looked into the pantry where adequate sugar supplies sat on the shelf. Enid looked into the pantry too for inspiration.

"Yes, dates," she said. "I haven't made a date cake in quite a while. I could make one for Mr Edwards too. It would keep well, wouldn't it?"

"That depends," Una said gravely.

"Depends?"

"Yes, on where it is listed," Una inclined her head towards an exercise book hanging from a peg in the pantry. Enid followed her gaze.

"Do you have it listed under cakes that keep for three days, cakes that keep for a week, three weeks, a month or until doomsday?"

Enid lowered her blushing cheeks over her writing, filling the page with washing soap, caustic soda, olive oil, sago, pearl barley, canned herrings, oatmeal and two rat traps.

"There!" she said tearing off the page and handing it to Una who made a crisp edge to the fold and slipped it into her bag.

"And if Ena has new bacon in, get me half a side as well," Enid said. "Then I can make soup with the ends we have."

"Are you sure that is all?" Una said, slipping her bag over her arm and sauntering off through the living room and out the front door.

Enid followed and drew the curtain stealthily to one side just as Una, on the road hunched under her cape, turned and waved. Enid withdrew and fled to the kitchen, pouring boiling water onto the crockery in the washing up dish, and having to curb an urge to fly into the other rooms and set them in order.

"I'll have this place looking like a new pin when she gets back!" she said, "I'll show her!" Thomas, who was back in the kitchen having decided to explore further this fireside sitting, and hopeful that it might be extended to food scraps from the larder, twitched his nose and ears. "Get out!" Enid cried, "Out!" She flung the back door to its widest. Thomas fled, tearing like an orange flame across the yard. "If the wretched thing scratches at my pansies, I'll murder it!"

She was giving her berries and ferns arrangement an extra jug of water when a noise outside on the road disturbed her. There were Edwards, his sulky and Una at the front gate, Edwards leaping down and running around the horse's head to help her. She made an arc in the air with her cape flying and he had to settle it at her waist, for her gloved hands were on his shoulders. Together they took parcels from the floor of the sulky and piled them on the roadside.

Enid fled to the bedroom where she tore off her apron. She tore off her dress as well and found a skirt that had been Nellie's. Una had altered it but there was no time to look for another. She put on a blouse that unfortunately had been made by Una too.

"She'll tell him she makes all my clothes!" Enid cried, close to tears and brushing her hair wildly.

By the time she reached the kitchen she had settled her face and arranged a smile. Edwards and Una were there, unwrapping the parcels, he following her example and folding carefully each sheet of brown paper.

"Now I have plenty of paper to cut the pattern for Small Henry's christening dress!" Una cried.

"I told you, dear, where the brown paper was kept," Enid said extending a hand to Edwards, who dusted some fragments of oatmeal from his before shaking hers.

"This is splendid, Una, I see you have everything!" Enid said carrying the hefty bacon to hang in the meatsafe.

Edwards sprang forward but Enid had the new bacon swinging from the hook and the old piece into a saucepan and on the back of the stove before he found tongue to beg to help.

"We shall make soup, and see that Mr Edwards get some!" Enid cried.

"Will that be quite soon?" said Edwards, his eyes on the large pot.

"Two days away!" said Enid. "Una, take Mr Edwards to the front room and give him a seat by the fire."

"I wouldn't mind staying to watch what happens next with that soup!" Edwards said.

"I'll set an extra place at the table," Una said, lifting her sharp little chin and flashing her eyes on Edwards, bidding him to follow her.

He did and was sitting up very straight in Jack's chair by the fire when Jack came in.

23

Jack had an armful of wood and looked over it on Edwards, his large face appearing to grow larger. Edwards sprang to his feet and extended both arms, whether for Jack or the wood was not quite clear.

At that moment Enid came from the kitchen and Una from the bedroom. Enid moved wood swiftly in the brass fireside box to make way to the new lot. Why couldn't I have done that? Edwards thought, scurrying for a seat on the couch, where he viewed Jack's solid, unrelenting back. Una took a seat beside him. How cruel that he could not put out a hand and hold hers, lying with palm upturned in her fawn silk lap.

Enid made her way around the table, putting the cruet to the centre, smoothing the cloth here and there. Then she sat, quite abruptly for her, on the other side of Edwards, murmuring to the room generally that dinner was only minutes away.

The two of them, the two of them! He should have gone on with that letter to his mother. He wrote on in his mind. Both these beautiful girls are mine for the asking. He saw Jack suddenly a lonely, sorrowful figure by the fire. He can see us, he's trying not to. Imagine flinging out his arms and crushing each to his side! (I did an extraordinary thing today Mother, I held them both.)

Una tilted her chin towards the kitchen. "Is there something burning out there?" she said.

"Thank you dear, if you'd go and look!"

Una did not move.

"Perhaps I — " Edwards said. Jack turned an astonished face on him, eyes bulging, jaws working, and snatched up his pipe from the mantel as if he had forgotten dinner was yet to be eaten.

Enid stood and made some more adjustments to the table.

"We're only waiting for Alex and George," she said, and as she spoke there were noises in the hall indicating that they need wait no longer.

"Come, Una!" Enid said, "and we'll bring dinner in." Una, with her gaze caught between the back of Enid's neck and Jack's jaw line, rose and followed.

Alex with the briefest nod in Edward's direction sought a magazine from the mail on the chiffonier and took it with him to the table. Edwards addressed a mournful George standing by the mantel on the coldness of the day outside, and George's answer was to turn and face the fire.

These rude, unfriendly, sullen men, thought Edwards, straightening his back as if a physical duel was not to be discounted. But wait! These girls coming in with downcast eyes, bearing hot and fragrant food were biding their time, merely playing a part, performing on a stage, beyond the wings a real life waiting. With him, with him! (Dear mother if you could see your son now.) He stood sweeping back the chairs for them, then attending to his own.

He made the necessary effort to revert to meekness to say Grace, not missing Alex's sigh as he stroked the magazine beside his plate. Enid fixed cold eyes on it, fingering her knife and fork, and Alex in a little while moved it to a small table within reach.

Authoritative! He would use that word to describe her next time he wrote to his mother. Strong, capable and authoritative. And I can have her!

A hand edged with a silk cuff moved the plate of bread towards him and he lifted thankful eyes. There were the pink cheeks, brown lashes and little creasing frown. Adorable creature! Tapping on his door and asking with girlish wistfulness if he would carry those parcels home for her sister. Loving, obedient, adoring younger sister. One for him, the other the adored sister-in-law.

Bravely he ran an eye over Jack, eating bread with the last of his meat, George waiting for his pudding, and Alex with his eyes on every part of the room, except on him, reminding him of the bulls of which he was terrified, who blinked their eyes on every other object but the one they planned to paw to death. He would return their hostility with a kindness that would surprise them. He would talk if they wouldn't.

"Mr Edgar's farm is to be vacant soon, I understand," Edwards said.

Jack's jaw stopped working on his meat, but stayed thrust out. That doesn't please him then, Edwards thought, looking to Enid for help. She gave it, of course!

"There will be plenty of families glad to live there. The Hoopers are quite old, and it was a kindness to keep them on."

"I must call on them before they go," Edwards said.

You bet he would, Jack thought, clattering his knife and fork together on his plate. Calling on people! What good does that do? He was overdoing the calling here, and he was lucky he wasn't told about it before he got his legs under the table today. Had Jack not come in cold and hungry smelling Enid's boiled beef it might have been a different story.

Enid had her eyes on the fellow's plate, anxious you could see that he liked it. Here she was now with a tray of puddings, giving the fellow his first!

"And yours, Father," she said, following his plate with a jug of custard. She had made his custard then. That was a little better! He would like to find out how the fellow got here with his horse and sulky. He appeared to walk one day and drive the next. Still on that christening business, he supposed. It wasn't to be here!

"Cream too, Enid," he said. That fellow was flooding it on his plate and there would be none for anyone else.

"Of course," Enid said, passing the cream his way. "But you do tell us too many rich things are not good for us."

"My sentiments, too," Edwards said. "The less we have of the good things, the more we relish the little we get."

He stared for a moment at the heaped spoonful of pudding on its way to his mouth, aware that Una's eyes were on it, starting to fill with laughter above her quirking mouth. He put his spoon on his plate and shook off half its load, then put it back to his mouth nibbling gingerly.

Una put her spoon down and spread her hand on one side of her face, turning it away from the table with her shoulders shaking.

Enid from long habit felt a small ache in her throat and an involuntary twitching of her lips.

Stop it, stop it.

A creeping softness invaded Alex's face and he pushed his pudding about unsure that his throat was ready for it.

Una laughed silently on, twisting her body now until she was looking backwards at the couch.

Stupid, said George's bulging eyes, watching the point of one breast jumping lightly under the silk. She would go off in a moment with a serviette wrapped around her face and leave all that good pudding uneaten. She did, and, Enid arranging her features into primness, went on eating with downcast eyes and Edwards, looking after Una, used his serviette to restore his face to sobriety.

"Dear me, I do apologize," he said with his face emerging more ruddy brown than usual and his eyes a very bright brown.

The laughter had been like sun on the table, going so swiftly you wondered when the bleakness returned, had it been imagined.

Edwards's eyes were on the doorway through which Una had passed. Come back and warm it again, he was thinking.

Jack saw. The fellow and Una! The pair of them giggling together. Wandering about and giggling. All they were good for! The fellow and Una. Of course! That's why he was hanging around on feeble excuses. They made a good pair. She was a flibbertigibbet, and he was a fool!

Enid was on her feet now, looking as if she wanted no part in that silly laughing business, setting out the cups and turning the handles in line with the teaspoons as Nellie used to. There she was, lovingly handling the silver teapot that had belonged to Nellie's mother. Enid, his Enid! All the things in the house she loved and cared for like her children. Her garden she loved equally as well. This was her home, a kingdom to rule over.

She handed the fellow his tea first, but that was only manners. His was next with a little smile, anxious that it was right for him.

Una came back and slid into her place. She had done something to her hair and the fellow was noticing.

Jack took his first swallow of tea. Just the right strength. His jowls relaxed and his eyes blinked a few times, chasing away the hardness. He looked as if he might begin a conversation. Well, really! thought Edwards, his own body losing its tenseness, if this is what a good meal does to a man, bring on more of them, is all I can say. He sipped his tea with relish too, almost feeling the warmth of

Una's body for she was close to him, and Enid within arm's reach. The two of them, the two of them! And one for him!

"Did you have sugar?" Jack said and held out the bowl.

Edwards nearly dropped his cup.

24

Enid was at the dressing table that afternoon when Una came bursting in and pressed her back to the closed door with her head back, pressing it there too. Habit caused Enid to look up, widen her eyes, and slightly shake her head before returning to creaming her hands.

"I thought I was being chased," Una said, still with her eyes closed.

Enid watched her face in the mirror for a change of colour. "You are so ridiculous Una. One grows tired of your nonsense."

Una flung herself full length on the bed throwing both feet together with a clamping of her leather shoes held high above the counterpane.

"I shall be washing the curtains and the counterpane soon anyway," Enid said getting up.

Una sat up too. "Oh dear, I thought I was doing something forbidden. Sin is so joyful!"

Enid rolled up her sleeves preparing to put on an old jacket to work in the garden until it was time to get tea. Una studied herself in the mirror of the wardrobe, daintily picking a few leaves and twigs from her skirt and jumper, for she had flung off her tussore dress when Edwards left and gone for a walk in the orchard. She lifted her hair clear of her eyes and pressed the great mass of it to the back of her head.

"See!" she said. "That's how I'd look with my hair cut! What do you think?"

Enid buttoned her jacket and left the room.

"She has no intention of cutting her hair," Enid said hurrying from the sharp edge of her fear towards her garden as if it were a friend certain to comfort her.

When she came inside two hours later Una was cutting the pattern for Small Henry's christening dress. She had turned back the green cloth on the dining table and had one eye on the dress she borrowed and the other on her paper.

Enid stared at the small white garment feeling a resentment that Small Henry wasn't inside it.

She imagined the puffing of the cloth for his body and his mauve feet turned outwards from the hem and the wrinkles of his neck coming out of the bound neckline. She had taken no interest in the girl's efforts to get a few things together for the baby and felt remorse that she did not know where the dress came from.

Una frowned from the scissors to the dress. "It's only the yoke that bothers me," she said. "I should unpick it, but I think I can manage." She flung the dress down and Enid had to suppress a wince. The sleeves were under the bodice and it seemed Small Henry's arms were carelessly crumpled and should be straightened.

"You learned draughting," Enid said.

"I did, I did," Una said, neatening an edge of a paper shape with her tongue in the corner of her mouth. "So I did, so I did."

She frowned some more, grinding the scissors blades together absently while she stared hard at an untouched sheet of paper. "But all this is different. Different."

Enid said nothing, fighting an urge to escape.

"You agree it is different, sister dear?" Una said with scissors poised.

"It's a small dress. Yes, that makes it different," Enid said.

"I see many differences. Many, many differences." Una began to cut. "All around."

Enid turned some flowers in a vase and a disturbed rose dropped its petals, some falling from the small table to the floor. She picked them up and with a hand closed over them went towards the kitchen. She heard the silent scissors at her back. She built up the stove catching sight of the soup pot with a softening of her heart. She put the lid on hastily when she heard the squeak of scissors and turned to find Una there.

"Will we be taking it to him in a basket like Little Red Riding Hood?" Una said. "I'll do the errand! It will be a lot easier than twenty pounds of sugar and half a pig!"

Enid began to bring things from the pantry frowning past Una to the kitchen clock, calculating the time she had to prepare tea.

"The soup?" Una said. She held the scissors with their points into the table. They were like two small swords digging into flesh.

"Do mind the scissors and the table!" Enid said. "As for the soup. George can take it in the sulky. Also it won't be ready until the day after tomorrow!"

"Quite a wait, isn't it? Quite a wait!" Una went off to the living room cutting the air with her scissors.

Enid went to the window to watch a wind running through her pansies causing them to nod for seconds after it had passed. Brown like his eyes. It's alright, it's alright! they said.

George came in as she was taking the remains of the corned beef to make it into hash for tea. He had a piece of timber for shelves for the closet and held it up, marking with his thumb a suggested width. These men, she thought with rising anger. Can't they talk? She nodded without speaking too. She watched George go, the timber slanted across his slight backside and his profile a wish-wash colour like poor soap suds. They were a hesitant lot!

"Show me where you want them!" he called from the lumber room.

"On the inside!" she called back. In the beginning the cupboard had been a source of great joy to her. Now she saw it only in the rectory, and she couldn't bear to look at it taking shape in the lumber room, restoring the room to order as she had wanted for so long. I need to stop this foolishness, she said to herself, knowing she had no such intention.

She was wearing one of her small soft smiles when Jack came in and she put down the knife she was using to peel potatoes and wiped her hands on a dishcloth.

"You're in for tea, Father?" she said, giving all her attention to scrubbing her fingers. "Go into the front room by the fire and I'll bring it to you there."

But when Jack took off his coat he sat by the kitchen table. "She's in there with all that sewing," he said, inclining his head towards the living room. He considered that Una sewed too much and there was unnecessary spending involved. He suspected when she asked for money for flannels and pyjamas for him and the boys she bought materials for dresses and fripperies, thinking he would not notice.

Enid now made the end of the table neat for his tea things and poured his tea. He liked watching her do these things, efficiently and not fussily like some women, but he wished she would sit and let him say what he wanted to and get it over.

He looked towards his hat where it hung, wishing he had it to turn between his hands. He looked down at his heavy thighs pressed near the table for they would not fit under it.

"Una and that fellow," he said.

He thought he heard an intake of breath but straight after there was a tinkle as she set her teacup on its saucer. Her eyes were downward, but he thought (he wasn't sure) that they might have run wide and wild around the room before she lowered them.

"She wouldn't be too far away there. She still needs you to keep an eye on her."

He pushed his cup forward for more tea. It seemed a long time before she poured it. He drank it quickly then got up and got into his coat and went out through the back door.

He tried to remember what expression was on her face. But this was impossible. He had not looked at it.

25

She went too, into the garden to weed a rose bed.

She had dodged the job for weeks, seeing the space too restricted to crawl into, but she was there now, tearing at soft cress-like growth, casting it backwards from her, unconscious it seemed of thorns plucking at her sleeves and digging into her back.

Some pierced her hands and blood was mixed with black earth, and she used the weeds to wipe her skin, and saw the red smearing the green as if bearing blooms.

Una, her cutting out done, wandered into the kitchen and saw the tea preparations halted, the fire low, and through the window her sister's crouched shape under the roses.

"Well, drat her socks!" Una cried. She threw the window up noisily, and Enid backed out from under the bushes. She stood holding the trowel against her skirt and seemed to grow taller.

Her head was back, her eyes on the sky and she rubbed a sleeve across her forehead, resting her face for a moment on it. A wind came and swooped the shrubs about, and made tracks through the flower beds, but nothing of Enid, her clothes or her hair, appeared to move. Weird, weird, thought Una. But beautiful, yes quite beautiful. I'm glad he's not here to see.

She went and poked among the coals in the stove, then went for the rice canister in the pantry, more than anything to pass the window again. Enid was now in a back corner of the garden where there was a trellis with a climbing rose. She had taken hold of the wood and was shaking it, stopping now and again to lay her face in the crook of her elbow and turn it from side to side.

Una, picking up a potato to peel, felt her mouth as dry as the skin offending her hands. She dropped the knife to look again at Enid, now with her face inside both arms upstretched, holding the trellis.

Una made the rice pudding, nutmeg on top, and had it in the oven when she remembered that Enid had been putting raisins in it lately. Oh, hang the lot of them! she told herself, giving the oven door a little kick with her shoe, as there was the sound of Enid's shoes in the hall. In a little while she came into the kitchen, buttoning the cuffs of a puce coloured dress that had been Nellie's. She seldom wore it and it didn't suit her, only the collar of rows of light coloured lace saved her face from taking on the same puce shade. She wants to look her ugliest, Una thought fighting a small gladness.

"I made a rice pudding without raisins," Una said. "You weren't here to ask."

Enid went for the raisins, chopping them so swiftly and finely it looked as if she had no regard for her fingers, then taking the pudding out, swirled the nutmeg out of the way, scattered the raisins in and returned it to the oven.

There, said the snap of the oven door, another of your mistakes rectified.

Una put her hands on her hips. "Well, I shall go and do some machining on Small Henry's christening gown, shall I?"

She was nearly to the living room door when Enid cried out "Una!" Una backed like a horse pulled with reins, until she reached the kitchen, where she stopped with rump extended and hands tucked under her armpits flapping them up and down.

A bird now, about to fly. Enid sank into a chair by the stove smoothing at her hands rubbing at the small bloody marks. Thomas came in and slid against her leg, and getting no response turned to Una who slung him like a scarf across her shoulder and set a tray with things for the dining table, pinning Thomas to her shoulder with a cheek. Thomas twisted about and twitched his whiskers hoping to get to the milk jug. She released him and he landed on his feet, hooping his back and trying to decide between a leap on Enid's lap and a watch on the woodbox out of which a mouse was known to have tumbled in the past. "Out!" cried Enid suddenly throwing out a foot, and Jack coming through the back door cried "Out!" too and swung the door wide to help Thomas on his way. Una with the tea tray rattling felt she was dismissed too and decided not to return from the living room but leave the two of them to the intimacy of the kitchen.

"Let them roll and toss before the fire and a shower of coals fall on his naked bum!" Una muttered making for the little room where the sewing machine was.

Enid was confused. Jack was in. For tea? No, there were the dirty cups and the clock hands, unless it had gone crazy, showing an hour past afternoon tea time.

She stroked the pot though in a distracted way, he thought. That other one was not giving her enough help!

"I'll wait for the hash," he said nodding at the end of beef under one of her gauze coverings.

"Of course," she said and taking the cover off it, stared for a long moment then put it back again.

She bowled some green apples towards her and began to peel them. She knew he liked a plateful of them stewed, sometimes before going to bed. He felt steadier. He didn't like seeing her unsettled, without her usual calm. The crack of the fruit as she split it startled him and he looked at the peel curling from her hand and dancing in a crazy way upon the table.

In a minute she had a saucepan full of slices, with sugar shaken through and some water thrown in and they were at the back of the stove.

"I see some of the apples on that tree are turning yellow," Jack said. "George can take a ladder and gather some for eating."

A basketful for him. The two of them admiring, she inviting him to run his thumb over the greeny yellow skin of the fruit to feel and wonder at the greasy surface. She knew his thumbs. They were long with a bluish tinge to the skin at the joint. Sometimes he sat with his hands on his thighs and the thumbs made deep dents in the black cloth of his trousers. She thought of her thumbs there, surprised that she felt no shame. She would press them deeper than he did and there would be a jerk of the flesh as he snapped his legs open and she on her knees would move her body till it was against his crotch and he could raise his knees and press them into her back and she would bring him even closer with her arms wound and crushed to his back.

Her elbows were amongst her apple peelings, and Jack, although he did not want to, was looking at her face with her fingers pressing the flesh upwards on her cheeks. Then she reached for a colander and put the peelings in.

"I think, Father, I will go to Percy's for a week. I feel the need for a little holiday."

He stood quickly and caught up his hat, holding it in a grip as if it was the hand of a friend who had unexpectedly solved a problem for him.

I'll give her five pounds too to spend at the shops there, slip it into her hand as she is going, he thought, turning his face from her with the odd and foolish thought that she might guess and spoil the surprise.

Una could be heard back in the living room.

"Tell her," Jack said and Una hearing the raised voice came with a small, creased, curious face into the kitchen.

"You sister is going to the sea for a week," Jack said as if it needed to be said very loud to be confirmed.

Una's face went vivid. Her whole body leapt and quivered inside her clothes. Jack looked from her to Enid who seemed shrunk inside her puce dress. She had got thin. She needed a holiday!

"Violet will come and stay with Small Henry!" Una cried bringing both hands together in a clap. "I shall have him here to fit while I make his christening dress!"

Jack had not wanted that. He had thought the flibber-tigibbett might settle to some serious housekeeping if she had the place to herself for a while. It would help prepare her when she and the fellow . . .

But he wasn't going to object. His Enid must get away for her holiday without disruption. She might finish up not going at all if there were arguments.

Enid was making the hash with mechanical hands. Small Henry! She had not thought of him for hours. His little shape rushed accusingly at her, and although his eyes were squeezed shut his face wore a hurt look. Small Henry, forgive me! Don't hate me. Please don't hate me! I'll make it up to you.

26

She did by thinking of him and talking of him all through the week she was at Percy's. Sybil, who was twenty and ripe like a black cherry, her body a piece of fertile ground ready for seed, raised the theory that it was Enid who bore Small Henry.

"Think of it!" she said to the ring of sisters in their attic room on their unmade beds, the air around them musty with the smell of scent and face powder, stained underwear and grubby linen and unwashed flesh. "We didn't see her for six months or more!" She narrowed her black eyes at a vision of Enid shut in a back room at Honeysuckle all day, walking about the yard awkwardly at night for exercise.

Sadie said this was nonsense. "Henry had a wife! Addie Brown was at the funeral and Enid was there large as life passing around the cakes and bossing Una about!" Thoughts of Enid immaculate in her room watching through the window the grey sea swirling, caused Sadie to get up and hand the jug from the washstand to a younger sister and order her to bring hot water from the kitchen, unbuttoning her blouse while she spoke. Sybil flung herself back among the tangled bedclothes raising both arms to exude more sweaty air.

"He's perfect, absolutely perfect. Wait till you see him!" she said, mocking Enid.

"I can wait — forever!" she said, giving her stomach a passing slap to discard any hint of fertility there.

Alex brought Enid home at the end of the week and

there on the verandah was Una with Small Henry in her arms. Enid moved forward in her seat holding her handbag very tight. Alex took the gesture as an insult to his driving. Silly, nervous female he thought glimpsing her tense face.

Enid saw Small Henry's head with hair thinned out at the back where the pillow had rubbed it away. It was getting lighter in colour. Una should turn him for her to see his face! She saw Una tipping her head to bring Small Henry closer to her neck, jamming him there and giving her no chance of seeing him.

It was deliberate! She left her suitcase for Alex to bring in, and with a hurt and angry face gathered up a bag of jams and pickles from the hotel pantry and cuttings from the garden. Una went ahead and was in a chair in the living room, unwrapping Small Henry and expertly wrapping him again and lifting him to her shoulder. Still no face for Enid to see! She sat on the end of the couch her luggage by her, waiting for the dimness to leave the room, wondering at the white blurr in one corner until it emerged as the christening dress in a near finished state.

Well, look at her there, Violet thought, putting a few of her things together for she thought while the car was on the road Alex might offer to drive her and Small Henry home. She does not look as if the holiday did her much good. She could look hang dog like George at times. Irritating. Give me a little brightness, I always say.

"How was it at Percy's?" Violet said. "Any of that lot caught a man yet?"

Enid might have given her head a little shake before standing abruptly and with her cuttings and jars went to the kitchen. Una buried a face deeper into Small Henry's neck.

Well, I can't hang around here for the Reverend's next visit to sort things out, Violet thought as she stuffed napkins in a bag. I've got to get home to Ned's mess. There was George stepping from one foot to the other, waiting for a bidding to put Dolly in the sulky. A little run in the Austin would suit her better! She might throw a hint Alex's way which was by the fire with a *Sydney Mail* which he had flapped open and was rolling the opposite way for easy reading.

But there was the money she needed from George for her hospital. Oh damn and blast it, Violet said to herself, plucking Small Henry from Una's arms to give vent to her annoyance, and laying him on the table she pulled the hem of his nightgown down around his feet, oblivious to the series of grunts he was starting and Una's woeful expression.

"I've got to start for home," she said loudly, the thought of Ned raising her voice several decibels.

Enid slipped into the room from her bedroom where she had gone to change into the puce dress. Small Henry's small and piteous face was turned towards her. It was a little fuller than she last saw it, a little more flesh coloured than that mauvish colour. Even the eyebrows, more defined now, were screwed into anger with the mouth a tear in his face showing wet and angry gums.

Violet, who had changed his napkin, rolled him up as if he were a parcel of meat and handed him to Enid.

"There!" she said. "You might as well finish off the spoiling for that's what he's had all week!"

Enid backed to the couch to sit on one corner. The comfort of the dry napkin smoothed the anger from Small Henry's face and the jagged hole that was his mouth closed into a small tight rosebud and he made a sucking motion as if food might be at hand and a little practice would do no harm. Enid smiled at this and bent low over his face so that his skin breathed onto her skin like warm silk, her breath moving the fine down like the wind bending low over her flower beds and causing a smell to rise, sweet as the smell of Small Henry's face.

Una caught up the christening gown and pinned it to her front with her chin. "See!" she said. "No lace or flowers. Imagine when he's grown up showing him something lacy and frilly and telling him he wore it. He would hate me!" She turned and tossed it from her and at that moment the back screen door banged and Enid lifting her face acknowledged the arrival of Jack. She stood returning Small Henry to Violet and slipped away to the kitchen.

Una leapt into a clear space in the room to pantomime the meeting between them. She thrust her body forward from the waist and pushed out her lips in the shape of a giant kiss. She held the pose, then as in a passion of ecstasy she flung a leg up and wound it around an imaginary figure. Alex turned to the fire to stifle his laughter by turning some logs. Violet's mouth twitched while she rocked Small Henry to silence. George saw only her softened face and wished he was close enough to touch her. Una's head was back and her arms stretched out and upwards, the fingertips just touching to illustrate the bulk of Jack.

Violet laughed outright and George moved up and touched her elbow. He tipped his head towards the back of the house, which in George's language was stating he would harness Dolly and bring the sulky around to the front.

Oh, well, I have to, I suppose! Violet thought, dumping a bag of Small Henry's things near the door with Una hovering near, arms poised to take Small Henry the moment Violet was prepared to surrender him. Alex there by the fire with his head in his paper was going to make no offer!

Violet trudged off to Henry's old room for her case.

Always the way, she grumbled to herself, those who have got it stick to it — meaning Alex's car. She would have to stay with George, dull as he was. There was the sulky in front now, and Una looking as if someone had thrown a bucket of cold water over her.

"Well, come for the ride," Violet said. "Take him and wrap him up well, in case he goes down with pneumonia!" Una plucked a bonnet from Violet's bulging bag and bore Small Henry to her bedroom, flinging him on the bed.

"Stay quiet there, you little turd!" she cried, crushing on her small hat and flinging her blue cape around her shoulders. "Keep still while I change my shoes, you little piece of rabbit dung. I need more time to get ready, but I haven't got it. He's seen me in this too many times already. Yell away, yell away!"

For Small Henry, fooled into thinking a change of position indicated a meal was on its way, arched his back and squealed, threatening to smother himself inside his blanket. She took him up at last, crushing his bonnet on, laughing because the white wool made his face seem even redder, and flew out and climbed in the sulky beside Violet, who was crushed against George, to his great joy.

Enid saw the sulky from the kitchen window. Speeding towards Wyndham. Towards him.

Jack had just finished telling her about the Hoopers. The son-in-law, finding himself with a free morning, decided to go and collect them, giving them no time to warn Ned or Jack, and driving off with pigs squealing for a meal, and cows trailing towards the bails, uttering an occasional pleading, mournful cry.

Both Jack and Horse reared their heads at the sound of the long blast of the horn. The son-in-law laughed for the first time that day and Mrs Hooper, sitting where she chose to in the back of the truck to guard her china from breakages, for the son-in-law had flung it carelessly on, broke down and cried.

Jack had seen her with her head down and a man's handkerchief to her face which was turned from the direction of the little grey house with the chimney still smoking.

Jack thought Enid was paying more attention to her garden through the window than to his story, but when he reached the part about Mrs Hooper's tears, Enid cried, "Oh, Father!" and burst into tears herself.

27

Mrs Watts had not disturbed the writing pad Edwards left on the table, the cover turned back like a bed turned down, waiting for occupancy. Mrs Watts, unable to read or write, dusted around it, aware there was nothing written there, but so deeply ashamed of her illiteracy she felt that even looking on it was equivalent to looking at a married couple in bed.

Edwards was aware of it too, lighting his lamp when it was too dark to see, and there was nothing to hear, after the sulky had carried Una back to Honeysuckle.

Dear Mother, the younger Miss Herbert was visiting this afternoon. It was totally unexpected. Passing my kitchen window I looked up and there she was.

He could not believe it. One minute there was the drab, empty front of Violet's house, the verandah posts drooping dejectedly as he looked on them, the patch of road so cold and still it might have been scraped from the surface of the moon. He took some bread and cheese from his safe and passing the window again there was the sulky pulled up and Una springing from it, her blue cape flying and her arms upstretched to take Small Henry from Violet. It was as if he turned his back on a blank wall and someone hung a picture while he wasn't looking.

"She's here!" he cried, taking a bite from the cheese, which he then flung down and walked rapidly into his living room.

He touched his writing pad as if he should write the

information down to make it more believable. Then he returned to the kitchen window and saw the empty sulky and the lowered head of Dolly.

He watched the house — surely it would open a door or window and show her to him! He threw up his window knowing the rattle had no chance of reaching those closeted inside. She had found a reason to call on him the last time she was at Violet's!

She was avoiding him, discarding him. He would have Enid then! He went to his living room again. Enid it will be! He fiddled with his writing pad and uncapped his ink.

Dear Mother, I have practically made up my mind. She is in your image, so very like you.

He sat sideways at his table, then got up again and returned to his kitchen window. Nothing. Only the chimney, with an air of mocking him, sent up a burst of smoke. They were making tea with never a thought of him. They could have sent George for him. It was the sort of thing George was used for!

He would go to his woodheap, his own fire needed lighting, if he was to have anything hot to drink before going to bed. He would not necessarily look their way. He stood looking hard at his wood.

Then out of the corner of his eye he saw. Una with Small Henry in her arms at the window. From out of his blanket she took a tiny hand and waved it back and forth, back and forth.

His horse under the big tree chose that moment to lift its rump while it rubbed the side of its head on a foreleg.

The wretched thing! He should throw a lump of wood at it. Then it decided to dance sideways for no reason that he could see and gave him back the entire window. He swooped upon a log of wood, a great thing testing his strength, and raising it, waggled an end, returning the salute.

Then Violet's great back filled the window and they were gone. He saw her shoulders working, she was snatching Small Henry from Una and pushing her ahead. He saw Small Henry's face, no bigger than a pinhead it seemed, dance away from him, and nothing of Una at all.

He dropped the wood and went inside. He saw shadows reach out from the corners of his room and dance quite crazily for a moment on the writing pad.

Dear Mother, If ever I should have a child of my own I would never have a nurse for it.

28

He dressed next morning to go to Honeysuckle with the excuse that he would welcome Enid back after her week at the sea, then changed his mind, put the horse in the sulky and took the road towards Bega. He sped past a surprised Violet dispiritedly shaking a mat on her front verandah.

He never said he was going anywhere, like Candelo or Bega, said her expression, fastened to his black back. He might have asked did I need anything! After all the kindnesses I've shown him! I'll be putting a stopper on the tea and cakes from now on.

She flung the mat into the front room when passing the door, not fussy where it landed, and tramped angrily to the kitchen. Ned was there, scraping his feet on the floor from his seat on the couch, and through Small Henry's closed door came the noise of his yelling.

"I'll make changes in this place before long, see if I don't!" She filled the big kettle for Small Henry's bath, needing to step around a stick with the end forming a natural handle which Ned had found in the bush, and now appeared to use all the time.

I thought it was his eye, Violet said to herself. I see now it's the other end as well. And what's in between is as good as useless too! She slowed her movements to punish Small Henry, who increased the volume of his bellowing, and Ned, who rose agitated and pointed his stick towards the bedroom door.

"They ruined him down there!" Violet cried, flinging a

wash cloth in a china basin that was Small Henry's bath. "I'm left to repair the damage. And repair it I will!"

Her shouting shocked Small Henry into silence for a moment, then he started up again, inserting a fluttery feebleness into his cry as if warning of impending exhaustion.

"And I might well dump him on them after all!"

Ned raised his head like an animal alerted to something that pleased him. She would wipe that look from his face!

"There'll be bellowing to take his place, make no mistake, Ned!" Ned looked about him, as if he'd received an order from a superior officer which he did not fully understand.

"I'm opening a hospital here, Ned. I've planned it all and I'm ready to go!"

Ned was in the kitchen doorway now, pinning a toe of his boot down with his stick. Violet saw his back and the edge of his face, the side with the lost eye. Enough! Enough! He heard, he knows, he knows!

She threw some cups and plates from breakfast into a tin dish and flung a towel over a limited space on the table, partly covering jam and butter and the teapot and not caring. She would have a girl from one of the farms helping when she had the hospital. Una could be here a lot of the time, since she was so fond of playing at mothers.

Violet had been, as she put it, sooling Edwards onto Enid. She decided now, with a small rush of pleasure, she would change to Una. Enid was too good a catch for him anyway. Going off like that without a word! She would let him know what real manners were. Not all bowing and hat removing and opening doors and gates the way she saw it!

She went for Small Henry, shedding his steaming napkin in the bedroom and returning to the kitchen with his bare behind defenceless, crushed like a peach, and not much bigger inside one of her large arms.

She laid him on the towel where his flaying legs failed to disturb his genitals, looking too like a smaller squashed peach. Lifting him into the water she saw Ned taking the track to the bush.

"You're one of them too!" she shouted to Small Henry above his new protesting squeal. She lathered his face and head with soap so that he looked like a small, angry Santa Claus. "You'll grow up just like them! No better! Give me a world without men! Free of the burden they bring, the worries they lay at your feet!"

She rinsed Small Henry as if he were a newly peeled potato and dried and dressed him. She screwed the cap on the powder tin after flooding his crotch and fished the soap from the water. "I'm meeting the cost of all of this!" she cried. "The dill water as well. And what about later on when he starts in on the gruel, the oatmeal and the mashed potato? And no cheque from Halloween every month!"

She sat and pushed the teat of the bottle into Small Henry's mouth and watched his last slow tear run into his ear while he drank.

"I must have that hospital, and the least you can do is help me get it! You've tied me down here, you're the reason why I can't go out on cases now! Hear that, hear that! I must have a better reason for being anchored in this hell hole!"

Small Henry's answer was an expansion of his chest as he took the first strong flow from the bottle, with eyes squeezed shut and fingers curled in ecstasy.

The room that had rocked angrily about Violet now settled down. The sun was warm on her back, and the fire in the stove snapped and hummed to say it was burning without attention. The only other sound was the scrape of

158

a fowl's throat from the pen, all the others reduced to a morbid quiet, since Ned had gone too long for even their optimism to hold out.

Violet, barely aware of it, rocked Small Henry gently with her eyes on the dresser. A dozen china plates and soup bowls, a dozen cups and saucers. Four bed pans, four enamel basins, four single iron beds and mattresses.

That wretched man! She could have given Small Henry an earlier bath and left him and a day's supply of bottles and napkins with Rachel, and taken the empty seat in the sulky. He would be going as far as Candelo. A missed chance of seeing what the stores there had to offer. One had a large parent branch in Bega through which an unlimited range of goods could be ordered.

That wretched man! She would have worn her black suit, looking every inch the matron.

She swirled the last of the milk in Small Henry's bottle but he shut his lips tight as a closed flower against the teat. She hoisted him to her shoulder where he broke wind at both ends.

"There he goes, farting like a bullocky already! Not one of them any different!"

She laid him in his bed and shut the door on him, going to the back verandah for a mop and looking into the bush for a sign of Ned.

"This quiet's a killer!" she said, missing Honeysuckle and Una rushing around, hair awry, bursting out with something unexpected, like a pantomime of Jack or George, or throwing her scissors down with a great clatter and a cry.

"I feel like some toffee! Let's make a batch of toffee and a mess while she's away!" Enid did not tolerate sweet making except for shows, where hers was usually the most professional of all the exhibits.

How would the reverend feel about toffee making when he was expecting the bishop? Hee, hee. Violet relished the scene with the same pleasure as a mouthful of treacly toffee.

She flung her mop about the bedroom floor, setting up a rattle from a small table in a corner displaying brass ornaments made from spent ammunition, which Ned carried home from the war, and Violet at first lovingly polished and arranged on a white embroidered table cover.

"Out! Out!" she cried, jabbing her mop towards them. "All of them out!"

She would have a closet in their place, similar to the one George was putting up in the lumber room at Honeysuckle to take the few things brought in by her patients. Not much in the case of Tess Skinner, whom Violet assumed would be confined there, since Violet delivered her other children in the house and she wouldn't be doing this any more. She felt an urge to move the big bed and wardrobe to the end of the verandah.

"In a couple of weeks it'll be warm enough to sleep there," she said hurrying the season along ahead of its time. "He might prefer old Phoebe's hollow tree and he's quite welcome to it!"

Banging the mop on the verandah rail and getting a view of the big gum under which Edwards's horse usually sheltered, she steered her thoughts back to him, bubbling away like a pan of sour jam on a too hot stove.

"I'll see him mated with the flighty one if it's the last thing I do!" she cried. "She'll keep him on his toes! I could have got a bolt of calico and started her on the sheets. How dare he go off, sneaking off without a word! How dare he?"

29

Violet's gaping mouth and angry brow was seen by Edwards when he passed the house, doffing his hat and raising the reins in salute. Guilt invaded him and he sent his horse faster as if he could leave the feeling behind this way. He should have called on Mrs Violet and asked if he could do any errand for her, a custom he knew to be practised in Wyndham when neighbours made a trip to a larger town. Well, what was done was done, and he hoped the farther he left Violet's accusing shape behind, the less troubled he would feel.

He could not bear another day spent without some positive step towards a future with Enid or Una. Una or Enid! He must have it out with the archdeacon. Marriage was normal and necessary. He wanted it! He could have either of those girls with a snap of his fingers. Snap his fingers he did, holding a hand high as he raced along, the crisp air chilling his face and deepening the ruddy colour.

"I can have either!" he shouted to the sky, a clear blue with only one puffy cloud racing with him. A pillow of cloud! He laughed up at it. He saw a streaming vapour like a girl's hair trailing the cloud pillow, and would have stood in the sulky and whooped except that he would lose his balance.

He slowed his horse. He could not wear him out this way. Bega was too far off to make the return trip in the one day. Where he would spend the night he did not know. The sky was his roof though, look at it up there! He felt he should be shouting to the sky as if the world was his house, and he could behave as he liked in it.

He was surprised to see Candelo come up so soon. The Anglican church and rectory set back from the road was several hundred yards past the first cluster of houses.

The Minister's wife, Mrs Palmer, had made a garden around the front steps, and bright cushions were tilted on chairs on the verandah.

Edwards having tied his horse to the front fence went up the steps, pleased at the sight of the front door open, a shine on the floor covering, a bowl of bright yellow flowers on the piano. He was staring at them thinking of Enid when Mrs Palmer answered his knock. She was fair, sturdy and strong looking, unlike many ministers' wives who were small with a cringing air, going about with downcast eyes, as if a reticent and humble front made their husbands appear powerful and authoritative, which Edwards knew, in many cases, they were not.

Mrs Palmer seemed pleased to have a visitor and offered Edwards a chair and tea. She kept up a conversation while in the kitchen, which was next to the dining room, through an archway separating it from the front room. A superior dwelling to his, Edwards had to concede with lowering spirits.

"Gordon is visiting the school this morning," Mrs Palmer said while her hands, visible to Edwards, buttered bread at a table.

Surprised at himself, he didn't mind. When he stopped (this was a day he was doing everything on impulse) he had vague thoughts of sharing his problem with Palmer, whom he considered approachable, though not as forthright as he would be, given a parish of this size.

He believed he saw now the reason for his hesitant manner.

Mrs Palmer was the stronger of the two, and he imagined now as she brought in the tea tray that it was her husband who lurked in her shadow. He hoped he did not come in soon. The Palmers had only two children, he remembered, and he wondered how they managed this (or she did) and looked foolishly for a solution in the vicinity of her hips and thighs, as if there would be something there to give her secret away.

I'll need to pray pardon for these kinds of thoughts, he told himself, blushing towards his teacup. She put hers down on the small table between them and asked about the health of Small Henry.

"A christening there quite soon," Edwards said.

"A sad affair," Mrs Palmer said, and Edwards, thinking of Enid as he swallowed his sultana cake, and of Una when he looked at the piano where he had seen her reflection in the shining wood of the one at Honeysuckle, and wondering where any sadness could be, was some time remembering the circumstances of Small Henry's birth.

"The young mother's death, yes," he said, making his voice sound pious.

He saw by Mrs Palmer's expression that it was not to be totally regretted. The mother had sinned and sin was for punishment.

"He's in the care of an aunt?" she asked next. (She gained this information from Rachel Holmes with whom she had occasional telephone conversations, the two having sung together in the same church choir as schoolgirls.)

"At the moment, yes," said Edwards, and felt her sharpish look upon him, allowing her to interpret a family intimacy, involving him.

"Is the father likely to return for him?" Mrs Palmer said.

"That is hardly likely," Edwards replied, putting his cup down with a crisp little clink of china.

"Perhaps the young sisters — ?", Mrs Palmer said. The reputation of the well dressed, gadding and unencumbered Herbert girls had spread far beyond the borders of Wyndham. Mrs Palmer, jealous of their freedom, and what appeared to be a generous clothes allowance, felt pleasure that here was something threatening to restrict them. Immediately she felt she should temper the thought with something more charitable.

"They are both capable, from what I hear."

Edwards needed to blink away the light suffusing his eyes and running down to tenderize his mouth. Capable! Indeed they were capable. And one of them his! He crossed his legs and Mrs Palmer's attention was caught and rivetted to his thighs, one squashing the other on the chair she had never thought so frail before. Ah, I see, thought Mrs Palmer. And I had thought this day as drab and empty as most of the others! Which one, I wonder?

She concentrated on a vision of the Herbert girls at a diocese garden party in Bega, so smartly turned out she was doubly conscious of her old navy serge suit, too hot for the warm spring day. Let it be Enid, the haughtier one. See how she manages on a miserable stipend. Edwards was smiling protectively, she thought, on someone envisioned. The younger one? She had looked shyly from under her hat trimmed with cornflowers and stood slightly behind her sister, with her half smiling lips, looking as if they had been coloured a deeper red. Paint on the face of a clergyman's wife!

Mrs Palmer now shifted her solid legs and raised a fair freckled face. This was interesting indeed! She refilled both their cups without asking, signalling a developing intimacy, aware that her breasts fell forward over his cup and rose and quivered when she leaned back in her chair. She sipped her tea with lowered eyes.

164

"Both charming girls," she murmured.

She saw his eyes bright as the gold rim on the cup.

"Is it too early for felicitations then?" she said. "Or quite in order?" She put her head to one side in coquettish fashion which Edwards observed, in spite of the train of his own thoughts, did not suit her.

He moved his cup and saucer to one side of the table as if it would be an obstacle in the serious discussion to follow.

"There are difficulties to overcome," he said. "They may be minor."

The father objects, said the pupils of her eyes, swimming in watery curiosity.

"There is a condition of my appointment to Wyndham that I remain single," Edwards said.

She remembered now. Gordon was at the diocese meeting and heard the matter discussed. When he mentioned it to her (mainly because he would no longer need to take a share of the responsibility of the Wyndham parish with other district clergy) she had snorted scornfully at this fresh evidence of the meanness of the church.

Not prepared to add even a few shillings to the already miserable stipend!

Her anger was heightened by the lean Christmas they were facing, her children unable to swap with schoolmates, tales on the toys they would receive.

"I need to have further talks with the archdeacon before approaching the father." He took up his hat and laid it on his kneecap.

"An engagement perhaps," Mrs Palmer said, still using a murmuring voice.

This was not what she wanted either. She wanted, in a fresh surge of jealousy, one of the Herbert girls in dresses and hats seasons old, losing her looks to a brood of children, in constant torment that she couldn't feed and clothe them adequately.

She had been plain and freckled and gawky and only Gordon had wanted to marry her. His face had never worn that soft, protective look and his thighs had never strained under the cloth of his clerical trousers, but fell away feeble and bony.

She had sat up in bed on their honeymoon, watching him undress. She thought he would hurry through, flinging his clothes off to leap in bed beside her. But he took his time, folding his clothes as he removed them and sitting down to remove his boots, even studying them before putting them down, looking for any sign of wear, frowning over them for a long time.

It seemed like a lesson to her on the kind of life she would have. She had let the blankets fall away to show her daring, sleeveless blue silk nightgown but he appeared not to notice.

He got up from his chair and put his collar studs and sleeve links carefully away, and all she saw was the back of his pyjamas, the cord so tight at his waist that the top bloused over, emphasizing his slightness.

She lay down then and closed her eyes, so she did not know if he looked her way, and when he had blown out the light she heard his hesitant steps to the bed, and was tipped slightly on the mattress when he got in, but moved swiftly back to her edge.

"Asleep?" he said after a while.

"Sound asleep!" she said. He appeared to be digesting this, then slipped under the covers. Her spirits rose with him when he sat up.

"You told them we would have early morning tea, didn't you?" he said. The dark put a thin and querulous edge to his voice.

It gave hers strength and authority when she said: "I told them!"

She waited with a beating heart, feeling him stirring.

"I forgot my prayers," he said.

She had forgotten hers too, and considered punishing him by remaining in bed. But she got up and knelt on her side with her face in the cold stiff sheet.

He knelt with his face turned away from her. She pressed both hands to her face to shut out the sight of him and the sharp tarry smell of soap on the sheets — the cheapest boarding house for their honeymoon! — and could not bring herself to say a conventional prayer. She could only pray for the strength of mind not to hate him.

Edwards's thighs had brought this back to her and she lifted her eyes to his face to return to the present. His eyes were asking gently about her own unhappiness.

I'm alright, said the toss of her sandy head. Her hair made Edwards think of tufts of pale grass growing out of sand. He had a fresh vision of Enid and Una. Una's hair was the more abundant, but Enid wore hers dressed neatly. Yes, Enid's hair in its way was every bit as attractive as Una's.

Edwards rose, taking his hat from his knee. He avoided looking at Mrs Palmer's disappointed face, but she sat on, not uncrossing her legs.

"I should go," he said. "It's such a long drive for my horse." He saw its mournful, drooped face through the open door.

"Why go on to Bega?" she said, eyes washing over him, like water too deep to see the bottom. "Wait till Gordon comes. He could perhaps put your case to the next diocese meeting. Rushing in is not always a good thing."

With me it wasn't. Stay the way you are a little longer! Visit me again like this!

Edwards sat. Here was a nice woman! Warm and kind, taking on the burden of another's problems, how wrong the gossips were that said she was hard and bossy.

A flush was on her cheeks and she had uncrossed her legs and was staring at the tips of her shoes close together on the floor. The toes of his boots were not too far from hers.

"Stay and eat dinner with us," she said.

"I could not think of imposing," he said, wondering about the state of their larder compared to his.

"There would be no imposition," Mrs Palmer said, seeing him part his legs and rub his thighs on the inside. A man is allowed so much, she thought, crossing her legs again, as if she needed to imprison a feeling there, and as a woman was denied the luxury of relief.

"I should complete the errand I set out on," he said. But looking towards the door, they both saw Palmer coming through the gate.

The men exchanged a greeting and Mrs Palmer left them to see to dinner.

Palmer had had a bad morning. He took a group of Anglican children for religious instruction, less than a third of whom had church going parents. His eyes, when raised above the book of parables he read from, accused them of these failings and the bold eyes of the children dared him to interfere.

For most of them the morning meant relief from the rigours of regular schoolwork, and they utilized the time in holiday spirit.

Palmer's nickname was Small Balls, and a row of the class this morning had passed along a paper under their desks, each one drawing a scrotum as they saw his. They were reduced in size as they went along, the second last being two dots, smaller than pin heads.

The last child made no attempt at a drawing, but wrote the word "invisible".

The others seeing this burst into laughter they failed to control, and Palmer asked for the paper. He looked at it and considered sending the group to the headmaster, but knew the large raw boned man to wield the cane without mercy.

After a long sad look at the drawings, some done so well there was no mistaking the subject, Palmer dropped the paper in a waste basket.

Relief escaped the children in a sigh that settled their ribs after the tight and fearful pain they bore, aware of what may be ahead of them. Palmer suggested they kneel and pray forgiveness for their wickedness, and they fell on their knees as one, grateful for the reprieve and grateful that the last few minutes before the bell clanged for dinner could be utilized in additional sly merriment.

"Our Father which fart in heaven," hissed the boy who wrote "invisible", and the others crushed their heads on the wooden desks, arms folded around faces, as if giving themselves up totally to piety.

Palmer saw their shoulders shaking.

Now he felt some slight resentment that there was a visitor at the house. Mavis may not be pleased at stretching the meal to fill an extra stomach, a hollow one if he knew Edwards.

A churchman calling unexpectedly was seen as his responsibility. Mavis could take it out on him subtley during the meal and openly afterwards.

He hung his hat on the stand and saw in the mirror there the reflection of her face, absorbed and quite soft as she set the table. She did not look resentful. Thank you, Lord!

Edwards wore a strained look. Something wrong at

Wyndham? Of course there would be! He got the dregs appointed to that backwater.

Palmer expanded in his chair feeling that Edwards was shrinking in his. Through the window he could see, beyond Mavis's neat garden, part of the solid old school he had just left. That was over for a week! Candelo, quivering nervously those mornings he went there, seemed settled now, snugly at peace, wearing a small and gentle smile like his.

A good place this! He had done very well. Poor, unhappy Edwards! What fresh trouble was that awful little settlement giving him? Palmer blinked his contentment while Edwards's head was inclined towards the window through which there came a volume of noise. Of course it would startle Edwards, unused as he was to anything but sleepy, silent Wyndham.

A muted roar was in the air, no words distinguishable, an urgent chorus, not from finely tuned instruments, no murmuring liquid background, but the beat of feet on earth, the final crescendo the crash of wood on wood, as a gate slammed to.

What on earth? said Edwards's startled brown eyes. There was Mavis flashing from kitchen to dining room with a bowl of freshly whipped potatoes, and there were other smells, fragrant and stomach stirring.

Palmer rose with patronizing energy. "The children out of school for dinner!" he said. "They're a high spirited, happy lot! Extremely intelligent as well. I quite enjoy my morning there!" He led the way to the dining room.

There was no point in Edwards making the trip to Bega after all. After dinner, Palmer, remaining politely uncurious during the meal (church matters were never discussed in the presence of wives and children), used the telephone in his study to confirm what he suspected. The archdeacon was away for a week, visiting a married daughter in Goulburn and only the curate was in charge.

Palmer sat with a flourish after clicking the receiver inside its metal holder and moved a blotter tidily before him. The room was neatly furnished, with no dust anywhere and some flowers on a bookcase.

Edwards thought of the table that passed for his desk in his living room, mostly strewn with his writing pad, magazines borrowed from Honeysuckle and socks dropped there after a search for holes, usually found in abundance.

Palmer motioned him to sit on the chair facing his desk, but Edwards remained standing, holding his hat, seeing a little frill developing at the edge, through the sun and rain beating upon it. He dropped it to his side.

There had been canned salmon for dinner. Edwards ate with relish and envy, believing it to be part of abundant delicacies in the larder, unaware that it was a treat kept by Mavis for rare occasions. He had noticed the children eating slowly of the tender moist flesh, giving silent credit to their mother for their good manners.

He did not know the unexpected treat had a soothing effect on their small troubled hearts. As it frequently happened, they had spent most of their playtime pressed together in a corner of the weathershed, sheltering each other from the jibes of classmates, isolating them, punishing them for their father's presence in the schoolroom.

Mavis came in with a tray of tea for the two of them to finish their meal in the intimate and male confines of the study.

Edwards said he could not stay any longer. "I must be off before the afternoon closes in," he said, looking at the sky through the window, as if instructing it to cloud over.

"Please don't get up," he said to Palmer.

Stay there and pretend you're the archdeacon for a while longer!

Mavis shook the cushion on the chair he had sat in with a light and tender movement of her large, bony hand. When he took it to shake he liked the supple feel and he may have imagined a curling of her fingers inside his palm. I'd like to sit and talk with her again, he thought, telling himself her face said the same of him.

"Thank you for all your kindness," he said in a low voice, for Palmer had come to the study door.

"Oh no, thank you," she said, puzzling both of them.

When he was gone she turned her back on Palmer and straightened the doily where the tea tray had been.

"Did he say what he wanted of the archdeacon," Palmer said, the let down putting an irritable edge to his voice.

She decided not to tell him. She should, if she wanted him to take the side of Edwards in the matter of an early marriage.

She didn't want an early marriage for Colin Edwards! She remembered suddenly she did not learn from him which Herbert girl he wanted to marry. Let it be neither!

"Perhaps his church roof is leaking," she said.

30

He might well leave the church. He would make a new attempt to see the archdeacon and tell him he could no longer bear the confines of his appointment to Wyndham. He was in the prime of life, he wanted marriage, he would not spend the next eighteen months celibate! He would find other work. He tried to see himself in an occupation of which Enid would approve. Una would not mind anything. But for Enid he would need to be a teacher, a bookkeeper, or a farmer although he could scarcely manage any of these.

The sulky bowled along the road towards Wyndham, dust flying around his horse's feet, the harness on the brown back tapping it gently, now and again a shake and a snort, a dipping of the head as if to say, this is more like it, be a sensible fellow and go home and forget all that nonsense.

Just ahead of him the Grubb children lined the road, let out of the little school a half mile down one of the turn offs, their classmates taking other tracks into the hills where there were three or four other farms.

The heart of Edwards softened at the sight of them, particularly the little girl he had nursed in the house during his first visit. There she was yards behind the others with the neck of her dress undone at the back, appearing too big for her, perhaps one handed down from an older sister. The hem brushed her naked calves and he saw her little feet were bare. Edwards thought of the road scraped with frost of a morning.

He pulled the horse up alongside her. She turned her face and there it was as he remembered it, under thick brown hair like Una's, remembering their intimacy with a sly, shy twinkle in eyes as brown as Una's were.

"Come up," he said, and she was on the sulky stirrup in a moment and the others, an older girl and two big boys came together in a little bunch, one of the boys embarrassed at the memory of delivering his father's message to the house and hastening Edwards's departure.

"Climb in, all of you," Edwards said, and they did, the guilty one keeping his eyes down and feeling obliged to take the worst place in the sulky, on the floor among feet, huddled there with a face pressed to scarred knees.

The sulky shafts tipped, and the horse's back broadened as both adjusted to the load, and after a few strained steps the horse settled into a trot, and the swaying sulky sent the little brown-haired one close against Edwards's arm, where she remained gripped to his flesh to avoid slipping down the sloping seat on top of her brother. The warm little kitten of a thing! He did not want to shake the reins in case his arm disturbed her, the chill of separation more than he could bear.

She pressed her chin into his shoulder to whisper: "Where is your baby today?"

The others heard and expected to be tipped from the sulky there and then. The boy next to her dug an elbow into her side, the girl next to him turned her head to give all her attention to the spinning sulky wheel, the boy on the floor pinned his head between his knees so he wouldn't hear if something more terrible was to come.

Edwards laughed, he couldn't help it, which in the children's view was worse than a rebuke.

The little thing had him confused in a relationship with Small Henry! There was gossip about Small Henry's future and this little sweet, innocent thing, knowing Small Henry was somewhere near him, associated him with fatherhood. The tongues that were long and moved freely in this place were coupling him with Enid or Una and this little one had added Small Henry. The little thing with her pink, shamed face crushed to his shoulder might well have spoken what could become a fact.

Small Henry should not grow up in the house of Ned and Violet, him with his neurosis and her with resentment against the role thrust upon her. And if the hospital came to pass, that was no place for a child. Women moaning in childbirth in a terrifying way. Once he visited the maternity hospital in Bega soon after his arrival from England, filling in for the curate who was ill with influenza. He walked in on a moaning women the nurse did not have time to get out of his way. He never forgot the woman's eyes begging him to do something. He looked down on the swirl of hair on the crown of the little girl's head, so like Una's. Una loved Small Henry, holding him as she did as if he were moulded to her own body.

He would take that baby in his arms and see what it felt like next time he was at Violet's. This very afternoon! He moved an arm a little sharply to hurry his horse along and the little girl looked up, thinking it a rebuff.

No, little one, I love you too. All soft, innocent things, I love. Una I love!

31

He went straight to Violet's to apologize for going off to Candelo without asking if there was any errand he could do for her.

"But I'm not troubled about any apology," he said to his honest eyes in the mirror, as he brushed himself up for the visit.

"It's Small Henry I must see."

He knocked for several minutes, seeing no sign of life through the open door down to the back where the fowls were picking in desultory fashion at the wire enclosure.

A little wind swirled the dust inside, ruffling the feathers of those crouched waiting near the dry troughs. Edwards waited too in the creeping silence for footsteps or a flash of Violet's dress in the bush or on the track made by feet, mainly Ned's, into the gully.

A great gully of silence there, the gums and the shivery grass and the blackened stumps waiting like the fowls, as if they too had a spirit locked up inside them, and eyes that blinked without expression, and voices that had no sound, but a power to deepen the menacing quiet.

Edwards glanced behind him across to the Post Office, closed against the cold, then along to the verandah of the store which no one crossed, and where the windows, hung with the hurricane lanterns, held the dusty china and garden forks and spades that were there when he came to Wyndham.

But it was less frightening than Violet's empty hallway

and what lay beyond, so he kept half turned in that direction while he knocked some more.

He was about to give up and leave for the rectory when he heard the cry of Small Henry.

Three grunts came first, then a small wail that was more of a question. Is someone there to get me? There was no cry following for a moment, then some more grunts, angry and peevish, then a vibrant yelling that told even Edwards's inexperienced ears there was no way he was going to stop unless someone came.

Edwards felt he was hung there, caught by some invisible thread, permitted to squeeze through the skylight if this were possible, but with no licence to open the door and stride in.

Just when he thought Small Henry's last cry was a death choke, there was the flutter of a heliotrope skirt through the gums and he saw Violet's head and waist attached to it, and when she was a little closer he saw her largish face pinched to a smaller size and her mouth anxious. Edwards, feeling partly responsible for her distress, had to be stern with some fluttering in his chest, and fold his arms and tip his head sideways, as was his habit when he combined meekness with authority.

Violet saw his shape in the doorway and beckoned him in.

"Ned's been gone all day!" she said, shouting above Small Henry's screams, which she appeared to be ignoring. Edwards felt it safe to do the same and sat by the dresser.

"Close that door!" she said and he obediently closed the hall door, reducing the volume of sound, but hating the miserable hand that performed the act.

"He's gone off to die like their old Phoebe did!" Violet said, to Edwards's astonishment, for he had not heard the story of the Herbert ancestor.

"They haven't told you that!" she said with a glance at his face, triumph erasing some of the concern from hers.

"Well, there's madness in them, I can tell you and it's well for you to know!" She went to the stove and stuffed it with wood.

"You can tell how long he's been gone, since the place is not roaring like a furnace!"

She shut the stove door with a shoe scarred and damp from her long tramping. Edwards saw the dead leaves and fragments of bark clinging to her ankles.

All your body speaks, he said to himself, seeing the wrinkles of worry on Violet's stockings, more vocal than the wrinkles on her brow.

"Yes, he might be dead! Already dead!" she said, snapping teacups on the table. "But I'm having a cup of tea!"

She went, however, and raised the blind on the window behind the couch, giving her a view of the bush while she made the tea. Small Henry's cries grew shrill.

"I could perhaps — " Edwards said, standing and putting out a hand towards the door.

"You can!" said Violet, taking milk from the safe so violently it slapped over the edge of the jug like an angry white wave.

Edwards went into Small Henry's room. There he lay the covers off him and his soaked napkin, which was so carelessly fastened that his navel, shedding moisture, was exposed on his rounded belly. His toes curled and his legs thrashed and Edwards saw an ear like a pink shell in wet sand. He mopped it dry with the edge of the blanket and the touch stopped Small Henry's wailing and stilled his limbs and he appeared to focus swimming eyes on Edwards for a moment, then squeezed them shut and pulled his mouth into a piteous shape to renew his wailing.

Edwards gathered him up, not too efficiently, unable to

arrange the blanket between his arm and Small Henry's rear, to save a spread of moisture on the thin stuff of his jacket. He held him away from his body to bind the blanket, as he had seen Una do, and when he drew him close, Small Henry was tight and still and at peace in his cocoon. Edwards smelled some faint odour from his hair, and the urine, not unpleasant, and shut his own eyes to feel his way to the door, rather than lose anything of the ecstasy. In the kitchen he sat and Small Henry at once gave his succession of warning grunts.

Edwards got to his feet and swayed back and forth, and Violet gave an odd little burst of laughter.

"You're his next victim! Thanks to that Una he thinks he can rule like a king. Well, I'm not one of his subjects!"

She went to the window and looked out, then turned her back sharply on it and sat down at the table. Edwards sat too, gingerly holding his body stiff in an effort to deceive Small Henry into thinking he was standing. Violet had dumped his teacup with a round dryish cake studded with currants on the dresser by him.

She sipped her tea, allowing herself some small pleasure in Edwards's predicament. Small Henry, worn out with weeping, had fallen asleep. Edwards dared not loosen his grip of the tiny body to his chest, and red in the face with effort, he brought his right arm close to his cup. No, he would not drink the tea! He sweated with horror at the thought of a splash on the tiny, tender head.

Instead he took the cake, ducking his head to take a mouthful and showering crumbs into a fold of the blanket. He brushed at them and Small Henry leapt in protest and expelled a long, warning breath.

"I'll drink my tea cold," Edwards whispered to Violet. "I often do."

Violet got up noisily, causing Edwards to rock Small

Henry to ward off the disturbance and he kept this up during the clatter she made mixing his bottle.

Parting is close, he thought, understanding the ache so often in Una's arms. But Violet dumped the bottle by the cold cup of tea.

"You feed it," she said. "I'll walk to the Burragate turn off. My legs will carry me without effort, since they've had a solid morning's practice!"

The gate had banged on Violet almost before Edwards realized what was happening. He watched, half believing she might turn back. Then he sat and Small Henry, rather than disturbed by the movement, used it to sink more comfortably against Edwards and sleep on.

Edwards looked at the cooling bottle and back to the fine streaks of damp hair on Small Henry's forehead, and under his nose a reddish purple around the nostrils, as if someone had painted a deeper colour there to distinguish the nose from the rest of the face. His lips, thin and purplish too, were pressed together. Those two small nostrils were all that allowed air into Small Henry's body. That was not enough.

Perhaps he had died!

Edwards moved him gently, but his weight settled back heavier. A dead weight, people said. Small Henry dead in his arms! He had cried himself to death.

Reckless now, Edwards removed an arm and tapped Small Henry on the cheek. He was still warm, thank God, but his head remained where it fell sideways and he did not close his lips after they had fallen open.

Edwards laid an ear to his mouth but heard no breath. He put his cheek there but felt nothing. He shook Small Henry who settled back after wobbling like a loosely stuffed doll. He pulled at Small Henry's blanket until he found his gown and raised it to lay an ear on a part of his chest where he thought his heart would be.

He heard no beat.

He had died.

Good God in heaven he had died! He stood and snatched up the bottle, now barely warm, and thrust the teat between Small Henry's lips. They flapped about lifelessly and Edwards pulled the teat away and held the bottle in shocked fashion in the air. Then he thrust the teat back between Small Henry's lips. He shuddered, a contented shudder, and pushed his legs down so that Edwards, back on his chair, felt their miraculous movement at his groin.

Small Henry swung his head and moved his mouth a little tiredly at the teat. Then he opened his eyes, blinked once or twice, squeezed them shut while his mouth came greedily to life, and gripping the teat he sucked with his tiny neck throbbing and his knees moving up and down as if there had been a long march and here was the end of it.

Edwards loosened his grip on the bottle and, tilting it, allowed Small Henry to draw gently upon it. He settled his own body and raised his thighs so that Small Henry's flesh flowed warmly into his as the milk flowed warmly into Small Henry.

Edwards too closed his eyes and breathed the most fervent prayer of thanksgiving of all his life.

32

When he set the bottle down, not quite finished, he worried about that and the wet and caked rear of Small Henry.

But he seemed oblivious to any discomfort, having curled his head close to Edwards's neck, causing Edwards to bend it towards the other shoulder, to keep his hard collar away from Small Henry's face.

He was in that pose when Ned came through the bush at the back, his arrival heralded by the fowls, who made a rush to the wire already picking at imaginary seed. Ned walked with the aid of his stick quite briskly across the verandah and into the house. He looked around as if making sure he was in the right house, his mouth round to match his round glass eye, heightening his vacant look.

Edwards, obeying instinct and training, stood and extended an arm and spread hand from beneath Small Henry's rump.

Ned looked to the stove, as if he too needed to obey an instinct and add more wood to it.

"Mrs Violet is out for a short while," Edwards said, speaking loudly as did most others when addressing Ned. He felt he should not say she was searching for him.

Small Henry shuddered at the noise, and Edwards set up a swaying motion, which caused Ned to stare in disbelief, then look with his mouth still hole-shaped, everywhere but in Edwards's direction.

Edwards felt he was failing badly in his duty, unable to take the opportunity of attending to Ned's spiritual needs, which must be great indeed. For all the long hours he spent in the bush, though, he looked far less affected by it than Violet.

At the back of Edwards's head the click of the gate and the sound of Violet's feet told him she was back. She had not hurried, having caught sight of Ned making his way through the gums, as she made hers along the road from the turn off.

She shed her warm coat in the bedroom and came to the kitchen rolling up her sleeves. Edwards found he could picture her getting ready for a confinement.

"Stove nearly out, Ned!" she said. "Has the bush dried up at last?" Ned tilted his face towards the ceiling, studying it, then, lowering his good eye, appeared to be taking a last long look at the room before he went through to the front bedroom.

Violet flung a clean napkin on the table and took Small Henry from Edwards, as if she was plucking a wasp's nest from a wall. Ignoring his sleeping state she lifted his blue feet and removed his napkin, roughly wiping at the caked excreta smearing his rectum. It reminded Edwards of a ripe plum with a deep incision in it. Violet, taking the soiled napkin to the wash house, returned with a dipper of warm water to sponge him, and Edwards felt relief for him although wearing a worried look for the slack genitals between the flaying legs, wondering if there was some deformity there.

"He'll grow into it!" Violet shouted, reading his blushing thoughts. "The time'll come when he'll be smaller there than anywhere else! No one knows that fact better than I do!"

She turned her eyes as she spoke on Ned coming from the bedroom, and had to snap her mouth shut and pretend she saw nothing unusual in his appearance.

He was wearing pyjamas and military trousers under a wartime greatcoat, and his digger's hat. He was not using his stick to aid his walking, but had more clothes bundled in a towel and the towel tied in a knot and slipped over the end of the stick which was suspended across one shoulder.

Violet found her voice when Ned reached the fowl pens and had to compete with their raucous din, more frantic than usual, for Ned was opening the gate and pushing his way through them, pecking at his boots, and stretching hopeful necks towards the bundle on his stick, some leaping on others' backs in a bid to reach it.

"Where's the cat?" Violet yelled. "You're a dead ringer for Dick Whittington!"

Ned took eggs from boxes and filled two pockets, making his way out, needing to unhook his bundle from a broken end of wire, while the fowls made a fresh onslaught on his legs.

Violet bound Small Henry in his blanket.

"He's taking up residence on the farm! It couldn't work out better if I organized it myself!"

She stomped to the bedroom to put Small Henry down. Edwards wondered about her voice. Did anger overrule the sorrow, or was it the other way around? He tipped his head sideways in his troubled pose. Marriage! What a state it could become. I want it though, he thought, suddenly anxious to return to the rectory, to picture Una there.

Violet was back and Small Henry quiet. "He's settled down then?" Edwards said, pride in the use of a new language he would have thought once strictly reserved for parents.

The closed door said yes, but Violet's closed face said nothing.

Edwards felt it his duty to offer some comforting words about Ned.

"I am sure he will miss the comforts of his real home and be back soon to them."

"Who wants him back?" Violet said. "The way's clear for me now to go ahead with my hospital!"

Una would never use words like that. His way would be her way. His dreams and plans hers too. He looked out of Violet's window to the sky spread with a furrowed cloud. Like a field, he thought, feeling his ankles bogged in softness, light as air, walking with Una. We will keep our eyes upwards and see no ugliness anywhere.

The clatter of a metal spoon on tin caused Edwards to look downwards. Violet had a basin of stew removing some for her own meal and pushing the remainder down the table.

"Take this home with you and heat it," she said. "It will only go to waste here!"

"Thank you, but I couldn't," Edwards said, holding his hat tightly, as if this helped him resist accepting it. There was nothing in his larder but bread and eggs, but that would do him until Mrs Watts came tomorrow and cooked him dinner at midday.

He moved towards the door with his bent face. "I'll offer up evening prayers for the safe return of Ned," he said.

Violet waited until the gate shut before she shouted a reply for only the kitchen walls to hear.

"God's will, they're fond of saying. When it's your will they don't agree with it! Let him rot in the bush, rot there for all I care, I'm having my hospital!"

33

He decided to go and see Jack next day.

Mrs Watts came and set his soiled clothes to soak in a wash tub, built up the kitchen fire to make him soup, and, as was her habit, put the chairs on tables and pulled the living room couch out to enable her to give the place a good sweep.

He told her he did not think he would be home for dinner, but he would appreciate the soup for tea. She had been to the church to shyly collect the two brass vases and began polishing them on the space left by the chair legs on the table.

He said he would not be leaving immediately but would read up for his Sunday sermon on the front verandah. (He was in fact allowing a decent part of the morning to get away before confronting Jack.)

His words filled her with a terrible inadequacy. Because she could not read or write, she felt she had less right to an existence than those who could, and wondered that he bothered to mention such things to her.

But had she known it, he had a deep admiration for her and would have liked to stay and watch her hands bring a lustre to the old brass, as her belly in a hessian apron jumped gently and rhythmically under the table.

How many children had she borne, he wondered. There were older boys who worked with their father on the farm, and some girls and then Wilfred. She was past child bearing age, he decided, wondering at his thoughts taking this trend, and looking away from her for a clearer vision of Una, trying to see her cleaning his brass.

He said he was leaving for Honeysuckle after his half hour's reading and he would not come back inside.

She raised sharp, intelligent eyes under straight black brows, and he thought she had been a handsome woman. Which one? the eyes said, and the hand slowed its polishing.

"The child's christening needs to be arranged," Edwards said. He should not be saying this! His father would never allow his mother to talk of anything but domestic matters with servants.

"The young one has made a beautiful dress, I hear," Mrs Watts said.

You and the rest of them hear everything! These little places with ears hanging on every doorstep, at every window! When Una is here we will close the doors to everyone. Or go and become swallowed up in a city. I hear! I hear! Don't let me hear it again!

She saw his angry face and bowed her own deeper over the vase. I should not have said that, she thought. But once something is said, there is no way of blotting it out. This I have learned without the help of books.

He took up his hat and showed her his stiff, cold back as he went out. I hurt the poor thing, he said to himself. I didn't intend it, but there's no way I can amend it.

He was miserable tramping along the road, but needed to transfer his thoughts to confronting Jack.

The walk seemed the shortest he had ever taken, and he was within a half mile of Honeysuckle with the beginning of the Herbert paddocks when he saw him.

Jack.

There he was by a horse in harness, staring hard at Edwards, and it was an amazing thing that resentment could show on a face at all that distance. Edwards raised his hat high to let the greeting be seen. Jack bent his head but it could have been part of a movement to adjust logs and stumps on a slide, in getting the new paddock ready for spring planting.

A crop of potatoes for Sydney, something he had never attempted before. Enid thought it a good idea. Alex saw it as added work, on top of running Halloween. George saw it restricting his visits to Violet.

Jack had his own dream. Henry was in Sydney. He might help him market the potatoes. Jack saw Henry with one of those fruit and vegetable shops, not stocked with the withered stuff he'd eyed off so scornfully when in Sydney, but carrying Honeysuckle produce, the summer crop of fruit, much of which was wasted, potatoes, pumpkins and melons that could be specially grown.

What was Henry working at now? They hadn't heard since he left. He had been putting bicycle parts together in a factory before he brought that girl home. Before that he worked for a grain merchant. He liked that better, and wrote about helping to haul bags of seed from a lorry, the corn inferior to that grown at Honeysuckle.

They should have bought a lorry, instead of that car, only useful for gadding. Enid did not care all that much for it. With a lorry Henry might have stayed at home and got some carrying work. He could have carried loads of produce to the railhead at Nowra, which would be even better than being in Sydney selling it.

Henry was the one he thought would love the farm best. He used to sit as a little boy in each furrow as he ploughed a paddock.

"I'm making chocolates, Farder," he would say, shaping the moist black earth into squares. Sweeter than chocolate it was in Jack's ears.

Would that new Henry grow to be anything like he was? Jack did not want the thought to settle in his head. He was quite frightened every time Violet came with the child to Honeysuckle that she might announce she was leaving it.

And here came that fellow! Barely a day passed without a visit. Jack tallied up the meals eaten with them since the funeral. Ten no less, not counting the morning and afternoon teas at which he ate abundantly.

Edwards on seeing Jack decided he would join him in the paddock, and giving himself no time to change his mind, ducked under the fence rail, scraping his back as he usually did, thinking of the way Una flew under them like that white tufty stuff that blew from the ends of grass. He walked to Jack, taking his hat off long before he needed to.

The horse, with a coat like toffee and big knobbly knees, appeared tolerant of the interruption, but not excited by it. He blinked great black eyes and lifted great black lips over teeth that looked like weather beaten clothes pegs, then decided a sneer would be wasted on the plainly agitated Edwards, and sought nourishment in some grass flattened to its sweet roots by the slide.

Jack sat on a log, and this made it hard for Edwards to execute his handshake, but he did, by bending down, then Jack rose and a passing car saw with amazement the two bobbing figures in the middle of a paddock.

The travellers recognized them both and said to each other here is something to watch! Something will break soon, keep your ear to the ground, here comes news to liven the old place up, and give us something to chew on apart from tough corned beef.

Edwards took a seat beside Jack, and the horse laid his ears back listening to the silence. Edwards felt Jack's were laid back too.

"You have probably noticed," Edwards said, "my fondness for the Misses Herberts."

The Misses Herberts! That sounded terrible, as if they were elderly spinsters. He looked at the horse and imagined Una grasping its mane and throwing a leg over its back, with her skirt falling back and frothy mysterious underthings showing.

"Miss Una and Miss Enid," he corrected himself, foolishly fearful that Jack saw his image of Una. He had put Una first too, which was not the proper way.

Jack might have noticed, for he lifted his large face and appeared to sniff at the air, as if this way he would detect how the wind was blowing. Edwards stared at the ground between his feet.

"They are fine young women," he said.

Jack brought his jaws together and his cheeks shook a warning. Edwards clenched his jaws too, sweating a little in the cool air.

He saw beyond the far fence smoke rising from the Honeysuckle chimneys. He longed to be there in the warmth and comfort of the house, but felt the stout chains Jack has used to bind the logs to the slide anchored him as well.

"Very fine women," said Edwards miserably.

"Both."

The smoke at that moment rose thicker and stronger stating that Enid was stoking fires. Enid stoking this fellow's fire? Jack got up and stood between Edwards and the house, as if this would put Enid farther from him. Edwards had the brief and terrifying thought that Jack might be shaping up for a fight. He stood too, so as not to be disadvantaged.

Their eyes met, Edwards's like those of a pleading

spaniel, Jack's coming forward so black you would not believe any expression could be in them.

They were like pools of oil that would drag Edwards to their murky depths, if he dared say the wrong name.

"It's Miss Una," he said in a low voice, even he puzzled at the soothing note in it.

34

They were married in January, just one year after Edwards's appointment to Wyndham.

Only weeks after the engagement was announced (a few days after the meeting in the paddock) the archdeacon came from Bega to confirm six or seven children, the first group in Wyndham for confirmation since the war. Edwards was proud of his achievement, the culmination of regular instruction in the church porch after school, with scarred boots banging the stool impatient to be gone, the road beyond the door a yearning thing, the bird calls far sweeter than Edwards's earnest pleas to believe what he was saying, although he himself held doubts about much of it.

The archdeacon almost fell in love with Una himself.

He watched her long hands in their frilled cuffs on the shoulders of the gawky, terrified children, gently moving in some cases a full hand from a mouth, the mouth refusing to close when the hand was dropped. The archdeacon would have a few words to his parish council after this!

That beautiful girl! An asset to the church.

Any man with support from a wife as beautiful and charming as that would do a better job for the church. A fool of a rule if ever there was one! Not only would he say so but he would suggest (insist!) on an increase in the stipend, small though it might need to be, there would be an increase.

What a home she would make of the rectory, if this

place was anything to go by! For everyone gathered in the Honeysuckle garden after the service for trays of tea, sandwiches and cakes. Here was the elder girl now offering cake. He pulled at a wedge, tearing it from the big, golden round, as if it was flesh cut gently to save a deeper hurt. He fancied he heard the girl wince and looked up to see her dart a smile to her lips, while her eyes stayed serious. She is anxious that everyone is being looked after. A fine girl too! An ideal wife for the church and why most of them choose mousey, drab women he would never know. Or bossy ones like the wife of the Candelo man, there in a dreadful hat looking quite boldly towards Edwards and Una together on a little seat as if their thoughts were already in unison, and they each needed a little spell, she from feeding the children moist tomato sandwiches and he from circling among shy farmers, ill at ease in suits and wives standing half behind them, shyer still.

"You do all this so well," Edwards said in a whisper when his mouth was inches from her ear.

Una chose the time for the marriage to adjust to Small Henry's timetable.

"In the morning after his bath and sleep when he's happiest," Una said, sending the wheel of the sewing machine flying, as she ran up a seam of a cream silk coat she was making for him for the wedding day. She clicked the thread from the needle and pulled at the silk to smooth out a little puckering.

Enid walked with her new step as if she was not certain the floor was safe, carrying plates to the dresser, for Una had moved the machine to the kitchen to work in a breeze from the back door, utilizing an authority that had come with her new status. She allowed herself a small glance at Enid's face now, and brushed fragments of silk and cotton from her front and if there was any stirring under the fine pintucks she brushed that away too. She'll be happier when I'm gone with the place to herself and more time to toady to her beloved Jack. Una trimmed a small armhole then clattered the scissors onto the machine.

Enid raised her head as if they had spoken, sharply and hurtfully.

"Do you agree on eleven o'clock?" Una said. "Then it will all be over by the time he is ready for his afternoon sleep!"

Una had proposed Small Henry stay at Honeysuckle the night before the wedding, and to her great joy he was there for nearly a week. Violet with her hospital only weeks old had two cases. Even Alex, drawn into the excitement of it, agreed to the drive to Albert Lane with Una to collect Small Henry, to leave the way clear for Violet to run between Mrs Skinner and an eighteen year old girl married to a Post Office worker at Pambula.

The fact that the girl, Florence, had booked into Albert Lane was a source of triumph for Violet. Pambula had a cottage hospital but the girl, formerly a Gough, came from one of the Wyndham farms and returned home to wait out her last two or three weeks with the Gough buggy ready to take her to Violet when her time came.

It was like a holiday although she had very little to do in her tiny Pambula house. As a girl at home she had milked cows morning and night and now, with her large stomach that left no room for a bucket between her knees, she stayed in the house empty of everyone but herself. She used to want to sneak back when she was a child to see how the rooms behaved with no people there.

Now twice a day she walked about the house, her round stomach, greasy with perspiration, rubbing against her thighs.

She walked between the beds and dressing tables, liking

the cool boards on her bare feet and the tickle of hooked rugs between her toes, glancing through the windows now and again to hear and see the activity beyond her peaceful isolation. There was the running between cowbails and dairy, cans of milk suspended between thin Gough arms, the clatter of gates opening and shutting as cows were released, the yells of pain and anger when a cow kicked, the bellow of calves penned away from mothers, pleading for moist milky teats in open mouths.

She could turn away when she liked and go to the kitchen and eat a succession of small soft cakes, putting the lid tightly on the tin after each, telling herself it would be the last. Her husband was a nervous city boy attached to a stamp collection, glad to have her out of the way, failing to look for means of visiting her, which she bore stoically, defending him on grounds of his busy and important life.

Ned stayed away from Albert Lane while the hospital was empty, returning and settling himself in when the two patients came and Small Henry was out of the way. Violet had not set their bedroom up on the end of the verandah as she planned to, Ned at Halloween and appearing to be dug in there. She moved a single bed into Small Henry's room for herself. Ned slept on the kitchen couch, his military overcoat for a blanket, rising suddenly like a pre-historic creature from a swamp when Violet came into the kitchen during the all night vigil with her patients, for Mrs Skinner and the Gough girl were delivered within twelve hours of each other, an event that set Albert Lane dancing on its stumps and all of Wyndham sharing the excitement and Violet's triumph.

"Goes to show how much we needed it!" said Rachel to the first customer in the Post Office after the births.

Rachel had been among those opposing the scheme. She was the businesswoman of Wyndham, superior to Ena

Grant (whose shop was in her husband's name although it was widely accepted that she was in charge). Rachel was proud of her efficiency at handling mail, telegrams and money orders, able to estimate to the half penny the cost of sending parcels, and her brisk and businesslike manner on the telephone amazing those customers who had never used one.

She repeated far and wide the praises of the postal inspector when he made quarterly visits.

Rachel was jealous of the intrusion of Violet, also with a business venture, and took the side of those supporting Ned, claiming Violet was abandoning him, and she would set the telephone tingling with her wrath. If only her Ernest had been spared, how she would have cared for him!

She slapped stamps on letters with pudgy hands, casting dark looks at the spruced up Albert Lane opposite, waiting for its first case the week it was ready.

But this case did not arrive. The wife of a telephone linesman living closer to Candelo than Wyndham, under pressure from Nurse Black ("I'd like to see her certificates," said Violet darkly), changed her mind and was confined in Mrs Black's hospital.

Violet crossed the road to pour out her troubled heart to Rachel. It had all been a waste of time and money. No one wanted her to do well, jealousy was behind it!

Rachel hid her blushing guilt behind the tea caddy as she made a consoling cup for them both. Afterwards she pulled the Post Office door to and crossed back to Albert Lane with Violet in a passion of newly unearthed loyalty.

Together they looked in on the ward, the beds immaculately made and on each bedside table nothing but a doily. Violet's drooping face spoke her fear that this was how it would always be. Rachel unconsciously took a step back as if she was not at home in this alien world.

She felt her stomach dry, her thighs lonely.

Violet went and raised the blind several inches to see out on the road where the world was more secure.

Rachel saw Violet's hips and waist lost in the shadows under the window. Alien too! The pair of them, another sex, not belonging in this place made ready for new life.

The room was holding its breath, the hard, clean floorboards ready to creak with feet made heavy with a bulk of living, breathing flesh. The air made ready to be shattered with a scream, the iron bedhead waiting for the grasp of a hand, the shaking in protest, then afterwards smoothed out, loved, thanked.

Only the sunlight blinked in the room. Violet turned from the window, smoothed her skirt at the hips and came forward, Rachel stepping into the hall to allow her to pass.

Both faces swung to shut the room away. Violet took the knob to close the door with a gentle click, drowning out any sigh that might have risen from either chest.

35

Small Henry was sick the day of the wedding.

He had been hot and his skin dry through the previous night and Una and Enid, as well as he, hardly slept. Enid, waking one of half a dozen times after drifting into a short, light sleep, saw Una, not bothering with a dressing gown, hushing him before the dressing table mirror. At the same time she was frowning on her face, anxious about the way it would look after hours without rest.

Enid felt a short, sharp, shameful revenge. Serve her right! Well, serve her right! To help put the thought from her she got up and held the clock to the window to see the time. Only four, too early to start the preparations for the day, but she could see no more rest for her.

"He's hot, really hot!" Una said, turning away from the mirror and easing her body onto a chair to avoid disturbing Small Henry, who leapt and quivered while she bound him more tightly in his rug and rocked him from her uncomfortable pose on the chair edge. As if forgetting the hour, Enid flung the bedclothes back to air the bed and remembering Una would not sleep there again began to change the linen. Una paused in her rocking motion to watch Enid tug the sheet from beneath the mattress with an odd, remote and sad expression that caused Enid to abandon the job and throw the pillows lightly together without removing the slips.

She pulled the curtains back to look out on the creeping day. A fine day, said her heart. Across the silvery paddocks on Hickey's farm were the still shapes of cattle, and it seemed that the fence running into the gully and up the other side was the living thing and the cows merely shapes carved from some dark grey substance. Mist hung low swirled about the tops of trees and the sky had broken into a thousand small pink shapes. It was almost warm already.

"Sun up yet?" said Una as if she should say something to Enid's back to make sure she too was not a frozen shape.

Enid went to the dressing table to gather up some tumblers half full of water and Small Henry's full feeding bottle and passed through the door.

"It hasn't, but there's no doubt it will!" she said.

Alone with Small Henry, Una needed to look on her wedding gown hanging from a chair back and her satin shoes on the floor beside it to know her wedding day was real.

"It's no use!" she said, coming into the kitchen an hour later with Small Henry, having sponged him in the washbasin alarmed at the small hot body and red ears and slack lips that refused to take a teaspoon of cool water. "I can't get married with him sick!"

His head lolled on her shoulder and his little rump was tense on her arm. "He's never been sick before!" Una cried. "He'll die!"

Enid, swirling icing on small cakes, took a fragment between her teeth that had splashed on her wrist. Her eyes remained lowered. Una, on a chair by the stove as if both she and Small Henry were cold, fixed blazing eyes on Enid.

"You don't care! My baby! He could die!" She burst into tears. Enid laid her knife down and came from her side of the table. She put her hands on Small Henry's waist to lift him from Una's shoulder.

"Let me have him," she said, but Una stood skidding the chair back, shaking Enid off.

"I'll lie with him on the bed for a while," Una said putting her streaked face into his neck and making for the bedroom.

"Una!" Enid called, as in the old days. And in the old days Una would have backed like a bird checked in flight, elbows flapping. But now she was still, a profile over her shoulder, so high it was clear of Small Henry's head. Enid might have called for Una the child to return to the woman's body.

"We must decide what is to be done," Enid said, and the profile turned a little more, waiting.

I have to assume the wedding will go on, Enid thought. Aloud she said: "Perhaps we should have Alex take him to Violet's in the car."

Violet would not want that. She had old Hetty Power, who had brought babies into the world in earlier times, to stay with Mrs Skinner and the Gough girl and free Violet to attend the wedding. A sick Small Henry would need to be isolated from the patients and old Mrs Power might not be able to cope. Violet would not want to miss the wedding.

"He's not going to Violet's!" Una cried. "I want him at my wedding!"

She walked with him rapidly to the bedroom and shut the door, Enid following her to the living room with a stack of plates for the sideboard.

The white cloth that had been used for Jack and Nellie's wedding was already on the big table, spread there after its meticulous ironing. No flowers there but vases of them at every high point in the room, on the little raised platforms of the chiffonier, the taller of the little tables and mantleshelf.

She remembered the funeral when the heady smell of stocks and wallflowers was mixed with the smell of food.

She had marvelled at the warmth then although it was winter, and now at the height of summer the roses curling back their outer leaves gave off a cool smell.

The wedding cake on its own small table was covered with a transparent cloth so that the silver beads trimming each tier were blurred like tears.

Enid flung the window up to let in some smells from the oleanders then shut it sharply. No, she said going to the kitchen to take a tray of her quite famous pork pies from the oven.

Let the room stay cold.

Edwards's face with a woebegone expression came to her while she was filling a platter of bacon and eggs for the men's breakfast at the kitchen table.

No, no, cried her thumping heart. I want you happy.

Jack saw the breakfast arrangements, having just come in, and expressed his displeasure with a snort towards the living room.

"The baby's sick," Enid said. "We are not sure what will happen!"

Happen? What did she mean? But she was rolling cut sandwiches in damp teatowels.

"Can't it go to Violet's?" Jack said. When he chose to he did not acknowledge the hospital's existence and certainly not the presence of patients.

He had to acknowledge it now. It should never have been allowed. It was a disruption. Ned wandering between it and the farm, no use at either place. His condition worse now. The hospital the cause!

And that child — Small Henry as they all called it but not him! — here this past week. Lately he had come in for dinner and there it was on a rug on the floor by the table, sucking on a bone from the roast joint, with all their necks craning to watch his every move.

When he had lost the bone once Alex got up and gave it back to him, and Small Henry rewarded him with a long blue look, as intent on giving it as finding the bone's way to his mouth. Then he rocked his body a little as if this was a language, still with his eyes on Alex saying I've seen you around here, you must belong. I do too, so we can get to know each other better. But don't take your size as the yardstick to measure superiority.

He rocked a little harder to emphasize this and Alex allowed his mouth to slip into a lazy, dreamy grin, and when he returned to his food he turned his potatoes over for the tops had grown cold. Many times he slid his eyes back to the little figure rubbing his heels together and flapping his arms up and down, still holding the bone.

"Oh, dirty, dirty!" Una had cried, running to him and picking threads from the rug from his bone, and closing his hand more firmly over it managed to get between him and Alex. Jack lifted the salt shaker up and slapped it on the table as he did when they were all young and misbehaving at the table.

Bugger him, Alex thought, and deciding against having pudding went and sat with the *Sydney Mail* on an easy chair at the edge of the rug, able to look at Small Henry all the time.

Alex came in now through the front of the house, asking with his tipped up head where the child was. He had driven the car to the front to polish it for the wedding.

Jack cut his bacon angrily. Things would need to get back to normal after this wedding! They would, mark his words, with the child back at Violet's and it close by for Una to carry on with it.

Enid was rushed off her legs, bathwater and clothes constantly in her way. She wore an anxious expression now, working swiftly as if she wanted to have this thing over and done with, her eyes raised in a frowning way every now and again towards the clock or the other part of the house. It was so still there he screwed his head around to make sure it hadn't vanished. Alex went to the car out the front with a tread that seemed to increase Enid's anxiety.

All this fuss about a wedding! Jack looked at the clock too, but only to estimate when it would all be done with.

Enid slipping gracefully about the ordered house again! The quiet, the peace. He had seen her doing her cooking at the little table, her basins jammed together, while the big table was used for bathing the child, Una taking all day about it and splashing and douching and calling out for them to come and look at ridiculous things like a roll of fat at the back of his neck.

"I'm going to paint him, yes I'm going to paint him! He's too beautiful not to be painted!" she cried, showering water over everything as she wrapped him in a big white towel Nellie had used for her babies. Well they soon would be spared the mess and disorder, it would be at that rectory when Violet (and he knew this would happen) passed the child to someone else when she had patients, in spite of all her boasting about how capable she was.

None was more capable than his Enid, look at her now closing the dresser doors with a cloth wrapped around her hand so that she would not mark the glass. Jack made a gesture towards the front of the house, and Enid brushed her cuffs unnecessarily.

"I'll see," she said and slipped away.

Soundlessly she opened the bedroom door and there were Una and Small Henry asleep on the tangled sheets. Her old kimono was awry and her hands tucked between her knees and Small Henry's damp head was on her damp hair. A virginal sleep, her face holding to her the last minutes of her girlhood, the face a little tense, as if she were hanging on, not ready to let go, not yet abandoning the old life.

Una by the edge of the sea, with a toe in the water.

I can't go in yet. Soon, but not quite yet. And she wrapped her arms around her body clutching it although the day was warm.

Enid now tapped the foot of the bed lightly and Una's eyes sprung open. For a second they held her new life in them, she was a little frightened of it too, a little less confident, questioning that it was right after all. She closed her eyes swiftly as if this needed to be kept from Enid who called her name.

Una sat up and propped on an arm looked down on Small Henry.

He slept on, a redness in his cheeks, a shine of sweat in the creases of his neck. His round head, now almost bare of hair, was touched with wetness too, a great round silvery head, ready to butt into life, no longer vulnerable, tender and uncertain.

Una stared at the wet mark his head made on the pillow through her hair, and then at his face. While she looked his eyes sprung open and he let out a breath and raised a fat leg and flung it from the sheet. He turned his head from left to right, swiftly and energetically, found Enid and grinned broadly, then flashed his eyes on Una and began to pump his legs up and down and flap his arms wildly against his wrinkled nightdress. It was soon raised to expose his belly which he pushed forward, bringing a smile to Enid's face and Una from the bed to lean across and scoop him and take him to the mirror to kiss his face, ecstatic to find it cool and moist. She found his light blanket and bound him in it and raced down the step into the living room called back to Enid.

"He can bathe in the tub with me! Mix a bottle for him to have when we're done. Hurry, hurry, hurry!"

Enid did not know if she was calling to her or instructing herself.

She flung the crumpled bedding to the foot of the bed, shutting out her sight of the wedding dress with its new low waist and sleeves just below the elbow, curling back like the petals of a great, creamy flower. The dress itself was like a flower there against the brown chair back, and seeing it at the side of her face as she made up the bed with fresh linen it seemed to open and bloom to the sound of Una's voice, calling endearments to Small Henry, racing with him tucked under her arm gathering his things. The living room as she ran through it came to life too, the roses opening wider and the silver and glasses taking on an added sparkle.

Enid on her way to the kitchen flung a window up to let the smell of oleanders in, mixed with the rich smell of her pies and the talcum powder Una was shaking playfully in the air, still running with Small Henry and calling him a sham, a put on, not really sick, just frightening her and never, never do it again, never pretend or it will kill her. She would die.

Jack was in the kitchen with relief on his face and his hands on his hips and George eating the last of the bacon with a mournful face, not having taken too kindly to the suggestion that he take the sulky in case there was someone in need of a lift back to Honeysuckle from the church. Violet would want a seat in the Austin, you could be sure of that.

Enid saw the hands of the clock moving towards eight. Three hours to go. It is going to happen after all. I thought it mightn't, but it will.

Nothing will stop it now.

205

36

The wedding went off smoothly until the end when Small Henry's temperature rose and there was a foolish attempt to keep it from Una.

"Put him in a room and tell her he's asleep and not to be disturbed," Rachel said, and Violet, holding him against her shoulder where his head was burrowed and his legs hung slack, snorted her scorn and turned him sharply from someone so naive.

Enid came up in her dark blue morrocain with a beaded collar and looked into Small Henry's face, telling herself he was merely tired after all the excitement. "They are almost ready to go," she whispered, for she had seen Alex take the luggage from the verandah and strap it to the rack at the back of the Austin. They were to have a week's honeymoon in Pambula, the suggestion of a room at Uncle Percy's hotel in Merimbula scorned by Una, who foresaw bedlam among the six cousins at the presence of a bridegroom.

Una had seen that all was not well with Small Henry. Dragged by Jinny Turbett to inspect and praise more liberally a china butter dish given for a wedding present, she had her head in its new blue hat raised so high she seemed the tallest in the room and her creased brow, turned from the table of gifts, asked questions of Violet and Enid. In a moment she was attempting to pluck Small Henry from Violet who swung him away, and Enid said not to disturb him, they would put him down presently.

"Down where?" Una cried, her eyes flashing towards a remote bedroom door where she pictured him shut away and left to fret and weep for her.

"Let me have him, please Violet," she said, as if her married state had increased her rights to him.

And taking him she sat on a chair, her blue hat sinking down over Small Henry like an umbrella. The guests craned their heads and their talk died to a murmur, although their new lowered tones failed to blur the edge of excitement that was there.

Something going on here! Just when things were winding down and thoughts had to turn to cows and bails, and manure slapped on stone floors, and flies buzzing around heads and no hands free to wave them off, and some dropping into the froth of milk and crawling there to the despair of the milker, who saw them then as enemies they would never conquer.

Just when this had to be the train of thought a crisis developed, and my goodness, supposing she wouldn't go off with him and leave Small Henry, or better still take Small Henry on the honeymoon!

The way her arms were bound to him now it looked as if she would never free them. Ah, this is interesting, said eyebrows raised high enough to move wedding hats, and eyes looking for Edwards so as not to miss his expression when he saw what was going on.

He came settling his coat after taking it off to wash, and he brushed the front now with his well shaped hands, the women admiring, some of them wondering how hands like that would feel on their bodies after the calloused groping ones of their husbands. One of the fine hands now drew the blanket back from Small Henry's face, and then Una raised her face to his and there was less than an inch between the profiles, making them look like a poster for a romantic and passionate moving picture. Many of the onlookers blushed and felt uncomfortable as if they were watching them undress.

Edwards put his hands under Small Henry on Una's lap and put him in Violet's arms. He took Una's arm and folded it over his own arm and it quivered there, half intending to pull away. But Una rose and the guests fell back, making a path for them.

"He's just a little hot," Enid murmured. Her eyes sought Edwards and he nodded in a way she knew and gave a small smile that said you are the wise one, I leave you in charge. He took Una with him to the door, her face over her shoulder, clinging to Small Henry rocked in Violet's arms.

"He'll be alright," Edwards said soothingly.

"Right as rain!" called a bold voice from a stout frame that had borne many children, not all of whom survived the rigours of childhood ills, but whose optimism remained unshaken.

The cry was caught up by the others. "Go off and enjoy yourselves, have a good time by the sea! Don't worry about a thing! Goodbye, goodbye!"

Alex had the back door of the car open for them and Una did not look back, for she could not bear to see faces that were not Small Henry's. All she could manage was a wan smile when she settled in the back seat. She dropped her head so that her hat became a blue mushroom and all an anxious Edwards could see was a piece of jawline which looked rebellious in spite of the anxiety occupying the remainder of her face. He put a hand on a fold of her dress on the seat, a blue silk she had made for the going away, not brave enough to take her hand seeing the tense curling of her fingers.

She turned large accusing eyes on him. "I left him sick," she said. "He won't get better without me."

Edwards looked away to the swiftly flying trees beside the road. All through the ceremony he had wanted to have his mother there.

God is wisest after all, he told himself. It is just as well she wasn't.

37

They were in a guest house high above the sea where they were taken to their room by the owner, Mrs Chance, who modestly lowered her eyes at the sight of the bed covered with a counterpane so white and crisply laundered it seemed a sacrilege to disturb it. But Una threw her hat on it and went to the window to gaze at the sea. Edwards saw with relief her hands linked behind her were no longer tense. Mrs Chance waited in vain for compliments on the room, for she had brought in a small table and covered it with a white cloth for them to have breakfast in private if they wanted it and she had two bowls of flowers on the mantlepiece, although heaven knows they were hard enough to come by in the January heat. She went off in a huff resolving not to put herself out further.

The moment she was gone Una flung herself around, her small face brighter than the yellow daisies.

"Did you see it?" she cried. Edwards didn't know what, except that she was happy again. "The telephone in the hall when we came in! A telephone! We can telephone Rachel and she can go across to Violet's and see how Small Henry is!" He hoped his face did not give away his instant thought on the cost.

"Jack gave me some money before we left," she cried, having read him correctly. "Don't worry about that part!"

"I wasn't worried about that part," said Edwards with dignity. "I'm pleased to have you set your mind at rest." He sat on the one chair, looking at his thighs, hoping she would come and sit on his knee.

A woman had never sat on his knees.

He felt his flesh creep a little now, ready to leap into contact with those round little buttocks in the slippery, flowered silk. He could put a hand up under it and move the hand around her underthings. He could do that if he wanted to!

He stood, hands on the chair arms, and saw her sink onto the window seat cupping a glum face in her hands. She raised her knees wrapped in her skirt and laid her chin on them, an untouchable figure rocking herself there with the blue sea, triangular shaped, seeming to sit on one shoulder.

"After tea we'll telephone," he said.

She looked at her feet in their new brown shoes rubbed carelessly together. She was casual with her fine things. He was ashamed of the thought that followed of Enid, taking scrupulous care of hers. "They will just say he is better,' she said. "They will keep the truth from me."

"The truth most likely is he is better," Edwards said, fighting an urge to be short with her. This was his honeymoon, for heaven's sake!

"Come for a walk by the sea before teatime," he said. He did not say before bed although he looked at it. Una creased her eyes towards it too, then rose with a sigh and smoothed her skirt.

"That's a good girl," he said putting a hand out to her.

"Should I put different clothes on?" she said. He dropped his hands. He had barely felt the stuff of her silk dress. She lifted her case to the bed and opening it began to take things out in little heaps. There was a shower of ribbons falling from the first heap and then a larger garment, white and lacy, which she tossed on the pillow.

"We unpack," she said. "That's what we do first."

His case was older and shabbier than hers and he was acutely aware of its lightness. He put it across the chair and with his back to her took out the shirts and vests Mrs Watts had ironed for him. He should have put his woollen jumper in. It would have taken up some of the space. He saw her hang her things in the wardrobe leaving a half for him. He did not need it. But how to tell her?

"Spread your things out so they won't crush," he said opening a drawer in a big chest. "I'll lay my things out in here." The drawer made a hollow noise when he shut it and he felt she could not fail to notice it was almost empty.

But I am a man of God, he told himself. It is only right I live more frugally.

But he remembered Alex's back in the tweed motoring coat, the crisp edge of his shirt and his jaunty cap. I haven't a motor, so those things would not be of any use to me, he thought. But he was not comforted.

Una took two dresses from the wardrobe and looked critically at each, then threw one on the bed and jabbed the other back. She crossed her arms and lifted the blue silk over her head and he saw her white neck and shoulders and the little crushed ribbons at the top of her breasts. So that's where they went!

He smiled at them but she got into her other dress quickly, new too, white dotted closely with navy blue and with a big white collar, a sort of sailor dress, suitable he supposed for the seaside.

The people were right. She was a fashion plate but he loved her for it, and it was too early to start worrying about where future clothes would come from. She had made herself enough, he supposed, to last a long time.

She snapped a small purse shut now, one on a long chain he hadn't seen before and this disturbed him too. The bag of creamy coloured leather shaped like a large envelope which she carried with her from the house after the wedding sat on the dressing table with some pots and jars. Goodness, he had thought it would be one bag for one woman.

He had a lot to learn, he could see, and felt terribly inadequate that all he could do in preparation was to brush at his coat with his fingertips and smooth down his hair with his hands.

She went out of the room ahead of him, sauntering down the wide hall filled with the smell of the evening meal cooking, something savoury, Edwards could detect with rising spirits.

Mrs Chance put her head out of one of the doors and her bold eyes asked if they had spent the time in the bedroom at you-know-what.

No, we didn't, said Edwards's bold eyes in reply.

And if you ask me, said his back passing through the front door and crossing the verandah to meet the sparkling sea, it's quite a way off yet.

Una had her small chin raised as they walked through the town which was a cluster of shops just past the wharf where the fishing boats came in. There was the smell of fish, tempered by the sharp salt smell of the water. A rough bank ran between the wharf and the first shop, which had a narrow front and backed over the water at high tide. It sold among other things sweets and fruit, the latter displayed in a glass dish in the centre of the window, wrinkled oranges and speckled bananas that did not look inviting and from which rose a cloud of little insects. There was a handwritten notice behind the fruit that said the shop also sold teas.

Next door was a shop with a similar front that sold harness and the smell of new leather wafted out as they passed it. Edwards was glad to reach it. He feared Una might have wanted to go into the other and have tea at one of the little tables.

His mother had sent him money for a wedding present, and he had saved only some of it to meet honeymoon expenses, having been tempted to buy a bathing costume while in Bega to arrange for the marriage and receive gratefully the modest increase in his stipend.

He looked forward to wearing the costume, a plain black wool, deciding something untrimmed was more suitable to his calling in life.

He had seen Una in her green one when they went to the seaside in the Austin for a picnic soon after the engagement. Enid had not changed but sat with him on a sandy shelf made by a jutting rock and watched the sea run eagerly up into the channels and back again, leaving foam like a long white moustache stained with coffee.

Una, unembarrassed at giving him his first view of her long creamy legs and arms and quite a bit of back too, stood dipping a foot into the water. Edwards was beginning to think the costume a waste of money when she took a sudden plunge in, splashing Enid's stockings and his clerical trousers, for the excursion had followed a Sunday morning service.

"Dear me, that was sudden," said Edwards, noting that Una did not call out an apology but went swimming off, turning her face from side to side, her hair streaming out like a mermaid's.

"She is given to doing things suddenly," Enid said.

"Of course," Edwards said. "It's part of her charm."

"Of course," Enid said, lifting her chin and looking not at Una but out to sea.

Now Una was up to her suddenness again. She stopped and he found himself a few paces ahead before he realized it. Turning he saw her staring at the Post Office, legs apart, hands on hips, her bag dangling carelessly from one.

"Look!" she said, frowning towards a recess in the porch front. He was a little slow but he saw eventually a telephone behind a glass door. She gave him a brilliant smile.

"We can ring Rachel!" she cried. She snapped open her purse and he heard coins tinkle as she dipped it to one side. He drew some from his pocket and stared at them. He was still holding them when she opened the door of the recess and stood waiting for the ring. She looked like a nervous boy in a sailor suit afraid he was not welcome at a party. After several minutes the postmaster, a rotund man with glasses well down on his nose, opened a door showing a small switchboard he was obviously tending and told Una there was no answer from the Wyndham Post Office. He looked Edwards over before closing the door as if undecided about connecting him with Una. Edwards was still gently shaking the money in his closed hand. Una heard the noise.

"There is nothing to pay," she said, running down the steps, sounding scornful. She walked rapidly off as if eager to get the Post Office away from her and appeared from the direction she was taking to intend returning the short way back to the guest house. He was blowed if he would follow like a chastened pup, he thought, stopping as she was about to plunge through a thicket of dogwood.

"We made a slide once we were here on holidays and slid down that hill!" she called, needing to shout, for the wind was humming around her and about to rise and sweep the slope with a tearing force.

"Come!" he shouted, inclining his head towards the road. "We can walk up the hill another time, if you insist on being blown into the sea!" She reached down before joining him and pulled burrs and twigs from her ankles, as if to say she was in agreement only to protect her clothes.

They walked for a while nearly side by side, and then he reached forward and took her hand, which was slack in his for a while, then warmer, then the tips of her fingers scratched gently at his palm and he considered swinging it joyfully but didn't quite dare. He saw her mouth stretched to deepen the indent at the corners and the wide brim of her navy blue hat — how many did she own? — throwing a lacy pattern on her cheek. Her knees threw her skirt in and out, moving so fast there was this continual whoosh, following the tap of her feet on the gravel. They were speaking. Her skirt on her knees, her feet on the road, her sharp little breath, all saying something. She glanced back sometimes over her shoulder and it seemed to him she was running from the past into her new life, charging forward with some misgivings but in the main prepared to meet it head on.

About them there was nothing. Nothing, nothing. Some white sky relieved by trees that went on forever. Someone was here once! They made this road. Edwards scraped his foot on it to make sure. She had stopped, and he stopped too, wanting to stride up level with her, but not lest it draw attention to his always lagging behind.

Will she always be ahead, he thought, or I those few paces behind?

They rounded a bend and a cart came towards them pulled by a horse whose feet made clopping noises, the cart rattling and the wheels squeaking. A man was driving. He may have been young, but he was grey with dust, blending into the grey cart which held, apart from him, a heap of slack corn bags. There was a shine on his trousers, with grease, not with newness and even the bits of scrappy leather tying his boots resting on the shafts were greasy too.

He stopped the cart and the myriad of flies rose in delight from the horse's rump and settled on the boots, running and darting, the sun twinkling on their wings and bringing a shine to the grease. Edwards put out his hand to shake the man's but the man gave his head a small shake and clung to the reins with his eyes clinging to Una. She had taken off her hat and swung it on her hand, the crown spinning so no flies came near her.

He ran his eyes over her hair as if it were food tempting him. She smiled and shook it then moved her hat up so that her eyes shone just over the crown and she rocked her body just slightly like a shy actor about to perform from a stage.

"Good afternoon," Edwards said, raising his hat, and the man jerked his eyes back to him as if he needed to be reminded where he was, and the horse took the movement as a signal to walk on, which he did, Edward needing to step back smartly to avoid being trampled on.

Una slapped the top of her hat onto her head.

"Let's run!" she cried and took off, he following, straining to keep up, his black trousers and her brown stockings quickly covered with fine dust. At the gate of the guesthouse, which swung freely, for the earth beneath was hollowed by wheels and feet, they stopped, dusting themselves down and laughing.

But when Una raised her eyes and saw the house she frowned. It sat there like a man fallen asleep with a pipe in his mouth.

She is thinking about telephoning, he thought. Well there have been some good parts so far, and for those I must be grateful. Keep it up God, and if it's not asking too much, spin it out a little. Thanks.

38

The cleaning up at Honeysuckle after the wedding obviously went on well into the evening, for there was no answer when Una rang the Post Office after tea.

Una flung herself on the bed and burrowed her head into the pillow without regard for her newly laundered nightgown resting there. She kicked off her shoes, raising her legs immodestly, and he wasn't sure whether he should look away or indulge the pleasure of staring at the white linen at her crotch and the lace showering her thighs. He decided to look away since she had clamped her hat on her face but was watching him with one eye.

He took his Bible from where he had it stowed in the corner of a drawer and opened it to read, rather at random, but settling the silk cord fussily between the pages, to give the impression of choosing a certain chapter.

She turned her eyes out of the hat.

"Will that help?" she said, in a quavering voice.

"It usually does," he said.

She put the hat back more firmly. "To make Small Henry better?"

"Small Henry is not necessarily sick," he said.

"He is. They have taken him to Bega hospital. I know."

"He is either at Violet's or Honeysuckle. And at either place he is in good hands." He had a vision of Enid's hands and bent lower over his Bible to push them away.

Una climbed off the bed and when he raised his eyes to watch, she smoothed her skirt down around her thighs. He went back to his reading. Just as you like, he thought. Keep it to yourself and see if it bothers me. Ashamed, he closed the Bible and put it away. She went to the mirror to brush and coil her hair.

"It's more than an hour since we rang," she said. "We can ring again."

She waited for him to accompany her, and in a moment he stood and followed her into the hall, seeing the back of her neck like the inside of a creamy shell, and cheered at the thought of walking with her on the beach tomorrow.

But they walked to Honeysuckle instead.

Rachel shouted through the phone that Violet decided to leave Small Henry at Honeysuckle in case he was coming down with something and would infect the two babies, still with a few days to go before discharging from Albert Lane.

Una, frightened and furious, rushed back to the bedroom and began to tear off her clothes. It's happening, it's going to happen! Edwards thought, beginning to part his coat.

"Small Henry infect their wretched babies!" Una cried through her petticoat. She threw it down after her face emerged pink under tousled hair. "Infect them with what? They would infect him more like it! Enid won't care for him properly running after Jack!"

Her brassiere came off and he saw for the first time her breasts with their little squashed nipples in the circle of brown. Like marble cake he thought, with saliva in his mouth. The breasts waggled with her efforts. She pulled her nightdress over her head and removed her pants and stockings by reaching up under it.

Edwards felt he was looking at a play where they had forgotten to raise the curtain. By George, she got through all of that in quick time! He had thought women took much longer at dressing and undressing. But he knew nothing much about them, he thought ruefully and his ignorance was certainly coming home to roost now.

He wondered if this was the time for him to start undressing, and saw with sinking spirits she had already curled herself under the covers very close to the bedrail and with her back to his place and her eyes squeezed shut.

"I'm going to go to sleep at once to be rested for our walk," she said. His question hung silently in the air between them.

She lifted her head and punched a deeper hollow in her pillow. "We'll walk to Honeysuckle in the morning."

He sat studying the floor between his feet. "Quite a walk that," he said.

"You walk a lot," she said. "You enjoy walking, so you always say." She sounded as if he said it more often than was necessary.

"Not twelve miles at the one stretch," he said.

"Fourteen," she said.

He stood and took off his top things first as she had and he kept his back to her, shielding his bare buttocks with the solid foot of the bed and ducking anyway below it to pull his pyjamas on. He had imagined them kneeling together to say the Our Father. He padded almost without sound to the window to look out on the sea like a great bare table with the moon hanging above it like a lamp. Cold, distant and lonely.

He felt like an unwanted guest at a table that would never be set with food to nourish him.

He crouched by the bed to say his prayers but they brought him no comfort either. Nor did the bed when he slipped cautiously between the sheets and thought of his bed at the rectory, unmade a lot of the time, tangled but welcoming, the harsh blankets mixed with the sheets and the pillow slip not slippery clean but smelling of humanity and comforting as flesh upon his cheek.

In a little while she turned and slipped an arm across his waist.

"Thank you for coming to Honeysuckle with me," she whispered.

Only his head turned. His hands were down between his thighs, pressed there to stay the quivering and leaping. "I'm fond of walking as you say."

She removed her arm and turned her back. Her little round bottom hit his like a tennis ball on its last bounce. "We'll need our rest, so I'll say goodnight," he said.

"You've said it," she said.

When he woke in the morning she was almost finished dressing and he got up and dressed too. The light was too dim for each to see much of the other and her eyes were down concentrating on lacing canvas shoes. He had brought his second best boots, clumsy things, unsuitable for the beach but all he had apart from his best. And this tramp will finish them off, he thought getting into them.

She took a writing pad from among her things and lighting a candle wrote something on a page, carrying it off on whispered feet to the dining room. He puzzled about it, his mind foggy with sleep, but on their way out he saw it propped up on the sideboard saying they left early for a long walk and would not be back until evening.

I can't accuse her of an untruth, I'll say that much, he thought on their way out. Three cows kept by the Chances to supply guests with milk and cream raised their heads in surprise to see them, then flung them down to chew at some grass, saying if this is your idea of recreation it wouldn't be mine. Edwards's eyes on them said it wasn't his either, be sure of that, and half their luck taking things easy on the grassy slope, keeping their stomachs full while his was hollow already and it not yet five o'clock. All they needed to make it perfect is the bull, he thought, not bothering with repentance as he opened the gate for Una. He saw her face fresh and dewy as the small wild flowers coming up through the grass to greet the day.

"We'll walk brisk, shall we? Then dawdle, then run, then trot. It will be fun!" she said, taking his arm.

"A mile of trotting, dawdling, et cetera? Is that what you

mean? We need to find fourteen different ways of travelling!"

"We'll find Small Henry at the end," she said and dropped his arm to rush ahead. She walked so rapidly he had difficulty in keeping up and difficulty too in disguising a pant.

"Is this the brisk part?" he said. "I doubt that I'll have the strength for the run. Or even the trot!"

"It's all that kneeling!" she called back to him. "Your feet have gone to sleep!"

"Kneeling's my living!" he said. "Our living!"

She stopped suddenly, a slender shape on the dusty road. He caught up with her, grateful. He wanted to take her in his arms, and when she turned her face to him, he did. No one was about. No sign of life. No car or dray or sulky. Only a belt of trees on one side of the road and a sweep of paddocks on the other, the farmer's house nowhere in sight for it was built long before the road was made, and not only was it two miles into the bush, but faced the opposite way with the dairy and cow bails in the front to the constant grumbling of the wife and growing daughters. All the farmer's cattle were out of sight too, so that clouds, rolled like great, thick white blankets, were all that moved. She laid her chin on his shoulder and looked up at them, and her body in his hands was like a bird that to his great surprise, though not wounded, allowed itself to be held.

"We'll dawdle the next part," she said into his neck. "So you need not take your arms away."

39

They reached Honeysuckle soon after midday.

"There it is!" Una cried when it came in sight, and raced forward with an energy that amazed him. Just as he was thinking she would reach it long before him and he would arrive dejected and rejected, she halted and sat down on a stump at the side of the road. She was plucking at little tufts of grey green dried up moss when he came up to sit with her.

"I am frightened of what we might find when we get there," she said. He took her hand and squeezed it. Things are improving, he thought. I can squeeze her hand now without having to decide if it's safe to.

"You'll find him there, happy and well. See if you don't," he said.

She got up. "The house looks as if someone is dead there," she said.

"If it looks that way it's because you are not living there," he said. But she was frowning too heavily to heed him.

"This is absurd," she said. "Knocking on your own front door!" A flash of her eyes accused him.

Enid opened the door. From behind her came the smell of roasting meat and another thinner smell, fragrant and sweet like vanilla. Whatever happened he must not fall down in a faint.

"Small Henry!" Una cried. "Where is he?" Enid moved to let her past and she flew around the dining table looking for him on the floor then on to the kitchen where, judging by her cry, she found him.

"Is he alright?" Edwards said sinking down onto the couch, thinking heaven might be like this. Enid sat there too.

"A tooth," she said and put a finger in the centre of her own bottom set.

"You walked all that way," she murmured in disbelief.

He felt a sense of guilt that he hadn't walked to see her. Una came in with Small Henry, her arms bound about him as if cemented there. He looked at Enid's arms lying with the inner part turned upwards on her lap and her fingers curled loosely as he had often seen them. Disturbed at their emptiness he stood and looked at Small Henry, Una craning her neck to see his face too.

Small Henry decided he would not cooperate immediately. They had been gone a long time to him and should not be forgiven at once. He stared down at a foot caught in the folds of Una's skirt. Edwards stared too and put out a hand and grabbed the foot. Small Henry with the start of a smile pressed it hard against Una and Edwards pulled at it tickling it gently. Small Henry laughed as he pulled it away. Edwards grabbed it boldly and Small Henry equally bold thudded it back into Una's stomach. He opened his mouth wide to laugh again and Una saw the tooth. She put a finger in and felt it and sought a chair to recover from the shock and the joy.

"A tooth! His first tooth! He has a tooth. He's grown a tooth for us!" she cried, swinging him back and forth with her face in his neck. When Edwards saw it the cheeks were flushed a deep pink and the eyes full of tears. Enid began to set the table and Edwards watched to take pleasure in her calmness. Una raced towards her old bedroom crying out that she and Small Henry would take a little rest.

Although Enid did not lift her eyes from folding two extra serviettes, Una balked at the step, then ran on and they heard the springs of the bed in Henry's old room leap to take the two bodies, Una's triumphant shout and Small Henry's chuckle.

After doing a few more things to the table Enid slipped to the kitchen returning with a tumbler of water for him, which he drank with his face turned from the direction of the room where Una and Small Henry were.

"Come with me into the kitchen," she said, "while I finish off dinner."

"Perhaps I could do something to help," he said, remembering.

Jack came in and found him on one of the kitchen chairs in the pose remembered from earlier days, his hands crossed on his knees. Jack's jowls shook and his black eyes snapped. He had thought the fellow was removed from the Honeysuckle kitchen forever! He looked to Enid to explain. "They have come to see how Small Henry is," she said. Jack had seen her face, as if there was a light under the skin and behind her eyes and darting about the corners of her mouth. He saw it that way when she began counting plates, then a frowning concentration take over as if the number wasn't coming out right. He put his hand on a chair back. Perhaps he should wait here in the kitchen until dinner time.

Enid's heart asked him to go. Give me five minutes with him. Can you spare me that? Three, two will do. He's here in my kitchen and I can't believe it yet. Stay and I'll never believe it. Go somewhere please. He may say nothing to me, or I to him. But you speak to me without words, don't you? So it's a language I understand. Let us have this silent conversation, this fragment, the last we may ever have. Go away, please. That's all I ask in return for all you have taken from me.

She went to the pantry returning with a jug of liquid, and slicing a lemon swiftly slipped the pieces in and Edwards watched them sink to the bottom like a pale swimmer then rise and bob about in a lazy float.

"Come somewhere cool," she said leading the way out. "And have this to drink before dinner. Both of you."

Alex drove Edwards and Una back to Pambula to resume their honeymoon. Una sat as she had on the first trip in a corner of the back seat and kept her face to the scenery passing the curtained window. Alex was not pleased about the errand. There was a tennis game at Towamba and he had intended going. There were people there who had not seen the car. There were girls who worked during the week in Eden, home to the farms for the weekend. Pretty, soft young things to tease between sets, and sit with for tea and buttered teacake, admiring the length of leg stretched on the grass, and the shortness of skirts, not folded piously at ankles, but spread out like the petals of a flower creeping higher as they moved, sometimes as if in energy and exuberance bodies wanted to leap altogether from the confines of their covering. The back of Alex's neck told Edwards that was where he wanted to be. Edwards turning for comfort to Una saw her neck saying she wanted to be back at Honeysuckle, holding Small Henry.

Well, blow them both, thought Edwards, letting the wind dig a deep path in his hair and send his coat collar flapping. He did not know how to draw the blind at the window and Alex was not going to offer any help. He remembered taking Una's hand to comfort her on the trip yesterday. Now he had no desire to. This must be how married people change, Edwards thought. It comes earlier than I expected, I must say. He took in great gulps of air for the wind was stronger as they approached the coast. He started to feel pleased to be free soon of the obligation to Alex, then had to change the feeling back to gloom at the thought of coping with Una's mood. The Austin stopped at the guest house gate to let them both out, Alex giving a curt nod as he swung the car around in a swirl of gravel as if performing on a race track. Edwards saw him go with envy. He looked with such certainty a single man. Una in her usual way went rapidly ahead, and he had to hurry so as not to be dragging behind in view of Mrs Chance, who was doing something at an upper window.

Una flung herself on the bed and Edwards took the chair and it occurred to him that this appeared to be the pattern of behaviour for them when they entered their bedroom. Una pulled half of the pillow across her face, as if closing her eyes was not enough. Edwards took his bathing costume from his drawer.

"There is time for a bathe before tea," he said. "Will you come?"

The pillow waggled. "Very well," he said in a voice as chilly as he expected to find the water. Awkwardly he draped the costume across his arm and went out passing Mrs Chance fiddling at the hallstand.

"A warm day for your walk," she said.

Not as warm as your curiosity though! Not as bubbling hot as that! Not as seething and boiling as your speculation! And false it all is!

He took the track to the sea that other honeymooners and holiday-makers had cut through the earth. Were some of the feet heavy and sad as his? Yes, they would be, he told himself. The pathway through life wasn't easy, as he frequently told others, but with faith the dark clouds rolled back and showed the sun.

227

I had better heed my own advice he said to his thudding feet, now on the descent to the beach, the track cut so deeply the sides almost reached his knees. By jove, some of those feet must have been heavy indeed! Well, he thought, springing onto a rock, I'll make mine light for a start! He took off his boots then sheltered by a large rock removed his trousers and pulled on his costume.

It reminded him of undressing with Una in the room.

I seem to be destined to keep this thing under cover, he said to himself, stuffing its slackness inside the black wool, then peeling off his top clothing. What has marriage brought me so far? To dress and undress in secret, to find a rock or a bed bottom to hide behind! To take a shameful view of this thing he imagined would get working at last, loosening the creeping sting at his groin, opening the flood gates, rushing as the wave rushed now and filled his toenails with foam. Flesh on flesh, lightly moist, a tickling of hair, a cushion of a breast, a nipple to gently bite, a knee to lift and stroke a hip, jutting gently as a rock jutted here, submissive as a wave flowed over it.

Edwards bound his arms around his hunched knees and bowed his face on them, letting the sea sing in his ears. A seagull squawked, flying low over his head, and he lifted his face and cried out, shut up, shut up! Shut out that body in the crumpled dress on the bed, the flinging arms, seeking a body, but not his!

He stood and jumped to meet the next wave, letting it swirl about him, his feet sinking into the sand when it receded, holding on to the wetness. He walked farther in and a strand of seaweed floated by his thigh. He flung it off. Limp like the other!

He looked at it wobbling like a stranded jellyfish under the black wool. He saw the fold of cloth, like a fold on nothing.

Oh damn and hell, he called to the swooping gull, swooping himself into the deep. He put his head into a wave, then turned and laid a cheek on it. He rolled over floating because he could not swim and shut his eyes against the stinging sun. The waves were small and gentle and he thought of the peace of Enid's arms, and when he was lifted light as the lemon that floated in her jug of drink, he thought of her breasts rising and falling. I am lying on her sweet, cool, soft body. Feel her rock me.

He opened his eyes to a line of pines on a ridge beyond the guest house, straight, stiff trees, not moving, trapping the wind inside them, remaining with heads proud and cold. That is she, the other one. Unconsciously he used Jack's term.

Enid the sea bobbed him about and after drifting a little he put a foot to the bottom, to find by stretching, a scratch of sand at his toes. She is not drowning me. She is the one, the one! He made for the shore, fighting the drag of water. "Don't worry, little one! I'll be back to you!" he cried out running to his clothes.

He remembered he had no towel. She would have made sure he brought a towel!

He dabbed with the outside of his coat his wet chest, and peeled the costume from his body, pulling his trousers on, drying his crotch with his hands, slapping affectionately at it. Wait, wait! We can wait!

He tore up the hill, his big boots wanting to pull him back on the slippery grass, and the wind flying about him, drying his hair. A crow in a large and solitary gum took flight crying *aah, aaah, aah* and he answered, null and void. *Aaah, aah, aah,* null and void!

I will sit quietly on my chair and tell her. She can bind her skirt about her ankles and I'll be glad. Yesterday never was. Null and void, null and void!

He tapped on the door and when there was no answer opened it. She was standing by the window holding a hat, a creamy coloured hat trimmed with bunches of red cherries. She held it above her, ready to drop it on her head.

Her lips were smiling, red as the cherries. "You've never seen this hat on me, have you?" she said.

When it was on she had to lift her chin to see him from under the brim. She put a leg forward and laughed and laid a hand on one hip, as if ready to be photographed. His eyes clung to her face for a moment, then slipped down to her feet.

They were naked as was all the rest of her.

40

Una was tired of the honeymoon by the middle of the week. She suggested taking the mail car home on Thursday, two days before the stay was to end. Edwards had paid for a full week at the guest house. He tried not to allow his expression to show a parsimonious streak but Una saw and gave her deep frown which was never far from her face since she began easing out of her exuberant state about Tuesday.

She was putting her hats one inside the other in the round hat case, and he saw with sorrow that she treated the one with cherries as if it were like the others. She is really going then, he thought. I must learn to accept the shortness of bliss, if that is the word for it.

He stood up from the chair and wished he hadn't, for he was developing the habit of adapting to her whims too readily. So he sat again and in reply to her raised eyebrows said he did not have much to pack.

"No," she said, and he felt she was acknowledging his indigent state.

"But I think I shall take a bathe in the short time we have left," he said. He did not ask her to accompany him.

He ran down the track to the place where he had bathed before. The waves he saw were brushing the sand tenderly and were unhurried in their wash backwards.

A different time, a different tide, a different mood.

He pulled off his trousers, more efficient now, having

put his costume on underneath his trousers and going without his boots.

The water lapped about him sadly as he floated. He could not find a wave rising and quivering like a breast. The water seemed heavy, sluggish. It had no arms to hold him. It was grey too, for the sun had gone behind a cloud and there were long shadows on the sand, streaking it with grey as well.

He left the water, but not wanting to return to Una too quickly sat on a rock to dry off a little, as he had forgotten a towel again.

I never got to do the thing properly, he thought, remembering Una getting her things together long before they set out, not forgetting cream for her nose, her bathing cap, and a comb all in a little bag she had obviously made for this very purpose.

Women are different, he said to the rim of the sea for he did not want to look at the part he had just left. I'm finding that out, but I've much more to learn. Much, much more.

He stood to pull his trousers on, keeping his back to the sea. Coward, coward, he told himself. Look back and say goodbye. No, don't. She is too cold and still, too sad. The water a billion tears. He began to scramble up the grass, not taking the track, pulling at tufts with his hands, his body sometimes only inches from the earth.

Crawling like an ant, he thought. An ant, no more than an ant.

A crow cried and he looked for it. Not in the gum where it was before. *Aaah, aaah,* it called again.

Edwards stood and watched the pines, but no branch bent, nothing black showed in the inky green.

Aah, aaah, came the sound again, and it was there deep in the tree.

I know you're there, cried his heart.

Aaah, aah it said again.

I'm coming, I'm coming.

He ran to beat the call should it come again, and only when he let himself inside the gate did he walk with dignity to the front door.

Una pointed out that it would be best to leave the mail car at Honeysuckle in case the furniture Jack gave them for a wedding present was not yet delivered to the rectory.

"Besides we will need milk and things for the larder."

How clever she is, he thought, sneaking a grip of her hand under the staring eyes of a pallid child on its mother's knee, suffering travel sickness and filling the car with the fumes from its turbulent stomach.

But Small Henry was not at Honeysuckle. With the discharge of Mrs Skinner and the Gough girl, Albert Lane creaked with emptiness. Ned disappeared after being underfoot the ten days. Violet, after loud and frequently repeated threats that she would have a few days to herself when her patients were discharged, found the quiet unbearable.

The melancholy air the rectory wore depressed her too.

She put on her mauve flowered voile and set off for Honeysuckle. It was a warm day but she walked happily, her best black shoes gathering a film of fine dust. Her excitement at two patients at the one time so soon after the hospital opened had not yet worn off, and she smiled up at the sky and the tops of the trees as if they were friends congratulating her. Another booking had been made for April, but you never know, someone could turn up before then the way the Gough girl did, two or three perhaps.

She was the best nurse on the coast and her reputation could only be enhanced with the opening of Albert Lane.

The Gough girl had paid too, and the Skinner woman would have to since Jack controlled the cream cheque, and could, if the need arose, deduct the hospital bill from the Skinner's share and pass it to Violet.

If Una conceived straight away there would be that to look forward to. Yes, I reckon he would know what it's all about for all that lowering of the eyes and brushing at himself. She wouldn't be backward either at flashing around the bedroom with her drawers off! A pair of leg cockers, both of them, if you asked Violet!

Things were not turning out too badly, after all (she would put Ned to one side for the moment) and she would have Small Henry back. Making his strange noises as he watched the birds hop down on the back verandah. Turning his blue eyes up at her when she came near him. Smiling with his eyes, like Ned when he had both of his.

She quickened her steps, getting a little closer to him. She hadn't seen him since the wedding. And he had a tooth. George had called to tell her when he was at the store on Monday.

And the Reverend and Una had walked from Pambula to see how he was!

Devotion like that was useful. She could pass him over to them when she had more than enough work at the hospital. Honeysuckle was too far away and Enid showing signs (from George's conversation) of getting overfond of him. He was safer at the rectory if he had to be anywhere but Albert Lane.

Una discovered he wasn't at Honeysuckle when she alighted from the mail car as Alex was collecting packages from the driver. She looked up angrily at the house as if it had betrayed her. Enid, coming from the kitchen untying her apron on her way to the bedroom, came upon her in the living room biting her lips and looking about her as if she suspected he was really there. But when Edwards was about to come through the door with the luggage she told him she would ask Alex to take them to the rectory almost straight away.

"We won't be staying," she said to Enid who had not so far seen into Edwards's face but was nonetheless trying to fix the image of it to her mind. She was quite pleased with her own face, seeing it in the mirror of the dressing table. Her eyes had gone bright and her nose wasn't red. I believe I'm inclined towards that red nose when Una's around all the time, she told herself, giving it a stern and silent warning to behave itself. She pinched and stroked it, pleased to see it return to a good natural colour, and putting it in the air she smoothed her muslin blouse down and tightened the belt of her grey linen skirt, thankfully not one Una had made.

"You'll stay for dinner at least," she said, flinging a white damask cloth on the table. Edwards had his hands on a chair back and his head at an angle that had the power to melt Enid's heart.

"That woman!" said Una, not attempting to help Enid with the cloth at the corner of the table where she stood, Edwards needing to fight an urge to pull her away. "She is allowed to get away with everything!"

"Do sit down," Enid murmured to Edwards at the drawer that held the cutlery. He sat and tried, she could see, not to look to Una for directions.

"The furniture came," Enid said.

"All the more reason for us to go at once and put it in place," Una said.

"I've done that," Enid said, measuring with her eye the centre of the table for the cruet.

"It still may need to go into place!" Una said. She picked up her bag from the chair and went coolly into her old room, tossing her head backwards should Enid be watching.

"I am sorry," Edwards murmured.

Enid, laying the table with an air of serenity, thought about how pleased he would be to see how she had arranged the things in the rectory. She had made the bed holding onto a dream that she would share it with him. Lavender inside the pillowslips. For him, for him!

"The Robertson's killed and gave us some beef," Enid said. "We're having it for dinner and there is some to take home for your tea."

"So kind," Edwards said, but looked partly distracted towards the bedroom door. "She will be happier when she sees Small Henry."

Enid stirred the sugar in the silver bowl and snapped the lid shut. A snap in her eyes too before she lowered them.

"It was hard for you to part with him," he said.

Always he says exactly what you want to hear, Enid thought, marvelling at the miracle.

"Violet has first claim on him," she said. She, too, would say what he wanted to hear. He was almost overcome by her saneness and goodness. Oh, perfect love, he said to himself remembering the hymn Mrs Palmer sang at the wedding. I mean, oh perfect woman, of course! He stood, determined to help her bring in the dinner however Jack may disapprove, and Una appeared and ran her eyes over the table.

"Just like old times!" she said. "It all might never have been!" She went ahead of them and the back door banged. Through the kitchen window they saw her walking in the garden, pulling the heads of roses to her and fingering the petals. In a moment she ran into the garden shed, returning with shears with which she cut the air a few times before slicing at the bushes. Enid winced but turned resolutely to the meat, sweating brown juice through its shiny yellow coat. Edwards was carrying it to the dining table when Jack came in.

That fellow again! said his undisguised expression. He is here as often as before.

I won't explain, said Enid's expression in return. I'm done with all that. "You can carve as soon as you like, Father," she said, for Alex and George were there and Una was putting her roses wrapped in wet paper with the luggage by the front door.

"So we won't go without them. Our first flowers in our first house!" She went to Edwards's side and flung an arm around him rubbing a cheek on his shoulder.

Enid saw him close his eyes to shut away from them the ecstasy there.

41

Una was not critical of the arrangement of furniture at the rectory but hummed a tune happily while she selected a wedding present vase for the roses. Head to one side she put them first on the centre of the table in the living room, then to one end grouped with the marble figurine of a shepherdess she had begged Nellie to buy her once when on a visit to Sydney.

"It's a suitable sort of ornament, don't you think, for a church house?" she said.

Edwards, helping in his braces, was never happier in his life.

In a little while he heard her in the room next to theirs moving things around and he went tut-tutting in husbandly fashion at the way women called for help in minor things and attacked major ones with a great display of independence.

"Look how she has put the stuff in here any old how!" Una said, pushing his old chest of drawers against the wall.

Edwards wanted to fly to Enid's defence. She had done so much and done it so effectively, but he wanted Una's good mood to continue.

"Take the bottom end of the bed and put your end of the rail in that little slot," she said. He did, managing it quite well, marvelling at her knowledge of these things and a little fearful too that she might be contemplating sleeping here apart from him.

Of course! It was their guest room. How wonderful if

Mother could come. Interrupting her as she was flinging sheets on the bed he took her in his arms and rocked her back and forth as she did with Small Henry.

He did not kiss her, just bowed his head, crushing it into the sweet flesh of her neck, feeling the rush of hair on his forehead. He lifted his face and felt he could shelter it there in her hair forever. But he glimpsed the dent at the edge of her mouth, a barometer of her mood, and reading impatience there went to the other side of the bed to help smooth out the sheets and blankets.

There was only a hooked rug on the floor and she straightened this with her foot and a frown and he knew she wished it was covered with a linoleum square like those in their bedroom and living room, which she had selected to add to the pieces Jack had agreed to buy for the rectory.

"Draughts will come up through the cracks and lay me low with pneumonia!" she had said in the Bega store during the purchasing. "It will be bad enough suffering boards in that cold old kitchen!"

Jack with a short curt nod indicated his agreement, but jammed his hat on and went out to wait in the car, the gesture stating there was to be nothing more added, and he would wait only a limited time for them.

Una now found a white linen runner for the top of the chest and plumped a cushion on a chair by the washstand which held a china jug, basin and chamber pot given as a wedding present by Rachel and secondary to the larger set from Alex and in the more modern commode cabinet in the main bedroom.

"Shall we share a jerry, or have one apiece?" Una said when, on the week of the wedding, she saw them taken out of their packages at Honeysuckle. "I bags the blue daisies if we have one to ourselves!"

Enid bent her hot face over the wrapping paper she was folding for future use. Una flung herself onto a chair with her legs stretched out before her, her head back and her eyes rolled towards the ceiling. Enid slipped away to put the paper in the lumber room. "We must try and believe she never pees," Una said. "Hard as it is this is what we must believe!"

Edwards now had the irreverant thought of his mother urinating in the pale green chamber pot then returning it to its little shelter behind a door.

He was looking its way when Una flung both arms around him from behind. "What do you think of it?" she said dreamily into his neck. He only thought of her as a soft and human burr he would never want plucked from him.

In a moment she moved to the chest of drawers, opening each one and checking, it appeared, to see that nothing was inside.

"Come!" she said, reaching one of her long white arms back to him. "We'll go and get him!"

He followed her through the kitchen that had looked so homely a half hour ago. Not any more. The canisters on the shelf too stiffly new, unmarked by hasty thumbs, the china on the dresser sterile, the stove cold and black as if it would never burn, the paper trimming a little shelf near the window cut into peaks, sharp as knives, the window too clean with too white curtains, the floor scrubbed to a hard grey coldness, resenting his feet. He was glad to leave it, following her straight little back and determined neck but grew afraid again when his horse by the sulky under the tree snorted loudly and shook his head, as if delivering some sort of warning.

As they came closer to Violet's house his heart slipped from its rightful place and beat somewhere up near his throat and he tried to be stern with himself and despise his weakness, but there was nothing, nothing, to dispel the feeling of doom.

240

42

"Alright," Violet said grudgingly. "But only for a little while. He has a bottle at five o'clock." She looked at the clock as if it had some way of confirming this.

Una wrapped her arms around Small Henry and peered into his face. It was already alerted to something going on for his benefit and involving the doorway, towards which he screwed his head and stuck out a hand.

"He knows so much!" Una cried. "He knows he's going somewhere!"

"Well, make sure he's back from somewhere in time for his feed and bed!" Violet did not see them off but took up the fowl buckets and went off on that errand, glancing into the bush for signs of Ned, her conscience troubled more than usual since he had gathered up extra eggs and the last of his war souvenirs when he found Small Henry back at Albert Lane.

"Oh, stay away, stay away, stay away!" she cried, able to shout as loud as she liked, the words drowned by the squawking of the fowls. Out of the corner of her eye she allowed herself a glimpse of the shrinking backs of Edwards and Una, with Small Henry's head like a small round sun between them.

She went into his room and remade his cot, turning the covers back ready for his body, and returning to the kitchen looked hard at the clock, doubting the slow moving hands.

Una took Small Henry straight into the room they had

set in order and laid him on Edwards's former bed, loosening his clothing, and to Edwards's surprise she unpinned Small Henry's napkin and pinned it on him again.

"Just as well she didn't have you all wet!" she said, gathering him up. "We'll show him everything, shall we?"

Edwards felt she was addressing Small Henry not him. She took Small Henry's hand and placed it on the foot and head of the bed and on the washstand, letting it run over the jug and wash basin and towel rail which he gripped and pulled at.

"That's where we hang his towel that wipes his beautiful face!" she cried. She took him to the window and tickled his face with the tassel of the blind. He laughed so loud Edwards found himself smiling and Una darted to his side and with what arm she could spare wrapped it around him, and Small Henry, not having paid much attention to him up to now, became shy and lowered his lashes to turn them into tiny fans on his cheeks and lowered the corners of his mouth as well.

Edwards took his foot and shook it. "I'll go and open up the church and air it," he said.

Una took a hand of Small Henry and wagged it at Edwards's back. "Ta-ta Papa! Ta-ta Papa!" she called.

There was just the slightest pause in his step, the smallest stiffening of the back of his neck, and Una might not have noticed for she found a peak of hair growing downwards at the back of Small Henry's neck which she could blow about with her kisses.

When Edwards returned to the rectory he heard voices raised in the kitchen. Violet was there telling Una it was nearly a quarter past five.

"We haven't wound and set the new clock yet!" Una was saying. He came inside to see Una making no signs of passing Small Henry over.

"That's something he can watch us do!" she said. "Come on, we'll fix up the clock since Auntie Violet has told us what time it is!"

She went off to the front room and Violet found a chair as if her frustrations were too much for her. Edwards looked at the stove as if surprised it was not burning since someone else was in the house now beside himself.

"I should get that going, I suppose," he said.

Violet with a hand on each of her large knees snorted. "You'll be the one to get it going if there's any hope of you eating tonight!" she said.

"Enid gave us cold meat for our tea," Edwards said, cold too.

"May she keep it up! That's all I can say!"

Una's voice floated in to them explaining the workings of the clock, and in spite of himself Edwards's mouth and eyes began to smile. Violet stood and shoved her chair under the table.

"If she stays there much longer he'll be old enough to tell the time himself!" Then in a louder voice: "Come on, come on! Enough is enough! He'll be looking for this every afternoon!"

Una sauntered into the kitchen with him, her arms wedged to his gown, her face pressed to his face and her eyes hidden from them. Violet clapped her hands together and held them out but Una swung Small Henry in the opposite direction and went through the back door saying she would carry him. Violet with an angry mouth followed, and Edwards went as far as the woodheap, kicking some chips together, then gathering them up to take to the kitchen.

Opening the stove door he found that Enid had laid a fire and all he had to do was put a match to it.

It leaped to life in a way that he could never achieve and

he was sitting watching it when the kettle, which Enid had filled, began to sing and Una came in.

He sprang up as if she had caught him out, but she kept her face averted and went to their bedroom and closed the door with a finality that made the house seem in two parts. When the kettle boiled he made tea and served himself a plate of meat and pickles and cut a round of bread and ate at the kitchen table.

"Like old times," he said aloud, picking up his knife and fork.

Una appeared before he was finished and he sliced her some meat too, noticing she had not bothered to comb her hair, used her fork only to pick at her food and shook her head at the round of bread he cut her which turned out more ill shaped than his own.

He would not mention Small Henry, he decided. There was something else to say surely! What would they do tomorrow? He would take the sulky and visit the Robertsons and the Grubbs. He thought with pleasure of her body falling gently against his as they sped along the flat part of the road.

They would take Small Henry. Yes, that would make her happy. She would have it to look forward to all morning until they set out after dinner. He would show Small Henry to the little Grubb girl. That was something he had always wanted to do.

He stole a look at Una's tight little face and wished it could have the innocence and peace of the Grubb child's. He put out a hand and closed it over the arm that supported her chin.

"We shall go and make a few visits tomorrow, shall we?" he said.

"A few visits! That would take us practically to Sydney, wouldn't it?"

"We wouldn't want to travel too far," he said. "With Small Henry." She moved her arm and allowed her hand to slip into his. When she spoke her voice wobbled just slightly.

"That woman drove her own husband from home with her bossiness!"

She rose with a sudden show of energy and took their plates and cups to the washing up dish, shutting the stove door with her foot after putting more wood on and looking through the window at Violet's house as if she had resumed ties with it. He came to her side and together they watched the smoke rise from the chimney, curl and spread out and in a little while it could not be distinguished from the transparent clouds.

"What did you do in the church?" she said.

She cares, she cares. Thank God she cares!

"Gathered up a few leaves that had blown in, otherwise it was alright," he said.

Una fixed her gaze on the tips of his horse's ears under the bough of the big gum it had rubbed smooth. "The dead flowers removed, the vases polished, and the altar cloths washed and starched?"

Yes, that's the way it was. He turned from the window and took up the kettle and poured water in the dish over their tea things, and thought this was foolish of him, she would want to do it perhaps.

But she sauntered off to the bedroom and when he hung up the tea towel she was passing the window with a spade that he had failed to notice in the shed.

From the living room window he saw her attack a strip of ground parallel with the front verandah. He saw her bobbing head with its long stream of hair falling over her face then down her back and the rise of her thigh under the thin stuff of her dress, then the rise of her breasts and he watched for her to tire soon, ashamed at the thought that he would have.

He saw someone in a buggy on the road slowing it down to watch too, and withdrew from the window, feeling his manhood in jeopardy.

Sarah Hart, who kept a small herd and a lazy husband six miles the other side of Wyndham, was pleased at the sight. That's what she had said to Albert, the young one was not as flighty as people said. She could settle down and do everything the older one did. Still on her honeymoon and making a garden. Beat that! He had made the wisest choice after all.

Sarah whipped up her horse to get home to her delayed chores. He had chosen the prettiest and the best. The cunning bastard.

Edwards was saying much the same in a letter he was writing to his mother.

"Dear Mother", he wrote, "I have certainly chosen wisely. My little bride of a week, where others might be fiddling with ribbons and laces and such fripperies, is out in the hot Australian afternoon making us a garden. We had a wonderful honeymoon. Bathing and long walks mostly. The guest house was very comfortable and the owner quite motherly. We got back today".

(He crossed out the date at the top of the letter and made it the seventh day after the wedding.)

"Tomorrow we go to make some visits neglected somewhat in the rush of the wedding and setting up the rectory. You should see the transformation. Everything fits in so well. Most generous wedding presents. Guess what we did as soon as we arrived? Fixed up the second bedroom. I live for the day when you will come."

(He spread a hand across the words with his head raised checking that the digging continued.)

"We just had tea, delicious cold meat we brought from Honeysuckle. You will be so happy that I no longer have to find my own meals. I will slip into the church before bed and thank God for his great blessings."

Tears came to Edwards's eyes when he wrote this and he put down his pen and hurried out.

When he returned it was almost dark and she was sitting on the couch with her eyes swallowed by the shadows.

"In that letter you wrote to your mother you did not mention Small Henry once. Not once did you say his name. Do you hate him?"

43

He tried his best to persuade Violet to allow them to have Small Henry for the afternoon, but Violet insisted the sun was too hot for him in the exposed sulky. He went back to the rectory to tell this to a mutinous Una.

"We could try her again when it is cooler," Edwards said.

"Then it will be his bedtime according to her! Did you suggest she go off and find Ned, which is what she should be doing!

"Those are the kind of things you should be doing I would think!" She slapped the new cushions she had made while they were engaged, tossing them back on the couch where they arranged themselves, Edwards saw, with the stencilled emus looking guardedly at each other.

"Well, what do you say?" she said when he did not speak. He went and straightened the pad and ink where his letter was still exposed. He should finish writing it. But it seemed, since she had read it, not to be his any more.

He folded the pages back and on the first blank one wrote the date of Sunday when he would give his next sermon. She saw with eyes like pieces of brown glass slanted suddenly towards the sun.

"What shall it be?" she said. Her amiable voice did not deceive him. He thought of eating a soft, sweet fruit, foolishly biting at the seed and filling his mouth with a bitter acid taste.

"I could make some suggestions," she said.

"Yes, I believe you could," he said. He stared at the white paper and felt his inside had the same emptiness. She slipped behind his chair and imprisoned his neck with her arms. He wanted to bite through the cotton of her dress and taste the flesh. She put her mouth on his forehead and flung her hair forward to cover his face.

"Love Small Henry," she said. "That's all I ask."

He stood and held her, kissing her through her hair, holding it so that it remained a shield for her face. It shielded his face also. In a little while she broke away and rearranged her hair swiftly with her fingers.

"Finish your letter," she said. "It's quite a nice letter." He sat again and turned the pages back to read his last sentence.

"This is a shorter letter than usual," he wrote, "but you will understand. Much love from us both."

He saw where the corner of the table dented her skirt and he noticed it pushing at her crotch as she slid gently back and forth.

"PS," he wrote, "Small Henry is growing nicely and has a tooth."

She straightened her clothes and caught up her little bag on a chair back. "We'll go for a little walk and post it, shall we?" she said. "I'll go and put my hat on."

She returned in her hat with the cherries and he as a token of respect brushed his alpaca jacket down with his fingers. He worried about the letter. It was very short for the cost of sending it, but to leave it and write a longer one would mean wasting the envelope. These things did not appear to bother her, he thought with envy. He expected that sometime in the future it would have to be a subject for discussion.

In the Post Office Rachel looked them over to try and gauge from their bodies the activity of them in the privacy of their room. Dear me, Edwards thought, perhaps we should tell them right off.

They crossed the road on the way home to come directly to Violet's gate. The ruffle at the neck of Una's dress, the brim of her hat narrow at the back, her bunch of hair all said she was trying. He caught her waist, not caring that Rachel was watching them from the Post Office window.

"We can call in if you like," he said.

She shook her head so violently the cherries wobbled. "No!" she said throwing the words behind her. "Five minutes with him is no use to me!"

What is it you want then? he said silently to her angry shoulder. Don't answer me! Don't tell me! Don't say it!

Inside he sat at the table and pulled the writing pad to him. After a while he raised his eyes to her hat. "Please take it off," he said. "It disturbs me." She was on the couch with her arms arranged as if she were in a drawing room full of guests.

Around them the house creaked in the stillness. The wind blew the curtain at the window so that for a moment there was a patch of bare road visible. She seemed, sitting there in her limp state, not to belong and he looked for some sign that she did, hastily past the vase of roses lest they bring Enid too forcibly into the room, to the outside where the spade lay slanted across the dug ground. It would be wonderful, he thought, if she would go out and take it up again and set up some sort of rhythm, as winding up a clock or lighting a fire brings a house to life. He looked about for something he might do, and would have liked to lay their new tapestry cloth on the dining table as was the practice at Honeysuckle between meals.

But he was not certain of the right side and it was sure to go on unevenly. He remembered the horror he experienced once when, turning back to the altar after the congregation had left the church, he saw the altar cloth barely touching one edge and hanging so generously on the other the hem scraped the floor. He righted it but imagined with a hot face the people tittering as they climbed into their buggies and Una looking for somewhere to collapse and laugh herself out.

He looked now at her face, so little of it showing below the brim of her hat, yet all that hunger and rebellion in the curve of her chin and mouth.

Would she never laugh again? Was it he who had wiped the joy from her face, like jerking a blind down on a sunny window?

He leaned across her and raised the blind for the day was fading. It emphasized the hollowness of the room and the blank walls, and at that moment a fading rose sent a scatter of petals to the table like a shower of tears. In one corner there was a little stack of her paintings.

"Let's hang those," he said, hoping she would have nails and things or knew their whereabouts.

It seemed minutes before the words registered. He saw the cherries duck then rise. "That is what I planned to do," she said, terribly mournful.

He waited. "Paint him," she said.

"Well you still can!"

She stood and lifted the hat from her head. He looked her down, foolishly believing she might be naked.

"Will you help me get him to paint him?" she said.

"Of course I will!"

She put both arms around him. "You are beautiful, kind and good," she said.

He gripped her shoulders quite hard to still the rocking motion she had set up.

The brim of her hat sawed gently at his forehead.

It isn't me she's holding, he thought, wondering if the chill of his body reached the flesh of her hands.

He released himself as politely as he could.

44

Violet refused outright to allow it.

"I've got him into a good routine now," she said to them both in her kitchen next day.

Her chair partly blocked off Small Henry's doorway, enabling her to guard it and keep an eye on the bush through the back door.

At the end of the table there was a mound of bread which gave off an appetizing, if slightly sour smell. It seemed to be waiting also for Ned.

Edwards began to think of their bread. They had brought some from Honeysuckle, but it would run out soon. Would she set a bread making pattern, baking on certain days as other Wyndham women appeared to? He saw her hands lightly holding her elbows. He could not visualize them buried in flour, and to his own surprise he did not care for the thought.

"When he's older, perhaps," Violet said.

Una lifted her chin with one of her small elegant snorts. Her long fingers tapped in agitated fashion her upper arms. She stood with a sweep of her hands on her skirt.

"I do like your hat," Violet said.

"It's quite my favourite too," Edwards said, fixing his eyes on the cherries.

Una went quite fast through the back door and Edwards, though he was quite unhappy about it, had only time to make a large nod in Violet's direction and follow.

"Come, walk a little slower and enjoy the scenery," he

said. At that moment his horse, tossing his mane to wave off flies, parted his back legs, raised his tail and from the dark wrinkled lips of his anus there flopped a pile of green dung moulding itself into a steaming heap on the ground.

Una stood like a tourist giving the scene rapt attention. Edwards looking for distraction saw their lavatory. Those wretched things! They seemed always to bend a little to one side like someone with a physical handicap of which they were ashamed. He would need to empty the can inside more frequently now. There is no end to my woes, he said to himself, seeing her little bottom quivering under her skirt in her hurry to keep ahead of him.

She went straight to their bedroom when they reached the rectory, and he to the church to say evening prayers.

He had dreamed of her kneeling in one of the pews, he at the altar exquisitely distracted, the moment coming closer all the time when he would turn and find her. He had to fight a feeling now that God had let him down as he knelt on the thin strip of carpet and averted his eyes from the abandoned birds' nests where the roof did not quite meet the wall.

When he stood and dusted off his knees she was there. She had made no sound coming in. Her face was bowed to such an angle he saw all the cherries on her hat at once. Her eyes were shut so he could allow the joy to wash over his face uninhibited.

The lovely thing! If only his mother could see this.

He tiptoed down the aisle until level with her, but she did not open her eyes or cease the rapid movement of her lips. He saw the passion in her trembling shoulders.

Outside beckoned him. It was a relief to be there. The sunlight was more honest.

As if he had no wife he set about getting the evening meal himself.

She gave the briefest glance at the dining table, which he was setting, on her way to the bedroom, and he wondered if she would go to bed without eating. Nothing would surprise me, he thought, putting their new cruet to the centre of the table, reminded of Enid. He studied the edges of the white damask cloth to see if it was level. Thank heavens I'm getting something right, he told himself, loving the shine on the cutlery and serviette rings. Elegance has returned to my life, even if I am in charge of it. He cocked his head on one side, seeing that the knives and forks were straight.

He looked in the pantry for some food. He opened a jar of preserved quinces and tipped them into a dish and found some tomatoes ripening on the window sill. They seemed too beautiful to cut, the skin smooth as a girl's, and in the end he arranged them on a plate and took them in with some cheese and the last half loaf of bread.

She came out of the bedroom then, shutting the door with a snap as if to lock her private thoughts from him. He waited, listening to her making noises in the kitchen, realizing after a while she was stoking the fire and getting the kettle to boil, something that had escaped him entirely. Dear me, dear me, he said to himself waving off the flies, remembering the sprigs of mint Enid scattered on the Honeysuckle table to deter those penetrating the back screen door.

When they began to eat, he suggested to Una that they grow some mint. No doubt there would be some to be dug up at Honeysuckle for transplanting.

"No doubt my sister will provide you with all the mint you require," she said, taking small bites of her quinces, obviously deciding this was all she would have.

"Could we go that way tomorrow?" he said amiably.

"What about the Grubbs and the Robertsons? I thought

they topped the list of those in need of spiritual guidance."

He took a nectarine from their bowl of fruit, running his thumb over some hard green patches, relieving the soft pinky red. You take the sweet with the sour, he thought, dragging it apart under her watching eyes.

"You will come with me, whichever way I go?" he said.

"I shall see," she said, getting up and taking up the silver teapot snapped the lid open and shut as she went to the kitchen.

When he woke next morning he heard her moving about in what he thought was the room she made ready for Small Henry. When he got up he discovered her in the room beyond, where she had put her sewing machine, a table from the lumber room at Honeysuckle and her easel. There were other odds and ends there and she was sorting these and obviously getting the room in order to work in. She had a sketching pad and pencils on the table. Working with energy, she seemed capable of, and indeed planning to, use physical strength to get Small Henry to pose for his picture.

But to his relief she said she was going to make sketches of him at Violet's and paint from those.

"I'll suggest she nurses him while I draw," she said.

He stepped over the suitcases she had taken on their honeymoon and put his arms around her.

"To hear you say that makes me so proud," he said.

She dug her chin so deeply in his shoulder he marvelled at her strength and needed all his to avoid sagging under the force.

She went passive soon afterwards and he released her body, waiting to leap back into its former activity.

He went out, trying to decide whether to go to the church for morning prayers or light the kitchen stove. "I'll do both!" he said aloud, reverting to his old habit. "And for the first time in my life I might make porridge without lumps! By George, I feel I can do it!"

He went alone to Honeysuckle. He fought a sense of uneasiness when they were parting, she with her sketch pad and pencils and he with his Bible. He was determined not to see it as a pointer to their future life. But it was best for her to adjust to visiting Small Henry, and who knows, she may come to be satisfied with that.

It was a sunny optimistic sort of day, and Edwards whipped up his horse, who ducked its head deeply and gave a great snort to say things are back to the old way, are they? And it's no surprise to him and glad he was to leave her behind. He threw out his knuckly knees and paced away with spirits akin to those of Edwards.

There were no Anglican families to visit between St Jude's and Honeysuckle, causing Edwards pangs of guilt. When I return though, I might persuade her to come with me to see the Grubbs, he thought. He could not face the little Grubb girl without Una to show her. He slapped his horse with the reins to race away from a vision of Small Henry placed tenderly in the little Grubb girl's arms.

Enid came down the steps at Honeysuckle with an expression on her face which he read as concern for the absence of Una.

"I have been banished while she does some little jobs on her own!" Edwards said, believing it to be the truth.

She swung the gate open to admit him. "But you won't be able to stay to dinner!" she said, running up the steps ahead of him and hurrying to the kitchen for she must have left her cooking pots at a crucial time.

He stopped in the living room, feeling a lesser right now to invade her kitchen. She was back with him almost immediately, with her apron off and her hair smoothed down, and he could see she was not unhappy with her appearance. Her dress was a fine striped cambric with a deep organdie collar which Una had made, but he was not to know this. She may have been expecting me, he thought. I mean us.

"We do thank you most sincerely for arranging the furniture and everything else you did," he said, crossing his legs and noticing her glance on his thighs. Then he saw her lifted brows asking a question.

"She was quite happy with it," he said.

The smoothing of the stuff of her dress on her knee was another question.

"We are settling in quite satisfactorily," he said, dusting off his knees unnecessarily. "There are no real difficulties. Except to grow some mint. For the flies, you know."

He saw her little smile in the cool and flyless room.

"In fact I had thought about starting a garden quite some time before —" he said. "I remember planning to come and see you one day for three reasons."

She looked down surprised to see no movement of the cambric over her rapidly beating heart.

"One was a cat to drink my spare milk." She smiled, loving this.

"Another was your advice on digging and planting."

He stood and she took in all his face, disguising nothing on her own.

He forgot for the moment the third one and when he remembered it was Small Henry's christening he could not find the words.

He decided to keep the image of her face to return to throughout the rest of his life.

45

Una was digging some ground by their tankstand to plant the mint when he got back. "By George, I'm glad I remembered it," he said hauling it from the sulky with some new baked bread, plums and peaches, some round oatmeal biscuits Edwards was dying to get his teeth into and a dressed chicken.

Una flung the spade down and planted the trailing roots of the mint to catch the drip from the tap, and inside, in a housewifely manner Edwards admired greatly, put the food away. She had made the place neat in his absence, and he inquired of her face, on which there was no trace of discontent, what had happened about the sketching.

"I made the drawings and she cooperated remarkably well," Una said, lifting a ring of the stove to put the kettle on the heat and hurry their dinner along. Things were taking an upward turn he thought, enjoying the sight of her back with her crossed apron strings and the tie at her slim waist, all remaining amazingly neat while she bent and stretched at stove and dresser.

"But you can't see, I must warn you," she said, closing the dresser doors with her tipped back head, for her arms were full of their new plates and cups. He did not mind.

"I will go again tomorrow and the day after to sketch some more, then do the painting," she said.

He stood and took the china from her and kissed her mouth. "I couldn't be more proud," he said tremulously.

One afternoon a week later he found her frowning in the

kitchen as she washed her hands in a bowl with her brushes lined up on the table to be washed too. The painting was obviously done. He was relieved, but all things considered, the week had not been intolerable. Only one bad patch and that was about midweek when they had chairs on their verandah and Violet came out of her gate wheeling Small Henry in a new perambulator.

Edwards saw the stiffening of Una's body and heard her breath being stifled in her throat while she wrapped her arms about her chest as if to stop herself leaping forward.

They watched Violet steering the pram carefully over the ruts on the roadside, not looking their way.

"She said nothing yesterday about getting that!" Una cried. Edwards said he had seen the mail car stop and the driver drop something over Violet's gate that morning. Dear me, he thought, I'm as bad as the rest of them! He watched Una biting her thumb then squeezing it with the other hand, narrowing her eyes on Violet's receding back. She rose abruptly and went to the room she was now openly calling her studio and closed the door with a sound that clearly said don't follow. She may well tear that painting to shreds, Edwards said to his distressed self.

But she didn't. In a couple of hours she was out of the artist's smock she had kept from schooldays and into the apron he liked and doing something different with their eggs for tea.

"By Saturday I will be done," she said, and he had to acknowledge a small chill of fear. How would she occupy herself then? He took up a magazine on loan from Honeysuckle to read while she set the table, deciding he would not worry about it until after Saturday.

"I will be the first to see it then?" he said, surprised at the surge of jealousy he felt should she say no.

The congregation improved on the Sundays following

the honeymoon, which did not surprise Edwards or excite him. Perhaps they are thinking of seeing a consumation on the front pew, he told himself. When it was no longer a novelty to see Una at the rectory the numbers would revert, he felt sure, to the few of pre-marriage days.

The door of the studio was not closed on the painting on the Sunday morning after it was finished.

But taking a look inside, passing through the little hall, he saw she had thrown a cloth over the easel.

"Patience, patience!" she said gaily to him in good humour, anticipating the attention of the congregation at the morning service, dressed for it in a frock of biscuit coloured fabric matching the hat with the cherries. Both were on show in church for the first time and she was giving the hat several little shakes, practising the wobbling of the cherries to raise envy among the plain Robertson girls in the pew behind hers.

George brought Enid in the sulky a good half hour before the service was to start, Enid with flowers for both the church and the house, spreading them out on the kitchen table with Una running for church vases and those given for wedding presents.

"Look Colin!" she called. "She has brought us half her garden!" He paused and smiled, dressed in his surplice ironed even more carefully than Mrs Watts's effort, liking the look of himself too and the approval in Enid's eyes, raised briefly from the roses and maiden hair fern. It took her hands a little while to get working again, affected as they were at hearing Una's free use of his Christian name.

George spent the half hour at Violet's, given grumblingly a cup of tea and a wedge of her orange peel cake, the dryness of which escaped him.

Ned was home, having established a new routine of spending three days at Halloween, then returning to Albert

Lane for food supplies. This time he brought sheets and towels, dumping them on the washhouse floor. She was torn between annoyance at the extra work and some small pleasure that Ned's hygiene was improving.

"It might occur to him to bring the water as well!" she said. "The tanks are low with the baby's washing — " Then she pulled herself up, fearing the complaint might reach Una's ears. George read her thoughts in part.

"Is she," he said, inclining his head in the direction of the rectory, "takin' him off your hands now and again?"

Violet's chair creaked with the stiffening of her body. "I'm not having him wondering where his home is!" she said.

George acknowledged the wisdom of this with a sweep of his eyes around the kitchen and a small and secret dream that it was his too. He asked a question of the closed door and it answered that Small Henry was down for his long morning sleep. He wouldn't have minded a game with the little tyke since Alex wasn't around to take over as soon as he got him laughing. Violet and him and the little bloke!

Ned came through the hall from the front verandah carrying a chair from the pile of discarded furniture.

"I see!" Violet said. "Just the thing for watching the night life from the verandah of Halloween!"

An arm of the chair swung downwards as Ned set it down, and George was shown wordlessly how a connecting piece of wood had broken in a socket leaving a portion embedded there.

Violet took up Small Henry's bathtub from the table and flung the contents on the roots of the lemon tree, causing the fowls to frantically throw themselves against the wire.

"Nothing coming your way that I know of!" she said, dumping the tub in the wash house. "But you exercise your vocal chords I'll say that for you!

"I'll tell you!" Violet said, back in the kitchen where Ned had the chair under one arm and George was standing too in mournful observation of it. "If it wasn't for the yelling of Small Henry I'd be taking myself off to Bega to get tested for deafness!"

"I'll fix it after church," George said. Violet was calmer. Ned would take himself and the chair off to Halloween and she and Small Henry could go to Honeysuckle with George and Enid in the sulky. That would be a way of filling in the afternoon. Una would not be there for this was the Sunday in four that Edwards took a service directly following the one at St Jude's in the Burragate school several miles away. Una would accompany him. Good riddance to her too. Nursing Small Henry for half an hour to get what she called "a feel of his little body".

"I'll do the nursing and you do the drawing," Violet had told her, letting his legs sprawl on her own thighs while she sat near the back door, able to keep an eye out for Ned should he emerge from the bush.

But she did not go to Honeysuckle, nor did Una go with Edwards to Burragate.

George in the end took Edwards in his sulky to save the time Edwards would have to spend in harnessing up his horse. This turn of events caused Dolly to snort with a backward swing of her head towards Edwards's horse, placidly sniffing at grass under his tree with nothing more arduous to do but switch flies from his tail and mane.

What happened in Violet's kitchen sparked off the change in plans.

After the service in St Jude's, Edwards and Una walked with George and Enid to Violet's with the picture in a temporary frame, wrapped in a piece of old sheeting Enid had thoughtfully added to the linen cupboard in the rectory.

Edwards carried the picture and Una held his other arm, her red lips smiling under the cherries.

Enid was not quite in line with the others, back a pace or two so that she could study undetected Edwards's strong jaw and thick dark hair. She thought of it lying on one of the pillowslips she had made fragrant with lavender. She saw Una with her chin raised to see better under the brim of her hat and marvelled that she seemed unconcerned with what was hers.

They trooped into Violet's kitchen with the exception of George, who went to work on the chair on the back verandah. His hang dog air temporarily banished, he walked with a spring in his step to collect tools from the wash house. Then he gouged at the wood in the socket, blowing out the fragments with puffed out cheeks. He would have the job done in no time. The pity of it was Ned would carry the chair off to Halloween and have it disintegrate in the weather beating onto the exposed verandah. He would like Violet in it, her round arms on the chair arms and her hands hanging loose as he liked to see them.

A cry from Violet shocked him into dropping the chisel. Ned sitting on the verandah edge swung around with his good and bad eye and his mouth forming three expressionless circles.

George went to see.

Una was at the corner of the table with the picture balanced there, her long white arms supporting it. The others were in various poses of horror and disbelief.

Small Henry looked from the canvas with large eyes black and pleading. A hand was stretched forward spread out to become a quarter of the picture. Violet's chin and mouth showed at the top of the canvas. Her great arms and thighs held Small Henry like logs of wood. They were a pen locking him in, and Una had given the flesh a greyish colour like ageing timber, hard as granite.

"The little bloke's eyes are blue," was all George could find to say.

Una looked down on the picture rather like peering with curiosity into a deep well.

"Paintings shouldn't be pretty," Una said. "They should say something. You agree, don't you Colin?"

Enid wishing she didn't, raised her eyes to Edwards from her seat on the edge of a kitchen chair. He put a finger inside his collar as if it needed loosening and stretched his brown jaw and she knew nothing else but that she loved him. She pleated between thumb and forefinger the material of her dress on her knee.

Edwards swung his head to see the time on Violet's clock. There was barely time to reach Burragate in time for the service.

Then Small Henry gave a shout from his room and all heads were jerked up but Violet's. Una loosened her hold on the picture as if there was another use for her arms. Violet allowed the smallest smile to touch the corners of her mouth. George saw. That's better, that's better. She had been standing holding a chair back and now her fingers loosened and actually rippled up and down on the wood as if it were a piano keyboard.

"Do excuse me," she said and went to the dresser behind Edwards, forcing him to duck to avoid being slapped with the suddenly opened door.

She took out a bottle and dumped it firmly on the kitchen table. "If you don't mind," she said, gesturing lightly with her elbow towards the painting. Edwards removed it swiftly and laid it against his trouser leg. That was a wonderful thing to do, Enid thought, and standing gave him the sheeting.

"Thank you," he murmured placing it carefully across the frame. Una looked almost disinterested, as if it was something done so long ago she had forgotten it. She lifted her head higher with Small Henry's yelling.

Edwards watched in agony for the tears to fill her eyes and run over her cheeks. He saw how tightly she held her little bag at the corner of the table.

Violet held Small Henry's bottle in a basin of hot water, lifting it out to shake a little on her wrist, then dipping it back in again, swirling the milk almost lazily. She wore the smallest smile, listening to the shrieking from Small Henry's room as if it were a favoured piece played on a piano.

She decided the bottle was right and, holding it aloft, left the door into the hallway and that into Small Henry's room wide open after she passed through them. Small Henry stopped a yell, trailed it off and turned it into a crow. The kitchen heard the cot rattle as he flapped his arms and pumped his legs up and down.

Una rushed from the room to tear across the paddock to the rectory. Two families beside their buggies saw her billowing skirt and frantically bobbing hat. My goodness! The women, who had been hot and irritated by the continued talk between the men, saw compensations for the delay.

This was a turn of events if ever there was one. A minister's wife racing like a furious boy, throwing out her feet in their good shoes, not minding the clods and manure and dead pieces from the big gum under which Edwards's horse raised his head in surprise, and amazed further to see Edwards running behind George to the front, where Dolly in the Herbert sulky was hitched to a telegraph post.

Edwards carrying something in a white cloth stopped and turned and cut Enid off in her run to the rectory, although she straightened up and slowed down in dignified fashion when she saw the buggies moving off with such reluctance the horses began to step backwards, wondering if this was expected of them.

Edwards passed the thing in white to Enid with a plea in his brown eyes to do the best she could to console Una. I will, I will Enid's eyes said back. Anything you ask. I am mad, mad!

With no one else in sight now she ran to the rectory, barely aware it was she who was left to carry the picture.

46

She found Una lying full length face downwards on the double bed. It was unmade and Enid, removing her hat, turned her sleeves back and began to pull the bedclothes from around the prostrate form.

"Come on," she said. "Sit on the chair. This is quite disgraceful!" She smelled his body on the sheet she held as close to her face as she dared. Una rolled over abruptly and Enid coloured, afraid she might have been seen.

"Now get up," she said, "And let me get this made!"

Una rose slowly and went to the window. Enid looking for a profile saw only her thick, rumpled hair and marvelled that it spoke so clearly her hurt and anger.

By the corner of the bed on the floor was the wrinkled heap of his pyjamas. She turned her back on Una to fold them, breathing in their warm and fleshy smell. His most intimate garments. Thank you God.

"Go and stoke up the fire for dinner," Enid said thinking of it as his dinner. She stuffed their nightwear in a bag Una had embroidered and laid it on the chair looking like a small cushion as Una had intended. Enid saw the look Una gave it, as if it was evidence of a hobby out of which she had grown. And how jealous I was of her when she was sewing that!

Una leaned closer to the window and pressed her head to the glass for a moment as if she needed something to cool her face, then left the room.

Alone here, alone, just for a moment! Enid dared to put

his collar box and brush to one corner of the dressing table, isolating them from Una's things. Did he miss his chest of drawers she had moved to the other room, she wondered. She would go and see, half angry at the thought that Una had probably buried it under things discarded from the other rooms.

Inside that room she found herself on the chair unaware that she had sat down. A white towel was on the rail of the washstand and a new cake of soap in the soap dish. A short lace curtain at the window gently brushed the sill. Like a wave, Enid thought reminded of the shells they had collected as children. They could be lined up there on the sill, some large and crusted with a rough and creamy coat and others small and purply dark with a curve defying the eye to see the secrets within. Alex and Henry and Una had called them bum shells because they were shaped like one side of a human behind. Enid had disapproved, but away from the others smoothed and stroked at the slippery surface believing it to be a skin and pushing her fingers shamelessly into the crevice.

Una appeared in the doorway now and Enid jumped, as if her sin was discovered. She raised her eyes from her quiet lap and caught a glimpse of the ceiling, the plaster there forming a pattern of shells too, heaped in each corner with more spread in a circular pattern in the centre. She imagined him lying counting them waiting for sleep with the twilight still in the room. A little shell boy, she thought.

Una laid a hand on the corner post of the bed. "I mean to have him, you know," she said "If I have to flee with him in the middle of the night, I will have him."

The innocent room slipped away from Enid. With it went Una running hard with Small Henry's face bobbing on her shoulder. Enid stood. Yes, go, go, go if you want to.

"Such foolishness," she said.

George did not wait for Edwards through the Burragate service.

Edwards insisted he drive straight back to St Jude's and take Enid to Honeysuckle. He was disturbed at the memory of her face trying, he could see, to believe he had no part in Una's painting. I don't want her discomforted further. Perhaps I don't want to face her too soon, he thought miserably, facing the congregation outside the school looking for Una and for reasons why she didn't accompany him.

George was miserable too. He leapt from the sulky outside Violet's and went to the back verandah where the door to the kitchen was shut and the house wore a deserted look. The chair stood with the dislodged arm swinging as if it were someone with a broken limb who was in need of help but had abandoned all hope of getting it. George tramped around the house looking for Violet. He saw the perambulator usually on the front verandah had gone. Violet had taken Small Henry probably across to Rachel's and the two women would be on the back verandah there with Violet recounting the story of the painting. He set about mending the chair with a long sad face. He should have saved Violet the shock and horror of seeing herself like that. He had failed her. All he had said was that Small Henry's eyes were the wrong colour. He should have shouted angrily at Una and Edwards and seized that picture and ripped it to shreds before their eyes. He should have put his knee in the middle of the canvas and thrust it strongly through. Violet would have loved that. He seized the finished chair to demonstrate such an action and stabbed his knee into the leather seat. The scrape of the chair legs on the wooden verandah boards alerted the fowls who began to race wildly up and down behind the wire.

Starve, starve! for all I care, cried George to his own hollow inside. He put the chair against the wall for the best shelter.

Then in a little while he took a dipper full of corn from the wash house and threw it to the fowls.

47

After dinner at Honeysuckle Enid drew the blinds to cool the front room and allow her to sit in the dimness to think. She should have looked directly into his face when Una threw the piece of sheet off the picture. She would have seen then if it shocked him too. Did he want Small Henry too? He might have married Una just to get Small Henry! Oh, foolish thought that!

She left the couch to escape it, and plucked the flopping head of a dying rose from a vase full to save it scattering petals everywhere. She thought about the flowers she had taken them. Him! Una would leave those in the church to die you could be sure of that. She should have seen them returned to the house to scent it abundantly for him!

She began to move in agitated fashion about the living room, smoothing at doilies, straightening magazines, rubbing with a finger at a smear on brass. As if it were his house she was tending.

She moved a crystal vase of asters and decided she would go to the rectory next day to start making his garden. He wanted her advice, he said. George could put Dolly in the sulky for her and she would load it with her garden tools and set off after dinner.

Two long beds by the front verandah where Una had started to dig. She knew by the angle of the spade it was Una who had begun digging and abandoned it. Then there was the back of the rectory. So much could be done to the back! It was fenced. Thank goodness it was quite well fenced from his horse. She would take her scythe and show him how to cut the grass low and neat for a nice piece of lawn.

She remembered as a child how church had been enlivened for her by keeping an eye on the kitchen door, open to show the harassed minister's wife getting a string of children ready.

He needed his privacy. A line of bushy shrubs could be planted to screen that back door. Honeysuckle over his lavatory. It was awful for him to go in there and people seeing. She had a use now for all the cuttings she had to discard. The sucklings that sprung up beneath her shrubs and had to be ruthlessly dug up and thrown away. Like destroying her children. Not any more!

She went rapidly to the kitchen and found Jack there and stopped cheated. It wasn't him! She did a strange thing then.

"Oh, Father!" she said and went and put her arms around him.

Jack sat, overcome, and held his hat looking at it, and she with very pink cheeks bustled about to start making him tea.

Jack said he had been to Halloween and Ned was there and told him about the row in Violet's kitchen.

"Ned said she painted this ugly picture of Violet," Jack said. Really now! said the new Enid inside the old one. Ned can talk when he wants to. These men! (But not *him*.) They loosen their vocal chords when it suits them. Other times they depend on gestures to have the women at their beck and call. She wanted terribly to push the round fat butter cake to Jack and tell him to cut what he wanted from it.

But she cut two slices with lowered eyes and put the tin back in its place.

"Violet is no oil painting at the best of times," Enid said. One part of her was pleased to see some of the real Violet in that painting. She fancied herself the best looking of the Herbert women in spite of the added years and extra bulk. She dropped remarks at times that showed she was the most handsome of the trio, in her opinion. Well that picture told a different story!

Jack was more pleased with her face now. It had the smallest smile starting up. And to his great delight she had decided to pour herself some tea and sit at the table to drink it.

"I may read for a while after this," she said dreamily. Jack scraped his chair legs approving. A little rest would be good for her!

She saw his face soft even while snapping at his cake. She thought of the lines from the Coleridge poem: "The lovely lady Christabel whom her father loves so well." *He* had loaned the book for her and Una to read but Una had not bothered. She would take it somewhere quiet to read this very afternoon.

Jack saw the smile deepen on her face and her eyes running around her kitchen. Yes, she was happy to have the place to herself. That flibbertigibbet made more work than she ever did. He always believed that things lying around like sewing and drawings and books made the place hotter!

"I'll take the *Mail* and read on the verandah," Jack said, believing he was in communion with her thoughts.

"Me too," she said smiling in a sweet way. "I'll take my book to the big rock and sit in the cool for a while." Like Nellie used to! She would take the children to paddle in the creek on Sunday afternoons sometimes and allow him the peace of the house for his rest. Life was good again after the worries of the past six months. She was happy again, that was the main thing. He put his empty cup and saucer to the middle of the table and tucked his chair under the table to tell her so before going out.

Enid buttoned her sleeves and put on a shady hat before the mirror in her bedroom, pulling the bun at the back of her head loose and laughing when her hair fell down her back. Quickly she removed the hat re-did her hair and put it on again before taking up her book.

She opened it to read again his name on the flyleaf written in his mother's slightly backward hand.

Sometimes on a Sunday afternoon he followed the creek from behind St Jude's to the part that ran through Honeysuckle and then he took the road home.

48

But not that Sunday afternoon.

He used the long walk from Burragate to reflect on the happenings of the morning.

He decided to concentrate on Una to avoid a recurring vision of Enid's face. Those eyes! Violet's black like coals with flames beginning to lick them, Enid's asking not accusing, and Una's near his shoulder with a coyness in their liquid toffee depths. Like toffee they could melt or harden as well he knew!

He would have a session with Una immediately he got home and tell her her behaviour was unacceptable. She must apologize to Violet to avoid a permanent rift that he quite likely would be blamed for. Perspiration ran under his collar and his boots were white with dust. This dreadful road, this dreadful little place! Likely as not there would be no dinner for him with Una in a black and frightening mood and Enid gone. Enid! He would tell her boldly he had no part in the wretched picture! Damn the other one, blast her socks, as she sometimes said! She would need to take a grip on herself.

He thought of his mother slipping quietly in and out when his father had business with church people. He remembered her anxious face telling the cook when the tea was to be sent in and feeling the scones with her little fat hand and her head up, wanting to be sure they were neither too hot nor too cold. Mothers needed to be around daughters-in-law. The daughters-in-law were quite frightened of them, he understood, and took pains to show how capable they were of caring for their sons.

He imagined Una with lowered eyes testing scones for their temperature. But a second later he had her tossing them from their plate as one tosses a pancake, catching some, with others bowling about the table and floor.

He walked faster from her merry face, rubbing his Bible on his trousers, for it seemed to be sweating too.

He began to dread the long blank afternoon. In earlier days he would take a walk after midday dinner along the creek bank, cooled by the sight of the green moss on the rocks, the willows trailing long green strands in the water and the mystery of dark waterholes, crinkled on the surface when a wind sneaked up on them and still as mirrors other times. Sometimes a bird flopped in them, a water duck he supposed. He loved the way the bird, having disturbed the water, rocked in its movement, as if this was its plan.

Sometimes he joined George in the Honeysuckle paddocks bringing the cows home, and finding Enid in the garden talked to her with an eye on the house, for Una usually threw up a window and leaned out, bright and lovely as one of Enid's blooms that bent over, tall and slender.

These times seemed far off now. He felt like someone looking back on a carefree childhood. He had not appreciated the freedom of it! Life worked that way he was beginning to realize. God held up a mirror for you to reflect on the way it was, and see it as clearly as he saw himself reflected in the creek water.

No doubt about You, he thought with Wyndham coming up, you know it all and show a man how powerless he is!

But he would utilize what strength he had to deal with

Una, he told himself, straightening his back and stepping briskly out in case someone was about. He would show Wyndham a long walk in the January heat was something he enjoyed if eyes were watching.

Inside the front room of the rectory, however, Una had succumbed to the heat. She lay on the couch under the window, slapping at a curtain to make it billow and hopefully raise a breeze. She was wearing a camisole with the ribbons untied and a pair of bloomers. They were made with a band at the waist peaked to meet her navel and gathered until they fitted into bands just above her knees. She was plucking at the bands now and waving both legs in the air.

"These are supposed to be my coolest bloomers! They are not doing much of a job, I can tell you!" she said.

He sat on a chair and laid his hat on the floor as if he were visiting a parishioner. He saw some of her breast was showing where the camisole was loose. He saw the table set and covered with mosquito netting, the mint in its dried state no longer effective. He suddenly felt quite faint with hunger, too faint for an argument.

Going through the kitchen to wash his hands in a back room that was both wash house and bathroom he saw the oven door ajar and his meal keeping hot between two plates.

She had obviously eaten although she appeared to be able to survive long periods without food. He felt grateful for the sight of his meal and lifting the top plate saw there was a generous serve of chicken and vegetables glazed over with a sauce. His heart melted with the melting sauce.

I will have to start praying for a hard heart and an ungentle hand instead of the other way around, he thought, admiring the arrangement of the food as he carried it in. An artist at work, though he would rather not be reminded of art just now!

Una sat up with her face turned to the window opened as wide as she could get it. Anyone passing along the road could see her near nakedness. He told her this quite mildly.

"Actually some one can see me now," she said and he stood greatly agitated, clattering his knife and fork on his plate.

"Your horse," she said in the mild tone she adopted from him.

"It hasn't a name, has it?" He had never thought about naming it and the omission gave him a feeling of guilt.

She left the couch and he had to rivet his eyes on his plate to avoid seeing her body, slender and white as a young gum and moving with the same grace.

"I'm going to go now," she said, flinging back the curtain which had fallen across the window again, and thus giving Wyndham a full view of the camisole and bloomers. "I'll name your horse!"

Like that?

But she went to the bedroom and returned in a loose housedress, tying the belt at the waist and tucking sand-shoes under her arm. In a moment she was leaping across the dug ground and running towards the horse under the big tree. It flung its head up, then made a half circle like a question mark in the air. He saw her drape both arms around its neck, patting, stroking and talking to it, then he went and found a plate of cold pudding under the mosquito net and took it to the window to eat and watch some more.

After some attempts at resistance, some head swinging and shaking and a front leg lifted and dropped two or three times, the horse allowed itself to be led off by the neck. I doubt it would do that for me, Edwards marvelled. He watched Una take the horse close to the fence that ran down the side of Violet's house.

Ah, I see.

He turned from the window not wanting to watch any more. That is a cowardly attitude, he told himself, taking his empty plates to the kitchen. From the window there he had a better view of Una and horse, now close to Violet's kitchen door. It flew up while he watched and shut down so fast he saw only a large arm and the bottom half of Violet's face, cruel and forbidding. My goodness, he thought, that window frame could have been the picture frame! Una tossed her head and the horse did too and cooperated by walking briskly by the fence until they reached the side gate.

There Una set up a rapid stroking of the horse's neck and what appeared to be an affectionate though one sided conversation.

So that's how you name a horse, Edwards said to himself. My baptisms are dull by comparison. After a minute the horse raised its head so suddenly it might have struck Una, lowered its rear and propped itself on two front feet.

It had been aroused by a sudden banging on the tank by an unseen Violet, who set up the din with a broom handle, hitting the part of the tank empty of water. Una clung to the horse's neck to stop it galloping off.

Edwards left the house and raced, unsure of his footing at times but plunging on to reach them. He leaned over the gate while Una was pacifying the horse, as wild of eye as he had ever seen it and spoke to Violet leaning on the broom by the tank.

"Violet," Edwards said as firmly as his scant breath would allow. "Never do that again. It's quite dangerous!"

Violet jabbed the ground with the broom. "Don't call me Violet!"

"Call her Vile!" called out Una, smoothing and slapping at the horse's neck, not totally brave, Edwards thought, although she intended Violet to hear.

Which Violet did. She ran from behind the tank and rattled the gate so hard the horse plunged again.

"Please!" Edwards cried, "It's scarcely the horse's fault!" He hoped he was not seen jumping too noticeably from the path of the swirling tail.

Violet gave an ugly laugh which said she was wise to whose fault it was. The top of Una's head showed over the horse's back and Edwards saw it suddenly tilted downwards. Well, he had better look Violet squarely in the face, he supposed, lest she think him a coward as well.

"Una would very much like to see Small Henry," he said, realizing at once how ill timed it was. Violet outsnorted the horse and using the broom as a walking stick jabbed her way into the house.

When she disappeared Una picked up a heavy stone at her feet and flung it, hitting the tank so hard Edwards expected to see a great hole and water gushing out. But the stone hit the empty rims and set up a great ringing clatter that was too much for the horse.

It reared and plunged and broke a violent volume of wind and galloped off, racing by the fence, letting them see it was the nearest thing to escaping. It swung around when it reached the corner of Violet's front yard and galloped back and Edwards thought if it found any rail lower than the others it would leap over it and be gone forever. Una put both hands to her cheeks and raced for the rectory. She had no apparent fear of being at any time in the path of the galloping horse.

Edwards felt it safer to stand his ground. The horse

circled the paddock twice more and Edwards thought at such evidence of boundless energy he would never again worry about undertaking the trip to Bega in the one day.

Eventually it slackened its pace and when it stood it pawed the ground a couple of times, lowering its eyes and turning its head as if embarrassed at the emotional display and already beginning to regret it. In a little while it ambled off and took up its old position under the tree and let the black wrinkled skin on its legs ripple a little before it was completely still.

Edwards decided there was nothing else for him too, but to go home.

49

Inside the rectory, Una had changed her dress and shoes and put on her hat with the cherries, announcing they would go to Honeysuckle for tea.

"But I have evensong!" Edwards said.

"Ring the bell and put a light there and no one will know the difference!" Una said.

"I'll do nothing of the sort!" he said. "Evensong is at seven and seven it will be!

"Besides it would be a terrible waste of kerosene."

He folded the mosquito net that had covered the table, gaining pleasure in spite of the day's trauma at the fresh sight of their cruet and sugar bowl.

"As well," he said, "the horse, I should think, would be hard pressed to raise the strength to pull us to Honeysuckle!"

"The fat useless thing!" she said. "The exercise would do it good!"

He pulled the linen cloth from the table (did she set it or did Enid?) and folding it put it in an empty sideboard drawer. The very place for it, he thought.

"By the way what do we call him from now on?" He could not resist giving the little brass handle shaped like a large fat tear drop a waggle as he closed the drawer.

He did not expect an answer and she gave none. She sat now on the couch, a heel on the edge and her chin on her knee.

He thought of his mother in her full skirted mulberry

coloured silk dress sitting in their drawing room on a Sunday afternoon with her Bible on her knee and her thumb between two pages. It had worried him as a child that it was not what she wanted to be doing, and he had wanted to ask her if she was having a game of "pretend" as she sometimes did when they played together.

He moved about putting the room in order, hoping he did not look too foolish, and looking often at her slender arms about her legs and hardly able to believe them capable of throwing that great stone. Going to the kitchen with some things from the table he wondered what his mother would think of her. I believe she would like her, he said to himself surprised and convinced.

But, dear me, I'm not deciding on any immediate course of action which I must do!

He went back to the living room to suggest they go to Honeysuckle, returning in time for evensong.

"Perhaps Enid will give us a five o'clock tea," he said. He told himself he was not giving in to her totally. There might be an opportunity of letting Enid know he had no part in the composition of that picture. She knows! said part of his heart. And he began to smile with warm eyes, knowing she did.

"Or we could eat a large afternoon tea, then have a bite of supper here before bed!" he said. The thought of bed did not cheer him. Her lovely body like a young white gum, still not moving there on the couch, was every bit as impregnable.

But the thought of eating heartily at Enid's table raised his spirits and he went to harness his horse, a little afraid she might see into his mind and perversely decide not to accompany him.

Dear me, he said to himself, to think there was a time when I thought wives simply did what husbands proposed!

He coaxed the horse into the shafts, telling it soothingly it was in a good position to know the difficulties of dealing with women following the experience at Violet's gate.

Una ran out of the house as he ran in to put his coat on and wish there was more time to spruce himself up. But he couldn't leave her too long with the horse, who shook the harness and lowered its backside at the sight of her, and he feared it might give a repeat performance of the paddock gallop if he didn't hurry.

Women and horses, Edwards thought climbing into his seat, flighty and unpredictable. And here he was caught between them.

Enid, back in the Honeysuckle kitchen after her walk to the creek, found the kettle singing on the fire Jack had thoughtfully stoked before riding off to help George bring in the cows. The ginger cat leapt from the chair as if inviting her to sit there. Kettles and cats, Enid thought. Are they to be my lot in life? And a long empty stretch like the creek she had just left? I could go to my room and lie on my bed and cry for an hour or two. There is nothing in the world to stop me, really, since I could serve everything cold for tea! I will not look at the garden, she told herself almost with her back to the side window, for if I do I might go there and work. And to cry is better.

But the side of her face directed towards the road caught sight of the sulky bearing Edwards and Una to Honeysuckle. She flung off the apron she had just put on and ran to the bedroom, wondering if there were loose floorboards to set the furniture dancing like that! She combed her hair and brushed her dress and stockings free of twigs and leaves. She laughed at her bright eyes in the mirror so far from tears. She slapped at her little collar to make it sit properly before running to fling open the front door.

She waved gaily to them climbing out of the sulky and

ran to the kitchen to bring a jug of water and a newly opened bottle of her lemon cordial essence, and when she had poured two glasses she set the bottle on the sideboard for them to take home and finish.

"Be sure and keep it in the cool safe," she said, for his benefit. She didn't want him drinking it lukewarm.

Una made a small face. It may be a little tart for her, Edwards thought charitably. Enid refilled his glass without asking.

"I can make an early tea for us all," Enid was saying. "Then go back with you for evensong. I can walk home for it isn't dark until nearly eight. I had a walk this afternoon, but it was only to the creek — and disappointing!"

She moved cushions on chairs to indicate that they should sit and went out to start tea. There was boiled beef and her new tomato chutney, lettuce, tomatoes, cucumber and some cold potatoes she would make into a salad. She would make pastry (she felt the temperature of the oven while her thoughts ran on) and fill it with ripe peach slices and serve it warm with thick cream. He would like that! She went to work glancing often towards the front room thinking he might come and join her. Of course he couldn't! He would never leave Una alone there in one of her huffs. Dear, good unselfish man that he was!

Edwards in the brown armchair he occupied in pre-marriage days listened hungrily to the noises from the kitchen. There was a refinement in the rattle of the dishes and crockery, not the banging and crashing that went on in some kitchens. He stood up as if sitting was unbearable. Una lifted her hat suddenly from her head and dumped it on the foot of the couch as if it too had become unbearable.

"Perhaps there is something we could do to help," he said, and opening a sideboard drawer he took out a white damask cloth feeling akin to Enid since he had found a similar place for theirs.

Selfconsciously he removed the bowl of roses from the dining table. She came in when he began to pull the green cover off. Wordlessly she took the other end. He held his end under his chin and she walked to him with hers, touching his shoulders when the two ends met. She caught the fold touching his knees and she touched them too. She brought it up to join the end still pinned by his chin. He lifted his chin and she slipped that fold in and her fingers touched the cushion of flesh on bone. For a second he pinned her fingers too. Deeply pink she took the cloth across her arm and flung it on the table to finish with two more rapid folds and, not knowing where Una's eyes were, laid it on a chair back.

When she turned back he had the white cloth in its folded state on the table and she opened it with revolving hands moving to one end of the table while he moved to the other. He took his end and she hers and they raised it above the table, then let it fall and she bent towards him and he towards her, his brown hands and her strong knuckly ones sweeping and smoothing towards each other, their bodies going backwards to smooth and stroke the table edges, then coming forward again with fingers dragging at tiny creases, then back to run eyes, never meeting along the hemline.

Faces turned from each other he took the cruet and set it in the centre, and she sorrowful and absent stroked a corner two or three times more then slipped away to the kitchen.

50

He did get there after all.

Una had jumped from the couch suddenly and before he had time to call her name ran down the back hall and he heard the door bang behind her.

He went to the kitchen to get a better view from a window there, pointing her out to Enid without words and an upturned hand.

Enid looked, gave no more than a shake of her head and returned to her pastry.

"She is off to the old racecourse," Enid said. "She hasn't been there for a while."

He knew she didn't intend it, but he felt chastened. No doubt it was his fault Una was deprived of her recreation of walking the racecourse fence, at which she excelled, as he was led to believe. He had gone there only once with her and she had clung to his arm and his side and showed no inclination towards the tomboy practice or any regret that it now belonged to a youthful past.

Enid lowered her head over the lettuce she was shredding so fine it looked like a pale green bird's nest. He would sit and watch her. Blow the Herbert men. He thought about Una throwing the stone and Violet banging the tank as something to say but decided he did not want any such intrusion. No words from either but a drift of petals from a shrub outside the window, bearing flowers like pieces of velvet, settled on the tins on her little table. They both saw. Enid went and found a full flower still intact, a centre like a cluster of caterpillar feelers and a stem like a piece of brown darning wool. She twirled it between her fingers and he thought it so much like her head on its slender neck he foolishly expected it to twirl too.

She dropped it out the window.

"There will most likely be some new growth I can dig up for your garden," she said.

Very swiftly his face said it was not what he wanted. She went to the window and cleared it of the branch and he saw her waist, small and tight, aching for an arm.

When her face turned around his said he would go to the front room and hers agreed, and he slipped away, she watching his back thinking he walked more quickly than he need have.

He felt no shame at his relief that Una did not return for tea. Enid was in charge, seeing to everyone's needs, talking of neighbourhood affairs, nothing that involved him, he was swift to notice, without hurt. Jack had greeted him with tempered curtness, having prepared himself after seeing Una striding out towards the racecourse. The fellow would be around somewhere, primed up for Enid's tea!

But she was not bothering too much with him, Jack could see, talking away about the Candelo show six weeks off. Her cakes and flowers would take most of the prizes, as they usually did. She had been asked to judge but had declined, wanting to be free to exhibit for a few years yet. That was his Enid! He had bought a glass fronted cupboard to hold her silver cups and dishes inscribed with her name, and she had it tucked away in a corner of the living room, slipping out of the room when he opened the door to show visitors, modest about her achievements, blushing shyly at the praise.

Hers was a happy face now, cutting her pie and serving them, his first — now the fellow was part of the family he no longer had priority which was something to be pleased about — and with the right amount of cream flavoured with vanilla and without sugar as he liked it.

She brought in the tea right after the pudding, and clearing her throat only slightly and glancing at the big clock said she was going to Wyndham with Edwards and Una for evensong, so if no one minded she would clear the table as quickly as possible.

Edwards sprang up first — the fellow would! — tea cup in hand while Enid took the things from the table that did not affect Jack. Off to church again! Well they had better make sure the other one was with them! A pretty sight, the two of them in the sulky and it getting towards dusk.

Enid, pinked over prettily as she gathered plates, said Una should be back from her walk by the time she was ready. The fellow with one of his endless excuse me's carried his cup to the kitchen too, and Jack bent an ear that way, not surprised at all if he heard him at the washing up. The fellow was more suited to women's work in his opinion!

Here was Enid back, taking the last of the things from the table, and the fellow springing forward as if about to help her fold the cloth but she did it on her own, thank you very much, and better and more efficiently that way!

She went to the bedroom returning with a hat on and buttoning her gloves and saying they would give Una five more minutes.

"She may have walked up the creek and will be at the rectory by the time we get there," she said.

We! Her and the fellow! This wasn't part of the bargain! He agreed to the fellow marrying the other one, he didn't give him access to Enid as well. If he couldn't tame that flibbertigibbet it was his lookout. Whoever heard of a wife wandering off like a schoolboy on holiday leaving her husband to a sister-in-law? And here was Enid dealing with a button that had sprung undone on her glove and that fellow looking ready to spring forward and help her.

Jack shook his jowls very red under a black scowl. The wonder of it was Enid, raising her face and looking full into Jack's, appearing to find nothing unusual in it and taking her handbag and prayer book from a small table saying George should drive Una to the rectory if she returned to Honeysuckle after they'd gone. George would be going to Violet's if she knew him, to squeeze out some words of thanks for the job he did on the chair.

The next thing she was climbing into the sulky helped by the fellow who raised his hat very high in farewell and slapped his horse into a smart pace under Jack's eyes, for Jack had gone to the verandah to stand wide of legs to glare after them.

When he went inside he could only believe it all seeing the cushion squashed by the fellow's shape and music not put away, for he appeared to have been looking through it.

Some Sunday evenings Enid played for him, as Nellie used to. She shook the rugs and swept away crumbs and made everything neat and the two of them sat through the twilight, her shape growing dimmer and the dark stealing her bundle of hair and deepening her brow so that she might have been Nellie. Nellie only left the room when Enid brought in the lamp to light it.

Now here was Alex hunting for his tobacco, dressed in his motoring coat, off to the Hickeys to play cards. Nellie never allowed them on Sunday nights. He was driving the car that short distance. A waste of petrol when he could have walked across the paddocks. Three paddocks to cross and he takes a car a mile up the road, then a mile along a cart track, more than anything to show it off to the Hickeys, and of course the girl Maggie, a schoolteacher home on holidays. Ladylike but too devout a Catholic, so devout Wyndham was surprised she didn't enter the convent.

Alex would need to marry someone though and get into the old house before it crumbled away. George was good for not much else than trailing after Violet, more so since he loaned her that money for the hospital. Just as well she didn't ask him, she would have been told right off her job was caring for Ned. Two patients in six months! Call that success! There was that row too this morning. It must have been something to get Ned talking! There were never rows in Nellie's time.

There was George coming to the front now with Dolly in the sulky and the other one still not back. She had better be back at the rectory where she belonged, and not start living between there and Honeysuckle. That would mean the fellow here more than before! He seemed to be getting the best deal. A wife and all that furniture, and here he was carrying Enid off as well. If the other one wasn't back there Enid would be alone with him in the church watching his antics, swinging around in those ridiculous clothes, singing with a great roar, looking upwards, closing his eyes, swooping about, and she approving of it all. He had let her go without a protest. She hadn't seen his glare.

"One look from you is enough for them!" Nellie used to say. He strode in his agitated state to the kitchen.

There he was freshly shocked.

Enid had the tea things stacked in a dish at one end of the table.

At the other end the ginger cat was eating a dish of butter.

51

"Feel that wind!" Enid cried as they flew along.

She held one end of the sulky seat and her hat with the other hand.

"Take off your hat!" he shouted, and she did, pinning it to the floor with a foot and allowing her free arm to rest along the back of the seat.

"I love the feel of your back!" she cried, gulping the words back with great draughts of air. She knew he didn't hear. But she imagined he did, and the softening of his profile was his reply.

About a mile from the rectory he let the horse slow down and she let her body sway with the swaying motion of the sulky, until the horse, with head down, dragged along, and the sulky seat ceased to jig and her buttocks ceased to quiver and her whole body was like a spring that had been pushed down by a powerful hand and was suddenly released. There was the rectory in sight! Oh, no!

"We could go for a longer drive," he said. "There is a little more time."

The movement of the sulky now was barely jerking her waist, as if a light and gentle hand was pushing it in and out. She felt like a child falling into a deep, sweet sleep with a dream awaiting. At the rectory gate he passed her the reins and leapt out.

"Wait here!" he said. Wait here! A command! She saw a curtain rise and fall at Violet's window.

"I should have waved," she murmured. Then she started

and Violet's curtain was flung boldly back. The church bell clanged half a dozen times. The horse, never harnessed when the bell rang, jumped to go forward and Enid had to pull him up and speak soothingly to his twitching ears.

Edwards appeared running, putting his arms into his short coat, evidently discarding his long one.

"Just to the school turn off," he said, unlooping the reins from Enid's gloves.

The horse began to trot and he lifted his hat as high as it would go to Violet on the verandah with Small Henry in her arms.

"He would love to come!" Enid said.

He slowed the horse to a stop. "We could go back and ask," Edwards said.

The horse turned his eyes in their direction, chewing at the bit, only obliging because it was the one he tolerated, not the other.

"Get along, get along!" Edwards said, in a voice he hadn't heard before. Stepping out smartly he stopped with a curved neck over Violet's fence, quite close to the jigging Small Henry who seemed in danger of leaping from Violet's arms with joy.

"We are out looking for Una!" Edwards said. "She is missing!" He frowned as severely as he could on Violet, who tossed her head and snorted so loud the horse looked about it, searching for a rival.

"For my money she can stay missing!" She took Small Henry's hand thrust towards Enid and pinned it to her neck. "Not that she will! She knows her way around, that one!"

Enid climbed from the sulky and in front of Small Henry clapped her hands together, then parted them. "Let me!" she said. "I haven't had a nurse for a week!"

Small Henry, sensing her connection with the sulky and

its connection with activity, swooped towards Enid, and Violet with a tightened face loosened her hold.

Enid sat tenderly on the edge of the verandah, wrapping Small Henry's nightgown around his legs, which were pumping up and down as if attached to bicycle pedals. He screwed his body to keep an eye on the horse. Edwards came and sat beside them. Enid put her face into the back of Small Henry's neck.

"I believe he loves me best of all," she whispered.

"Me too," he whispered back.

Violet heard, but couldn't distinguish the words.

Enid's head flew up and Edwards was very still, his face and Enid's face in the wash of the last of the day's light, as if drawn by someone who could only manage one expression.

"You rang the bell for church!" Violet said in reprimand.

"I must ring it twice a day for the Boyds!" Edwards said. "Their old clock won't go any more, Mrs Watts told me, and they have to tell the time by the bell!"

"We should give them a clock, shouldn't we, Small Henry?" Enid said. "Tick, tock, tick tock, tick tock! There would be a clock to spare at Honeysuckle!"

Edwards smiled a small, dreamy smile imagining the two of them delivering a clock to the poor Boyds, who lived with their ten children in an old tumbledown house on the roadside a half mile from Wyndham.

Violet stood frowning, waiting for Small Henry to be returned to her. Though Enid held him loosely, there might have been steel inside the soft flesh of her arms. She had her head laid sideways on his head and it was a leap from him that dislodged it, for there was the clip clop of Dolly's hoofs bringing George in the sulky.

He had barely finished tying Dolly to a telegraph pole

and just escaped a clout on the side of his head, for Dolly questioned the presence of Edwards's horse there ahead of her, and swung her head to ask why, when Jack cantered up on Horse, swinging through the church gate, having recklessly jumped Horse over an obliging panel of staggering fence here and there.

Edwards's horse stamped, snorted and broke wind, saying he was there first and wasn't going to be crowded out.

"Woa!" Edwards called when the sulky tipped.

Dolly backed excitedly, her sulky wheels grinding against Edward's wheels, and Horse, tied by Jack to Violet's gatepost, lifted his head and whinnied, letting the others know he was the least encumbered of the three and able to make the easiest get away if the occasion called for it. Horse pranced in a half circle to demonstrate he was practically free.

My goodness, Rachel said to herself from the gap in her curtains at the front window. There's something going on there. She could take something across perhaps to Edwards, but had dropped the habit, since the Herbert girls were the better cooks, and Edwards was looking sleek and plump from two larders. Her curiosity sent her looking at her kitchen shelves, and seeing nothing there she went out the back to her vegetable garden, in a state of wilt after the day's heat.

She found a watering can on the tankstand and trotting to the front began watering a clump of geraniums near the Post Office steps, an action that caused Enid's dreamy smile to deepen.

"Come and sit by me, Father!" she called to Jack. "And say hello to Small Henry. He grows more beautiful every day!"

Edwards took hold of one of Small Henry's flapping hands to indicate his agreement and let Jack know he would not be giving up his place and Jack would have to squeeze himself on the other side, verandah post or no verandah post.

But Jack remained with fists on hips, a whip dangling from one. Violet decided to take a verandah chair and leave Small Henry where he was. She had been lumping him around all day, upset as they both were over the morning's trauma.

She didn't mind having a longer gander at the Reverend and Enid. She knew from the start Enid was the better catch! Rachel should be in on this!

"Come across!" she called to the stooped shape with the watering can. "Half Wyndham is here anyway!"

Rachel dropped the can and came. She sat near Violet's feet with her hands in the silk lap of her Sunday afternoon dress.

"She's missing!" Violet cried. "As you can see, we're all out looking for her!" Rachel ran her eyes over the assembled group to work out who she was.

"Nonsense!" Enid said getting up. "Una has merely gone for a walk to the old racecourse!" Then she sat in confusion with an apology on her face for Edwards, remembered it was he who had said Una needed to be found and he and Enid were out looking for her.

"I thought by the way the sulky was heading she was somewhere on the road to Candelo!" Violet cried.

Jack stirred the whip and Edwards crossed his legs quite firmly.

"Take Small Henry if you like!" Violet said. "The air will do him good after the morning we had!"

Enid stood, pulling Small Henry's gown around his feet and shifting him in her arms to shut Jack off.

Edwards stood too. "For a very short run then," he said.

He took Small Henry while Enid climbed into the sulky, then handed him up.

Small Henry flung his round head downwards to the sulky wheel and then to the horse's rump, and slapped a hand on the back of the sulky seat and rubbed a foot on the leather by Enid's lap. His body was like a tight, slippery barrel inside his clothes and Enid held him on the knee nearest Edwards so that his head touched first one shoulder then the other as the sulky bounced along.

"Sit down. Jack!" Violet cried. "Let your blood cool down in the breeze!" Jack dug his whip handle deeper into the earth.

"All you did wrong was to marry the wrong one off!" Ned's measured tread could be heard crossing the back verandah. "It's happened before and will happen again! You can be sure of that!

"George! Come and sit here on the verandah! That pole will stay up on its own!"

George came. He sat in the doorway and miraculously Violet skidded her chair back on the boards so that his stretched out legs were by the chair legs.

Ned came through the hall deciding to lean heavily on his stick, and when he reached the doorway George had to move to let him through and he moved towards Violet, so close his face brushed that loose hanging arm and he could have gently bitten those twinkling fingers, playing away at an unseen piano.

He would too one day. One day he would!

Ned stabbed his stick on the verandah and Horse turned to look at him and sent the flesh on his back quivering like a ripple on dark water. He raised a foot and stamped it, alerting Dolly to something new. Dolly sprawled her legs and the sulky shafts were raised pointing like gun barrels towards the sky.

"Woa! You fools!" Jack called.

Ned plunged off the end of the verandah and beating Violet's lilies away with his stick fled down the side of the house towards the back.

"Show him more than one horse and he's back in the front lines!" Violet cried. "He never fed a horse, watered a horse, rode a horse or probably saw a horse, but he wants you to think he rode them into battle!"

"Poor Ned!" Rachel said. "He doesn't get any better!"

"Do any of them?" Violet said. "Show me one that does!"

George bent his head so that an ear brushed Violet's waist. Me, me, he cried silently. Give me a chance to show you!

Jack went to Horse and untied him. Horse curved his neck in the direction of Dolly, who put her neck over Violet's fence and snorted inside a withered rancid geranium.

Jack without raising his hat to the women turned Horse thoughtfully towards the road, letting him dance and slide among the dust and stones reined tightly in.

Then he kicked one side, threw both elbows out and galloped Horse down the road.

"So he should!" Violet cried. "Leave them be, I say. Surely he can light the lamp himself, for once in his life!"

52

Edwards let his horse pace smartly until they were out of sight.

Small Henry moved until his head slipped under Enid's chin and there it lolled approaching sleep when the horse slowed and stopped. Enid rocked her body gently so that Small Henry would be fooled into thinking they were still moving.

The horse flung its head up in surprise, but said no more, just rubbed a nose gently down a leg and left it lowered. When Enid gained the courage to lift her head and look at Edwards's profile she saw it stern and sad against a sky pale and thin like separated milk.

Around them the bush was slipping into dusk. A little wind brought a sharp and cruel edge to a day that had been all warmth like thick sweet custard. She saw the flesh over his jaw move. Words were inside there. She waited, breathing leaves and dust and dogwood and Small Henry's sweetly sweated head.

He pulled the reins and the horse, not knowing what was next, backed, and Enid with her awkward gloves groped for support and clung for a second to Edwards's thighs. Small Henry looking for a pillow threw his head about until he found the softness of Enid's breast.

Edwards turned the sulky with the horse threading its legs in and out and the wheels making great furrows in the dust. The horse was still, waiting.

Both of us, Enid thought.

"I have to go back," he said.

"Of course," she said.

Violet went ahead into Small Henry's room and turned the bedclothes back for Enid to lay him down.

Back on the verandah finding her hat and smoothing her sleeves she said she would go home with George when he was ready.

George rose at once from the doorstep.

"George is always ready!" Violet cried.

Edwards walked his horse to the big tree and unharnessed it. Enid saw the horse's rear with the tail swishing about the deep dark seam separating its buttocks.

The seam in Edwards's trousers separated his, moving busily while he unbuckled straps and hauled the harness off.

Enid thought of the shells, feeling the seam, pushing her fingers at the crevice, searching for a blemish and finding none.

Edwards held the sound of George's sulky in his ears, allowing himself only one glance, and seeing the two white blobs of Enid's gloves flying like white moths through the dusk.

Inside the rectory Edwards called Una's name and ran through the rooms half expecting to find her on the bed in the room she had fixed for Small Henry.

Then he started off down the creek.

The racecourse was about a mile along, one corner so close to the creek bank the races had to be abandoned one year when floodwaters spilled over the track.

She would have left there by now, he thought, and would be wandering up or down the creek.

First he would check the waterhole where the Herbert males swam. The activity was forbidden the girls, a rule of Nellie's that Jack upheld. Una defied him, trailing home dragging a bathing costume with her blouse clinging to her damp skin and her hair in wet strings on her sunburned neck. Enid usually succeeded in getting her wet things out of the way and saw her bathed and changed before Jack appeared. Inheriting many of Nellie's rules and habits she would have earned Jack's wrath if Una was caught, just as Nellie would have.

Edwards knew Una had taught herself to swim in the hole and appeared to him to do a good overarm. His plan had been to watch her closely and see if he could work out her method.

But she had flashed into the water on their honeymoon, bobbing up between the waves quite a way out and he had walked about in agitation looking to others on the beach for assurance that she would not drown. When she raced out finally and flung herself on the sand her wet body trembled, not with cold, vibrating with the power it held to battle the sea, whatever its mood. He sat beside her not going in, ashamed that he could not manage to get beyond the second breaker and out of his depth.

He found her now lying much as she did on the beach, only she was on the big rock that rose with a sheer face out of the water and levelled at the top, smooth as a table. A wattle with its trunk wedged against the rock at one side gave shade and a long stout rope was tied to a branch just above the spreading roots.

The rope now lay coiled on the rock and Una on her stomach was playing idly with one end. An early moon washed her with light, making him remember briefly the long summer evenings at home in England.

Una was in bloomers and camisole dappled with reflection from the tree. Her dress was flung among the branches, making the tree look as if it bore one large tawny coloured flower.

"There you are!" Edwards called, and she rose on her hands then dropped down again and laid her face on the rock. He felt with her, the hardness meeting her cheekbones and hips and knees and squashing her breasts.

He could cross to her by going several hundred yards downstream to a crossing of rocks through which the water poured, but were raised clear of it, making it possible to step from one to the other.

She could well fly off while he was about it.

"A shame I can't walk on water!" he called.

"Are you sure you can't?" she said. She sat up and wrapped her arms around her legs. The ribbons tying her camisole were reduced to thin strings in their wetness. He thought of the feel of her breasts, bluish white porcelain, cool to touch, chillingly cold, but heating under rubbing fingers.

The water near him lapped his boots, but ran deep in the centre where he knew it was several feet over Alex's head, the tallest of the Herbert men. It was dark and still, no ripples there, speaking in some strange way to him of the space between them.

More sheer rock rose on the upper side of the creek helping form the waterhole. The hole was kept full by a steady flow of water through crevices at the bottom. The water spread out on the top side and here it was waist deep on an adult.

The Herbert boys and their cousins and friends learned to swim in what became known as the kids' hole. It was a positive step towards manhood when they could slide down the rock face and stay afloat in the big hole. Manhood was established when they could grasp the rope and swing wide over the water, dropping in neat as a stone and rising to fling wet hair from wet eyes and throwing the floating rope out of their way and strike out for the bank.

If Edwards removed his trousers he could wade through the kids' hole and reach Una with terrible lack of dignity and not knowing whether to get into the trousers then or fling them on the branch beside her dress.

Perhaps Una up there like a white bird newly landed, uncertain whether to stay or fly off and look for something better, was watching for this.

Damn her then, he said to himself and took off his boots. He set them on a log and rolled his trousers to his knees.

He waded into the big hole, surprised at the warmth of the water than feeling it cold when it slapped the cloth against his thighs. Colder still when it ran into his crotch, failing to cool the heat there, fiery as a branding iron. No relief, no relief, he thought wading on. He saw his white shirt turn grey and limp, felt the sting of the water under his arms and the cut of his starched collar into his neck like a wet knife.

"Here!" she called, standing. "Take the rope!"

She flung it and he had to struggle from a hole taking a draught of water when he reached for it and it bobbed past him. He would float. He would show her how well he could float! Pray to heaven he didn't float over the deep part.

She hauled the rope back, coiling it with an expert hand. She threw it again and it slapped heavily his floating face. He seized it but it was a feeble thing weak as a twig. He gulped more water, slipped under the water — is this the way you drown? — pedalled wildly with his legs and got his head out again. He blew out his cheeks but his hair remained plastered to his eyes, limiting his vision. There was a blurr of white, her legs dangling down unconcerned. He pulled at the rope, hand over hand, but it seemed never to become taut. He would die this way, bloated and helpless, dragged towards the rock but reaching it too late.

"Wait!" she called, and his ears must have been out of the water for he heard. Wait? For what? He was drowning! What did she mean? Wait for a quick and painless death? He couldn't tell her for he was choking as well as drowning.

Then there was a splash and she was beside him. He must not hold her too tight and drown them both, he knew that! She held the rope high — it went taut for her! — and he throwing away his shame bound his arms around her and his mouth miraculously free of water was pressed to the sweet flesh of her breast. Gently they bumped the rock together and she with a cry kicked it hard with both feet sending them out again, the rope twirling, and her with both legs around his waist, a heel digging and rubbing at one of his buttocks.

They swung back to hit the rock and she with a practised foot found one of the small steps hollowed below the surface of the water and guided his foot to another.

"I'll scale up," she said. "Don't drop back!" Drop back? Fall into that black, watery ravine? The air was sweet as wine, the moon was balanced up there, rocking like him, but safe, safe! He pressed his face to the rock, his knees were torn by the rock, his hands scratched by the rock, but the rock held him until he slipped, and was almost gone again. He heard her chuckle above him and the rope tickled his nose. He grabbed and he heard her feet running back and her breathing laughter and he was hauled up, ashamed he did so little for himself, wanting to shout and laugh when he at last rolled over, arms and legs flung out and her dress on the tree so close he could have touched it.

She sat beside him in her old pose, arms wrapped around her knees. One side of his face saw her narrow feet and her

304

ankles hollowed beautifully, faintly blue where the skin stretched over the bone, like the pointed end of an egg-shell.

He reached up and squeezed some water from her bloomers. She slipped a hand down the front of his trousers and taking a handful of cloth turned her hand so that water trickled down his belly and ran off, the way a stream runs into reeds. He stroked her wet hip and she turned her body and laid it on his hip, pressing so hard she wrung more water from them both. She rubbed her wet legs on his wet trousers and he undid them so that she could rub and push them off, he helping, and she pulling at his wet collar too and putting her face there, sticking to his skin at first, but soon fanned dry with her warm breath.

In a very short time the furnace of their bodies had dried them both.

53

Lanterns were bobbing around the rectory when they climbed through the fence of the church paddock.

"Carry me!" Una said. "Pretend I've hurt my leg!"

He bowed his head partly to hoist her on his back, partly to shut out the frowning face of the church.

Violet's face was below the first raised lantern.

"There you are!" she cried. "Frightening everyone half to death!"

"It's my turn to be frightened now!" Una cried. "Looking at you!"

Violet dropped the lantern to her side as if her face did offend. Then she jerked it up and swung it so that Una had to crush her face into Edwards's shoulder away from the blinding light.

"Your poor sister!" Violet cried in a burst of passion.

"Help me to bed," Una murmured to Edwards. "I must get my leg up."

They passed Jack and Enid in the kitchen, Enid by the table with cups set out and Jack a dark shape by the dresser. A lantern gave the room its only light, Enid having lit the best lamp and placed it on the living room table. Edwards saw and thought how beautifully Enid placed a lamp.

"I am too exhausted to undress myself," Una said closing her eyes.

Edwards, sitting on the chair, decided he wouldn't undress her.

When does a man revert to a beast, he thought. At the height of his passion or when it has subsided?

Enid slipped into the room with a cup of tea for each of them. So beautifully chaste, he thought, watching her move a candle to make room for Una's tea.

Mercifully she went out almost at once to rejoin Jack in the kitchen drinking tea on one of the chairs that seemed far too small for him.

"I saw that painting," Jack said. "When I went looking to see where they put the furniture. I paid too much for it!"

The ghostly light in the kitchen swallowed Enid's ghostly smile. "It's a poor specimen of a man who would allow a wife to paint a picture like that!"

Enid, who took no tea, rolled down her sleeves and packed some plates she had brought food from Honeysuckle on. She was going then. Good! He got up and found his hat, so there would be no delay. He had put Dolly in the buggy, which got little use these days, to give Enid a better ride when she insisted on going to the rectory to see if Una was safe.

She had always loved a buggy ride, her gloved hands folded in her lap and her slim body assuming a dreamy quality even while she kept it erect with her chin up. The other one rode a horse well, but Enid was better in a buggy.

"I'll untie Dolly and wait at the gate," Jack said. It got him out of goodbyes. The fellow had nodded to him going through the kitchen, that would be good enough. But Edwards was upset to find Jack gone and wanted to go to him and thank him for bringing Enid to the rectory.

"No, no," Enid said. "I'll tell him goodbye for you."

He took her hand, thinking with pleasurable surprise that he would always be free to shake hands with her.

"I'll write and tell mother all about you," he whispered,

and realized it was an odd thing to say, for she dropped his hand and almost ran across the verandah and down to the waiting Jack.

He went to the kitchen looking for something to do, but Enid had made it neat and had brought in kindling wood to start the fire next morning. He had missed evensong for the first time since coming to Wyndham, so taking up the lantern still in his damp clothes he went to the church to pray for a while.

It was several weeks before he wrote to his mother.

By that time Una was reduced to a rag doll of a figure and on this late summer afternoon was without shoes and in an old kimono on the couch flapping the curtain to make a draught, between bouts of retching.

He offered tea and a drink of water but she flapped her head from side to side as if a spring inside her neck had come loose.

She became still and Edwards thought she might be sleeping so he stealthily took his pad and sat before it, one eye on the raised knee on the couch with the kimono trailing on the floor.

It took him quite a while to get started.

When he did he wrote: "Dear Mother, I most definitely must learn to swim."

54

Rachel brought the news to Violet of Una's pregnancy, going there without shame straight from the rectory where she had found Una, pale and with uncombed hair, head on folded arms on the kitchen table.

Edwards had filled a cup with some of his pale blue tea and was putting it by her elbow when Rachel came to the back door with a colander of newly gathered beans.

"Oh poo! I wouldn't want her here screaming and carrying on the way she would and upsetting all the other patients!" Violet rose rapidly from her chair and attending to the big kettle on the stove, so Rachel could indulge in a broad smile (all the other patients!) and rehearse the words to be repeated to Ena Grant when she went for cheese and sugar before she opened the Post Office.

But less than an hour after Rachel had gone, Violet wiped Small Henry's mouth of toast crumbs and carried him across to the rectory.

She hadn't, as she frequently said, put foot inside the door since the day Una showed her the painting.

Una had raised her head by this time and was holding a wan face in one hand. Edwards sprang from his chair by the open kitchen door when he saw Violet, his head on one side in his characteristic cleric pose, not used so much since his marriage, and looking on Violet as if she were a new parishioner, one newly defected from another religion.

Una sprang from her place too and covering her face with her hands fled to the bedroom and slammed the door.

"Well she looks as if she'll make a great success of it, I must say!" Violet said, taking the chair Edwards had vacated and moved forward for her.

She adjusted Small Henry on one thigh, raised with the point of her shoe on the floor.

By jove, Una was spot on, Edwards thought. She does have limbs like logs of wood.

He was reminded to stoke the fire, which he did, Small Henry's bright gaze following his every move. The little fellow! I would love a nurse. Why do women hold babies as if they were in a steel trap?

Small Henry rocked himself back and forth indicating a need to escape. Violet scooped him up, squashing his rump with another bind of her arm and went to the window to look across to Albert Lane and down the back to the gully and bush. Edwards watched her profile aimed at her tank-stand with the eyes sliding around to take in as much of the back as possible.

Dear lady, he thought, give Small Henry to Enid. Her arms ache for him and her heart is broken. Ned will come home and stay. He will be happy, you will be less tormented, Small Henry will be happy and Enid ecstatic. Why not give it a try?

But Edwards knew people seldom took the course that created happiness. Not even for themselves. They kept the soft bladder of their feelings inside a hard leather covering, pumped tight like a football. They preferred to hang onto the tightness and the hardness, not caring that it was reflected on their faces. I think many people are frightened to be happy, Edwards decided. If it means being generous, they'd rather be miserable.

Violet went and sat on her chair again. Edwards remembering that it was several weeks since he had seen Small Henry, and although Violet was not his natural parent, she would probably be like all others and look for complimentary remarks on the child's progress in the interval.

Edwards was just about to say that Small Henry was coming along very nicely and looking most healthy when his horse whinnied. Violet swung sideways in her chair to see through the window and Edwards went right up to look. Dear me, I am as bad as the rest of them, he thought. A horse's whinny is an event.

Violet hoisting Small Henry to her shoulder looked past his round swivelling head.

A buggy was at her gate and there was a man running around the horse to lift down a young woman shaped like a giant vegetable marrow.

"It's the Tasker girl!" Violet cried. "She was going to Bega! Wyndham wasn't good enough for her!"

Edwards held the poker about to attend to the fire again, an activity of great interest to Small Henry, and the next moment he had flung it from him and had Small Henry in his arms crowing and jigging in triumph.

They both watched Violet make her way across the paddock, unhurried, head up, straight of back. Only the starched uniform was missing.

Inside the house she got into it, wordlessly and sternly, leaving Mr Tasker and his terrified moaning daughter to wait on the verandah.

Edwards saw it blinding white at the window which she raised. Then she straightened a chair and swept an arm across a counterpane, and going into the hall stood with hands folded below her bust.

Humbly with hat in hand Mr Tasker helped his daughter into the room. The girl bit back her screams at the sight of Violet's face and holding the head of the bed rubbed her sweaty face in the hollow of her sweaty arm. She screamed freely when Violet was out of the room, and Edwards, now on the back verandah gathering up Small Henry's napkins and bottle to stow in the foot of the perambulator, paled at the sound.

Small Henry held the sides of the perambulator with fat, dimpled hands.

"We'll go! You're needed here!" Edwards shouted, hoping this would urge her to go to the desperate girl.

Violet at the kitchen table was setting out a little stack of enamel basins. They still had their shiny newness, and it might have been the shine from them giving Violet's face its dreamy shine.

Edwards manoeuvred the perambulator over the edge of the back verandah, not daring to invade the sacred territory of the front.

The girl's screams followed him to the roadway, and speeding away from them he felt the eerie quiet of the rectory, in sharp contrast.

But no less terrifying.

An hour later, Jack saw him, approaching the Honey-suckle paddocks.

He was hoeing the newly sprouted potatoes, and put his hat back to see the better. Edwards thought it a salute and raised his own.

He stretched well back behind the perambulator, so that from a distance he looked to Jack like a large black grasshopper.

Jack threw down his hoe in disgust and put his hat back on his sweating forehead. That topped everything.

But look what his beloved Enid had been spared.

55

George had to go next day in the sulky to collect most of Small Henry's things, for there was no chance of Violet having him back with the Tasker girl bearing twin sons. (She was respectably married to a transient telephone linesman but sharing her parents' home.)

George came away unhappy but impressed. Violet had no time to do other than jerk an elbow towards Small Henry's old sleeping basket filled with his napkins, nightgowns, rompers and woollen jackets, rather matted for Violet was not the careful washer Enid was. Violet was bathing the two rabbit-like creatures and dabbing at their bleeding navels with a heavy frown.

She's got an important job there, very important, George said to himself, putting the basket in the sulky and wondering how long he should linger on the chance that she would rush to the doorway and call him back for tea and her peel cake.

The Tasker girl and her twins stayed nearly a month. Violet thought it wisest to keep the babies until they gained enough weight to be the size of average newborn infants. The girl's husband, in regular work, could afford the extra.

Ned was there most of the time. He passed through the hall several times a day and stood about the front verandah, scaring the Tasker girl when she looked up and saw his glass eye in an opening between the window curtains.

He made enormous fires in the kitchen stove, turning the room into a furnace. Violet cursed him loudly once as she pulled half burned logs from the firebox and threw them on the hearth, covering them with a kettle full of boiling water which hissed and spattered, sending a great shower of black ash over her clean uniform.

Oh go to the bush, she cried silently. Go, go, go!

But when he went and the Tasker girl and her babies had gone the quiet had a chilly edge that Violet could not escape. She saw no reason to build up the fire in the stove since there was no one but herself to cook for and no further use for great quantities of hot water.

She had made up her mind to go to Honeysuckle and bring Small Henry back when Ned burned Halloween to its chimney, surrounded by some sheets of blackened corrugated iron, formerly the roof.

He had fallen asleep on the chair that George had mended and a spark had settled in the fuzzy wool of his khaki trousers and he had felt the sting and stamped a foot, sending a shower of sparks to ignite the paper pinned down by his chair leg. Both trouser legs were well alight when he got outside and rolled himself in the grass that grew abundantly by the sagging wire that once enclosed Mrs Hooper's brave but struggling garden.

George saw the flames and smoke from the Honeysuckle calf pens and galloped Horse to Ned, who was staring in fascination at his wounds while the Halloween timbers burned away under their load of iron.

All that work I did on that chair, George thought as he hoisted Ned onto Horse and bore him off, leading Horse with a finger hooked through the bit.

Ned's thin white legs and half burned boots dangled by Horse's side causing confusion. Horse would jerk forward when an empty stirrup hit him to be pulled up by George, only to step out smartly when Ned's boot scraped his belly.

He stopped abruptly once and set up a quivering of his flesh, asking for an explanation.

George dealt him a clout on the side of his head in reply.

"You wouldn't be much bloody use in the war either," he muttered.

Violet put Ned to bed in the labour ward and he seemed quite pleased to be there.

She set the kettles over the heat, then bustled off to get into a uniform. "Why not?" she said to the mirror, neatening the pieces of black hair either side of her cap.

She said she must clean Ned's wounds, setting a tray with tweezers, antiseptic and two basins of hot water, but if George liked to wait she would make them both tea when she was done.

George did wait and had to watch while she set another tray, this one with a cloth and cup and saucer from the new lot (George paid for them!) to take to Ned. George felt the starched edges of her dress and cap would cut his flesh if she came near enough.

Her words did.

She told George the Taskers paid their account with a little extra and she was now in a position to give him back portion of the money she borrowed to start the hospital. "I'm most grateful, George," she said, cutting thin bread and butter for Ned's tray.

He rode Horse home to Honeysuckle with his mouth working.

Jack's was too, on the verandah after riding from the ruins of Halloween and scorching his fingers looking under the iron for Ned.

Enid brought Jack a strong cup of tea, leaving instructions with George, sitting mournfully on the edge of the verandah, to watch that Small Henry stayed on the rug.

Jack after a draught of tea said it was a pity the windows

and doors of Halloween could not have been salvaged to be used on the old house or barns at Honeysuckle.

"Let's not talk about it," Enid said. "Ned got away thanks to George."

George not sure that this tribute was to his liking drooped his head a little lower.

Enid put her sewing aside and clapped her hands to Small Henry rubbing his heels lightly together on the rug.

"Show Grandad and Jaw-Jaw what you can do!" she cried.

Small Henry decided to take his time and chew a little longer on a wooden peg. He transferred the peg from one hand to the other, opening his mouth to receive the un-chewed end and misfiring, jabbing it into a fat cheek. Then he cast it from him and rocked himself on his bottom still, with his delicately coloured heels together and his toes curl-ed so that they appeared like a scalloped edge to his feet. A small smile settled thoughtfully on his face while he con-templated the next course of action. Like a runner starting a race he put his forehead forward until it nearly touched the rug. He spread his hands and heaved his bottom up. He wobbled for a moment. Then he undertook shakily but with no thought of failure to separate his body from his thighs and sent it upright. It was there, level with George's screwed round head, with Jack's knees, Enid's sewing basket close enough to dash to the ground, the wrinkled rug fathoms away.

He put his head back to crush his yellow curls on his neck and laugh, then fell sharply on his bottom.

Enid gathered him up and held him. Small Henry, my beauty! He stands by himself! Soon he will walk. She wished for a million ears to hear the magnificent tidings.

56

But she did not keep him.

Henry came home unannounced with a wife and they moved into the old place.

Henry could scarcely believe Small Henry was real. He carried him everywhere about the farm. Henry's wife was a short black haired girl with a fringe across her forehead. (Another wife with her hair cut, thought Jack, looking hard at her middle, expecting she would probably be already in the family way like the other one.) She was plump and pretty and shrewd and decided not to lose out to Small Henry on affection from Henry, whom she genuinely loved. She would take on Small Henry as well.

She begged to be allowed to carry him some of the time, and he stretched arms very straight and stiff towards Henry at first, then found tiny pearl ear rings which she allowed him to finger, then when she wore a jacket with a trimming of fur on the collar he dropped his face in it and looked for the ginger cat connecting the two in his little mind.

Edwards wrote about this and other events to his mother.

"We always say nothing ever happens in these places, don't we?" he wrote, "But I have several things to relate on top of the news a few weeks ago about the new little life. Have you digested it yet?

"My poor, dear Una is not really well though. We succeeded in finally getting her to the Pambula doctor and he says she will need a long rest following the birth, maybe in a Sydney hospital. Don't distress yourself. We will manage.

"There are changes at Honeysuckle. Small Henry has gone to a new home with the return from Sydney of Henry and a new wife. It was tragic for dear, sweet Enid. (No sister-in-law is greater loved.)"

He crossed out the word loved and wrote respected in its place.

He wrote on: "I was quite nervous for her that Alex, the elder brother courting Maggie Hickey (they say "going with" over here), may have claims on the little fellow. They constantly took him for Sunday afternoon drives. She is a Catholic too, no marriage for me to perform there, a depressing fact. I feel responsible (foolishly I know) and am quite dreading my next meeting with the archdeacon who will no doubt remind me of my failing.

"He has visited us only once since my marriage. It was to take a service on the anniversary of the opening of St Jude's. By great good fortune it was also the anniversary (or near enough) of the opening of St Peter's in Pambula so he had time only for a brief meeting with parishioners and morning tea in the rectory before going off. He mistook Enid for Una and to my everlasting shame I did nothing to rectify the error. Enid made a perfect hostess. Una had taken her bathing suit to the swimming hole, although the middle of winter. I was terrified she would appear looking like a deep green football sprouting arms and legs."

He wriggled on his chair to rid himself of cold and cramp and then wrote on:

"I have this plan. So far only God and I know of it and I now share it with you.

"When the new little one is born I hope to carry it off and place it in Enid's arms. If a boy Small Colin, if a girl Small Enid. I will insist. Una I don't think by that time will raise any objections, simply allow herself to go off for the long (very long) rest cure.

"In her state I think Una will allow herself to be confined at Violet's, although the two still do not speak. Violet wants it desperately. She has few patients owing to this limited population (of adults) and for her own niece not to be confined in her hospital (and next door) would be taken as a social blight.

"Ned recovered from his burning accident, and now walks with two sticks. He goes to the bush less and less which is easier on Violet. My prayers in that area have brought results, although I have to admit, since he burned the farmhouse down, shelter is unavailable and nights spent in the open during an Australian winter would have limited appeal.

"But to say more about my plan. It was I who took Small Henry to Enid when Violet had to handle the unexpected birth of twins, followed by Ned's burned legs. I took great delight in the happiness he brought her. Then she lost him and I feel somehow I failed her. This way I will make it up to her. (Please God!)"

He laid down his pen and rubbed the finger that held it. A noise startled him. Una had returned from her walk carrying a long branch and trailed it along the windows of the church, then around the tankstand. The noise was like a bell tolling, a light ringing on the surface above a deep and thunderous sound.

He went swiftly to the kitchen, tearing off the written pages and folding them.

He lifted the ring of the stove and laid the pages on the coals. Flames ran from the corners curling them as they went. Some of the words leaped up blackened and with letters enlarged.

Then the pages turned to transparency, and when he last looked reminded him of frail waves breaking up on some strange, metal coloured sea.